HEARTBREAKER

HEARTBREAKER

LAURENCE GOUGH

M&S

Canadian Cataloguing in Publication Data

Gough, Laurence
Heartbreaker

ISBN 0-7710-3438-5

I. Title

PS8563.O84H43   1995   C813'.54   C95-931941-7
PR9199.3.G78H43   1995

The publishers acknowledge the support of the Canada Council and the Ontario Arts Council for their publishing program.

Typesetting by M&S, Toronto
Printed and bound in Canada on acid-free paper

McClelland & Stewart Inc.
The Canadian Publishers
481 University Avenue
Toronto, Ontario
M5G 2E9

1 2 3 4 5   99 98 97 96 95

This one's for
Charlotte
Spencer
Charlotte's brother Alexander
Liam

1

Shelley was cruising along just fine until it came time to get dressed. Did he look sweetest in the diagonal-striped yellow and red suit or the solid colour electric-blue model? He was wearing the blue one now, as he preened in front of the mirror. Did he look good? There was no doubt in his mind that he looked *very* good. But he wasn't sure that he looked *right*. Plenty of scorchy August sunbeams were waltzing in through the leaded-glass bedroom windows, but even so, it wasn't the same as being outside. The quality of the light was different. Not as lively. To his eye the blue suit should've had a certain iridescence, like a peacock's tailfeathers, that just didn't seem to be there. Maybe the material was getting old, fading . . .

He wriggled out of the suit, hung it on a doorknob, and daintily crammed himself into the yellow and red model, reached down in there and got himself comfortably arranged. Getting all his ducks in a row, so to speak. He turned sideways to the mirror, squeezed his butt muscles tight. The blue was cut a little higher in the leg. Was that a good thing? Yes. Shelley flashed a smile. What a hunk. Man, he was almost too good to be true.

But was it gonna be the solid blue or the train-stopper red and yellow? He just couldn't get his brain straightened out. Was life full of tough decisions, or what? He grabbed his jeans off the bureau, gave them a shake. A few loose coins tinkled merrily. He

ferreted out a quarter, flipped it high into a shaft of sunlight and
let it bounce on the pale green wool carpet.

Queens.

He shucked the red and yellow Speedo and reached for the blue.
Was it electric blue or neon blue? The salesgirl had told him but
he'd been too busy looking deep into her big brown cow-patty
eyes to hear a single word she said, until she politely told him that,
yeah, she had a boyfriend. And she wasn't done with him yet.
Reminiscing instead of paying attention, he'd somehow got
himself tangled up in the Speedo. Stretch fabrics could be such a
pain. He hopped gracelessly around the huge bedroom until he
lost his balance and tumbled onto the kingsize bed. He shut his
eyes. Wouldn't it be nice to take the day off, lie there in the drowsy
sunlight and dream sweet dreams . . . But nice didn't cut it. He
had work to do, money to steal. He got his legs straightened out,
rolled over on his back and pushed himself into about half an
ounce of fabric. In front of the mirror again, he cocked a leg, bent
an arm, turned and checked himself out full face and profile, left
side and right.

What it came down to was mood. Was he in a red and yellow
mood, or was he in an electric or maybe a neon blue mood?

Standing there in front of the mirror, Shelley looked anything
but an indecisive petty thief. He was twenty-six years old, just
edging into the prime of his life. He was a couple of inches over
six feet, almost always the tallest guy in the elevator. He weighed a
solid one hundred eighty pounds. Had nice, even features. A great
smile. Charm aplenty. And he was smart, too, a real quick learner.

He'd never in his life held a full-time permanent job, but it
wasn't as if this was an ambition he'd aspired to or planned but
failed to achieve. Sometimes things just happened. He certainly
wasn't what you'd call a lazy or slothful guy. Rain or shine, every
day that he got out of bed was a day he drove to the gym and spent
a solid two hours working out. On the bench or machines.
Sweating. Not lounging around or hitting on women, like a lot of
the guys. Or if he did strike a pose or help some woman do this or

that, showed her how to work a machine or whatever, he always kept close track of the minutes, and put in extra time to make up for the time he'd lost. In the gym, there was nobody who worked harder than he did, and it showed. Every minute he'd put in lay there just beneath the surface of his skin, smooth and hard, for all the world to see.

He turned to face the window. Looked over his shoulder at the stunner in the mirror. Was that him? No, really. Could that be him?

Shelley was wide in the shoulder, narrow in the hip. Plenty of women had told him he had hair like Superman. Lots more had insisted that his eyes were a lot bluer than Paul Newman's. His skin was absolutely flawless. He had high cheekbones and a strong chin – the kind of bone structure plastic surgeons dream about. Dimples, when he smiled. His teeth were perfect.

If he looked into the mirror and fell in love with what he saw, well, who could blame him?

He slipped into a pair of fairly clean black Levi's that he'd cut the little red patch off, because he didn't think much of the concept of unpaid, involuntary advertising. Nobody rode for free, and a butt snug and tight as his was worth a heavy dollar if it was worth a dime. The Levi's were the 501 model, tight leg and button fly. He rolled aside one of the mirrors, reached in and grabbed a silk shirt in a kind of burnished gold colour that looked terrific with his tan. He put the shirt on, buttoned up and tucked it into the pants. The shirt was a size too large and a little on the baggy side, but it would do. He pushed his feet into a pair of Birkenstocks with anodized buckles and suede straps. The borrowed sandals were a half-size too small, but they were a lot more comfortable than bare feet.

He went into the ensuite bathroom with its black slate floor tiles and black plastic jetted bathtub, more mirrors and rows and rows of lights. It was like being backstage at a ritzy nightclub or theatre, except quite a few of the bulbs had burnt out and not been replaced. Shelley flossed and brushed and rinsed, gargled with a mouthful of blood-red liquid that was a guaranteed plaque- and bacteria-killer, spat into the sink. He pumped mousse into his cupped palm, spread it on good and thick and combed his hair. As he was doing this he idly wondered how guys like him kept their hair looking good before mousses and gels and sprays were invented. Kept it cut real short maybe, or so long you could pony-tail it. He'd learned in school that Indians used bear grease. Slap on the bear grease, ease into the Birkenstocks. Speaking to the mirror he said, "Hey babe, like my scent? That's bear grease, sweet-heart. You looking to get chased up a tree, I'm your man!" He laughed, not so much at his little joke as the opportunity it gave him to scrutinize his smile. Eye still on the mirror, he let un-bridled jollity segue into sincere good humour . . .

He pulled a neatly folded, pale blue beach towel from the tidy stack of towels in the heated storage unit, slung the towel over his shoulder and went back into the bedroom. He charged his Magic Flaming Wallet with lighter fluid, checked to make sure he had a couple of dollars and his driver's licence and the only card he ever needed, which was basically any card at all that had somebody else's name embossed on it. He stuffed the wallet in the back pocket of his jeans, the fit so tight he had to cock his hip to slide it in there, and then randomly snatched a fat paper-back off the bureau.

The Birkenstocks made hardly any noise at all as he trotted down the wide, artfully curved oak stairway that led to the clerestory-type entrance hall dominated by the tasteless but glit-tery crystal chandelier, which also had a lot of bulbs that needed replacing, but still burned brighter than a thousand suns. He grabbed his keyring off the row of ornate brass hooks beside the door, spun the keyring around on his little finger.

Magic wallet. Beach towel. Pulp. His keys. What else did he need? He disciplined himself to think about it *now*, not when he was a couple of blocks away, stuck in traffic. It was a red-hot, blue-sky, happy-go-lucky day in the middle of August. What could go wrong, aside from arrest and incarceration? He made his fist into a gun, turned and aimed at the hall mirror. "You'll never take me alive, copper!" But it was all talk, wasn't it?

The Datsun 300sx was out on the street in front of the house, parked beneath a streetlamp. Shelley knew that nowadays, in this modern world we live in, there is nothing that can be done to stop a talented thief from boosting a vehicle he or she is determined to steal, or a vandal from setting a car on fire or turning it into a urinal out of meanness or stupidity or whatever motive was lying around and looked good at the time. Sitting in the car twenty-four hours a day with a shotgun in your lap was a good start, but still a long way from an ironclad guarantee. But Shelley did what he could, which was park directly in front of the house, under the streetlight. Since he parked not far from the end of the block, a thief or vandal might, hopefully, worry about a cop coming down the cross street and turning the corner, catching him by surprise. Shelley took other measures as well. Despite the nigh-intolerable throb from the airport, he made a habit of sleeping with his window cracked open. Plus he'd installed a high-end Alpine alarm system, and had a steel bar that locked onto the steering wheel and made the sx impossible to drive, except as the crow flies. The car's CD player was in the trunk. Out of sight, out of mind.

In the first few days after he'd moved into the house, he'd met several of his new neighbours and for the most part they were a bunch of nosy, prying bastards who had no compunction about grilling him right there on the sidewalk, smiling sweetly as they quietly but forcefully demanded to know who the hell he was and exactly what he did for a living. The guy who owned the house on the upsloping lot across the lane, directly behind him, was particularly intrusive and obnoxious. Fortunately the guy, a fisherman, was only in town for a few days, while some repairs were being made to his boat's engine. As soon as the work was done, he'd be gone.

Shelley always told his interrogators the truth, even if it wasn't the whole truth. He said he was a house-sitter, didn't do much of anything when he could help it, sometimes worked as a

Skull-Crusher. If that drew a blank, he'd try Dome-Disintegrator
or Tooth-Trasher. Knuckle-Buster was his favourite euphemism,
because of its elegant simplicity. If the neighbour still didn't get
it, Shelley explained that he was a bouncer, worked various
downtown clubs. Adding that he also did private parties, he'd
give them his embossed business card, a rectangle of shiny gold
with his name printed in heavy, boxy black letters and the two *l*'s
in Shelley made out of arms bent at right angles at the elbow,
hands curled into fists. No address. His phone number pencilled
in below his name.

Kerrisdale is an upper-middle-class 'hood – large imported cars
and small imported dogs. It didn't take long for his neighbours to
decide to let him be. In fact the only problem he'd had with anyone
was, predictably, over the sx's parking space. A woman in her early
thirties, youngest daughter of the people next door, not bad
looking but still living at home after all those years, who drove a
green Miata ragtop with genuine leather upholstery, had staked
out the prime spot under the streetlight, and didn't want to give it
up even though Shelley made it clear he felt the spot was his, since
it was located in front of his house. He'd tried to be nice with her
but she wasn't the kind of woman who responded well to soft
talking, or warmth, or what logic he could muster about the sx
being worth ten of her cheap Mazda trash. It was a bad situation.
What they called an untenable situation. Sometimes he'd drive up
and the spot would be vacant and he'd take it. Other times she'd
be just getting out of her car, give him a smirk as she walked away.
He spent a full week glowering and pec-flexing and spitting on
the sidewalk, but to no avail. Thirty years old and still living at
home, but she was a tough cookie. Feeling aggravated and unjust-
ly dealt with, he jogged over three blocks to Dunbar and up the
hill and down the other side and into the Home Hardware, where
he paid cash for the cheapest hatchet they had in stock. It was as if
she'd been reading his mind. That same night he learned from her
mother that the woman had moved out of the house. Taken a job
in Nova Scotia, if that was possible.

And then, a month later, yesterday morning early, she was back. Still driving the Mazda, still parking in his spot. Shelley talked to her just the one time. Starting out polite, moving at his own pace into pissed-off-but-still-reasonable, then downright angry, snarling and spitting. He'd gotten nowhere. She'd laughed in his face! Brain pulsing red, he'd stormed down into the basement for the hatchet, spent most of the afternoon caressing it with a file until it was sharp as sharp could be.

This flash of temper was a sign of what was wrong with him. A clear symptom of an undiagnosed disease. But for now, the important thing was that he had four months left on his lease. Where he stayed next, $600,000 west-side house or tiny, hunch-ceilinged basement hovel, depended, as always, on his references. So it was important that he remember not to spill stuff on the rug, and that he tend the garden and try not to annoy the neighbours. He *knew* all that.

Even so, last night, he'd watched infomercials and cranked out pushups until it was so late it was starting to get early, then slipped into his black jeans and gone outside and driven the blade of the axe right through the driver's side of the Mazda's windshield, and left it there. Walked down the block and stood under a big maple tree, for a different perspective. The axe sticking into the Mazda was kind of weird. Artistic, even. He visualized a massive oil painting of the stricken car, an ornately framed, gigantic painting hanging under soft lights on a corporate wall. *Sports Car with Axe.*

Still chuckling, he'd strolled back into the house, showered and gone straight to bed and slept like a newborn until about eleven, crawled out of the sack, taken another shower and washed his hair, dithered over the Speedo. And now it was past noon and here he was all set for another day at the beach, and nobody'd kicked his door down yet. So maybe he was going to be okay.

But when he opened the door to leave, there they were, like magic, two of them. A skinny young guy and an old fat guy, both wearing pale blue short-sleeved shirts with big VPD flashers, dark blue pants, shiny black shoes that were almost boots, a wide black

leather belt that sagged under the considerable weight of a functioning law officer's bare essentials – MagLite, Mace, handcuffs,
radio, spare ammunition, nightstick, donut pouch, semiauto. The
young cop believed in God, but his pal had a bulletproof vest
under his shirt. Both of them stood there on the porch, trying not
to look surprised.

Shelley gave the coppers a slow up-and-down look. Assessed
them and found them wanting. Finally said, "How long have you
two dopes been standing there? Talk about initiative. Didn't
anybody train you to knock?"

2

All week long, at every opportunity, Annie had been pressuring Willows to pack a lunch and enjoy a lazy Saturday afternoon at the beach. Relaxing in the sun, swimming, reading, tossing a Frisbee around. Stuff like that. Classic picnic stuff. Willows had eventually caved in, but only on condition that Annie do the preliminary work; round up the blankets and towels, shake the dust and spiders out of the wicker picnic basket, and perform without complaint any other minor tasks or chores that were necessary but that he might have overlooked. Friday evening, Willows and Claire Parker and Annie had driven to the local Safeway and bought a mix of cold cuts, a whole roast chicken, the various ingredients needed to put together potato and Greek salads, a loaf of French bread and a six-pack of Diet Coke. Annie had spent the rest of the night in the kitchen, working hard while at the same time watching "X-Files" on the small colour television perched on top of the refrigerator.

Willows' son, Sean, had left the house as soon as he'd finished dinner. He'd spend the next few hours hanging out with his pals at the local 7-Eleven, then head for a party he expected to last most of the night. He'd casually told his father he'd be home very late, if at all, and firmly refused to commit himself to the following day's picnic. No surprise there. Sean's habit was to do his best to avoid commitment of any kind, wherever and whenever he could. Unlit cigarette dangling from the corner of his mouth, the gangly teenager patiently explained to his dullard father that he was a video-games, not a picnic kind of guy.

Willows was an early riser, even on his days off. Saturday morning he was up at seven. By seven-thirty he'd showered and shaved and was out on the sundeck, working on a cup of coffee and the morning paper. An hour later the sun had burned the dew off the lawn and he was sweating lightly as he worked the hand-mower he'd bought at a garage sale a couple of weeks earlier for a paltry twenty-five dollars. A steal!

He paused to wipe the sweat out of his eyes, and heard the telephone, and wondered how long it had been ringing, and why Annie hadn't picked up. Flipping the mower's handle away from him, he started towards the house. The ringing stopped, and a moment later the door banged open, as playful Annie shouted for all the neighbourhood to hear that there was a beautiful young lady on the phone who desperately wanted to speak to him.

Willows went inside, picked up, said hello.

Parker said, "Are you okay, Jack?" She sounded genuinely concerned.

"Yeah, sure." Willows frowned. "Why?"

"You sound a little short of breath – as if you've just run a couple of laps around the block."

Slightly wounded, he said, "I was mowing the lawn."

"Moss," said Parker. "I know what your yard looks like, Jack. You were mowing the moss."

Annie was watching Willows from the kitchen table, a concerned look on her face. Her father had been a cop all his life, and she knew as well as anyone how the job had a way of pushing everything else aside. Willows gave her the thumbs-up sign, trying to reassure her. He said, "Was there something you wanted, Claire, other than to make disparaging remarks about my gardening abilities?"

"The picnic. Is it still on?"

"The ants are counting on us." Willows winked at his daughter. "Annie wants to go to Spanish Banks. There's a particular section of the beach that's very good for swimming. Or looking at boys."

Annie mimed throwing a cereal bowl at him, and Willows feigned panic. He said, "You going to meet us there, or here, or should I pick you up?"

In a low, exaggeratedly sexy voice, Parker said, "Pick me up, Jack," and then giggled like a schoolgirl.

"Eleven-thirty?"

"Eleven-thirty's fine, see you then." She hung up just as Willows was about to tell her not to forget her bathing suit. He wondered if he should call her back – not that he was wild to go swimming. *Jaws* had killed his enthusiasm for any body of water larger than a bathtub. But Parker had recently bought a new swimsuit, a one-piece model cut low in the back and high at the thighs, in a skintight, very silky, *clingy* material that drove him absolutely crazy, knocked his lust-o-meter right off the scale. A glimpse of Claire in her new swimsuit was definitely worth risking a shark attack, being torn to shreds. Belatedly, he heard B.C. Tel's tinny, recorded voice advising him to hang up and please call again. Should he hit the redial button, call Parker back? He glanced up and caught Annie watching him. Smiling, he said, "I must've drifted off, huh?"

Annie nodded. Her eyes were dark, thoughtful. She said, "What were you thinking about?"

"Mowing the lawn," said Willows with a sly grin, and went back outside to finish the job.

He cut moss and grass until the mower's bag was full, and then paused and was engaged in conversation by his elderly neighbour, Eric Watkins, who was eager to discuss a decision recently made by a "pack of idiot politicians" to risk the quality of the city's drinking water by logging an environmentally sensitive area of the North Shore watershed, and to dump huge quantities of chlorine into the water, in case things didn't quite work out the way they should and the reservoirs became contaminated. Eric pointed out that the city should have the best damn water in the world. He firmly believed that politicians were elected primarily for their entertainment value, and Willows tended to agree. How else to explain the vast legions of fools and clowns and outright buffoons who, the moment they were elected, suffered severe brain damage through self-inflicted asphyxiation as a consequence of burying their snouts too deeply in the public trough?

Unburdened, Eric limped off to decapitate a cluster of dandelions. Willows emptied the mower's grass-catcher onto the black plastic compost bin he'd bought at a subsidized rate from the city. Immediately, Eric was back, leaning against the fence that separated their two properties. The compost bin was another thorn in his side. Vancouver was a port city; it already had more than its share of rats. The compost bins were ratproof, but only if they were properly installed on a flat surface. If they weren't on a flat surface, they'd warp. A warped bin was gravy to a rat. Eric had made a point of strolling up and down the lanes and damn near every bin he'd seen was warped. Willows had to admit, didn't he, that his own bin was bent all out of shape? Just look at it! Probably it was stuffed full of nesting rats. Eric shook his head, disgusted. The idiot politicians had gone to considerable expense to ensure that the city's rat population had plenty of comfortable new homes and all the garbage they could eat!

Willows returned the mower and rake to the garage, and went into the house. In the kitchen, standing at the sink in his stockinged feet, he poured himself a tall glass of chlorinated water, and drank it down in one long gulp.

Annie said, "We should leave in about half an hour, daddy." Willows nodded. In a tone of voice that was obviously intended to be tactful, Annie added, "Are you planning to take a shower?"

Willows rinsed the glass and stood it on the drying rack. "I hadn't thought about it. Think I should?"

"Definitely."

Willows walked down the hall and knocked lightly on Sean's door. No answer. He knocked again, waited a moment and then opened the door a crack. Sean's bed was unmade, empty. The air was stale and dry, and smelled of cigarette smoke. But then, it always did. It was impossible to determine if Sean had spent any part of the night at home, but Willows doubted if he had. The boy had never been an early riser. Now that he had a job – working the graveyard shift three nights a week at a local gas station – he finally had a legitimate excuse for sleeping in.

Willows smiled inwardly. Not all that long ago, his son had insisted on getting up at seven o'clock sharp every Saturday morning, so he could watch cartoons on television. Willows and his ex-wife, Sheila, had tried everything they could think of to break him of the habit; sneaked into his bedroom on Friday night after he'd fallen asleep and turned back his clock an hour or so. Once, Willows had gone down to the basement and flipped the breaker switch that fed power to the electrical outlet the television was plugged into. Sean responded to the challenge by patching together a couple of extension cords and plugging the TV into an outlet that still worked.

Willows' smile faded. He shut the bedroom door. Sheila had left him. Sean had long since lost interest in Roadrunner and his pals and was already trying his wings. How much longer would Annie stay? Five or six years at best, maybe less. He tried to imagine being alone in the house, day after day and night after night. It was a gruesome thought. He found himself wondering about Parker. She had never mentioned a desire to have children, but even so . . .

He walked rapidly down the shotgun hall towards the front of the house, checked his watch as he jogged up the wide oak-planked stairway to the second floor. In the bathroom he turned on the shower, adjusted the hot and cold mix until the temperature was to his liking, stripped out of his work clothes and stepped into the tub. Twenty minutes later he was standing in front of the mirror in a loose-fitting mock-Hawaiian shortsleeved shirt, lightweight khaki-coloured cotton shorts and a pair of battered white leather Nikes, no socks. His hair was damp, but it would dry. He strapped on his Timex Ironman. The perfect beach watch, it was waterproof to a depth far beyond his capabilities and had cost him only forty dollars – no great disaster if he lost it.

Downstairs, the front door was open and Annie was impatiently waiting for him on the porch, perched on the old wicker picnic basket that had once belonged to Willows' grandmother. Annie wore a pair of cheap rubber thongs, a pink and white and green vertical-striped T-shirt and baggy, sun-bleached jeans. She looked cute as a button.

Willows said, "You all set?"

"C'mon, let's go. Hurry up, or we're going to be late!"

Willows shut the door and locked it. The deadbolt shot home with a satisfying thud. He tried to take the picnic basket from Annie, but she wouldn't give it up. He slipped his arm around his daughter and gave her a quick hug. Together, they walked down the sidewalk towards his car.

Parker lived in a modest one-bedroom apartment on the top floor of a small three-storey block on West Eleventh Avenue, just off Burrard. She'd taken the apartment eight years before, for no reason other than it was available, priced right, and less than a twenty-minute drive from her desk at the Public Safety Building at 312 Main. Due to increased traffic the commute took half an hour now, sometimes longer. Eight years was far too long for a single girl to live in one place, and Parker knew it. She'd been putting money aside for the past few years, for a down payment on a False Creek condo or even a small house on a small lot, on the East Side of town. Then Jack's wife had left him, and Parker had started dreaming again, hoping that she wouldn't have to spend the rest of her life living alone after all.

She checked her watch. Willows and Annie – and Sean, in the unlikely event that he'd wanted to come – were due in about five minutes. She went into the bathroom, snapped on the overhead light and ran a quick brush through her jetblack hair, touched up her lipstick. She wore a loose blouse and a colourful lightweight cotton peasant skirt over her bathing suit, basketweave Mexican sandals. She turned her back to the mirror, glanced over her shoulder and, not minding what she saw, smoothed the skirt over her hips.

It'd be kind of a kick, stripping in front of Jack on the beach. If she waited until Annie had gone for a swim, she could have a some fun with him, maybe drive him a little bit crazy . . .

The buzzer sounded. Annie's happy-go-lucky signature tune – *shave & a haircut, two bits*. Parker smiled. If there was one thing you could say about Jack, it was that his daughter was punctual.

3

The cops had rectangles of black plastic pinned to their shirts, their last names chiselled out in white. The fat cop's name was Mungari. His partner was Dent. Mungari tilted his head so his RayBans slid down his nose. He jerked his thumb. "We got a call from the young lady next door . . ."

The porch was hot, a sun-trap. But Shelley, blocking the doorway, was nice and cool in the shade. He said, "You guys care for a Coke or a nice cold beer? Fresh orange juice with maybe just a splash of ice-cold vodka?"

No way. Their tongues were hanging out but they were all business. Dent was impatient. He said, "Do you know the young lady next door, owns the green Miata down there?"

"The one parked directly under the streetlight, in front of my house, has got an axe sticking out of the windshield?"

Mungari said, "Yeah, that one."

Shelley said, "I know her. I mean, I know who she is. Nancy? I see her in the yard or on the sidewalk, I usually say hello."

He gave the cops a wide-eyed, innocent look. "But that's it, that's as far as it goes. I don't care what she told you, I'm not humping her and I never did, except maybe in her dreams." He raised his voice a little. "And that goes double for her mother."

He started to shut the door.

Mungari said, "Hold on a minute." He reached out, put his hand against the door.

"And I deny chopping up her car in a lover's rage, or anything along those lines. So if that's what she told you, she lied."

"Hold on a minute," said Mungari again. "We're investigating a crime. Nobody accused you of nothin'."

"Not out loud," said Shelley. "Not in so many words."

Mungari pushed his glasses back up his nose, as far as they would go. The two cops looked at him as if he was something laid out on a plywood table with folding legs, to pick over at a garage sale or flea market. Dent had a narrow, funnel-shaped face. His ears were set too close to his head. He'd left his hat in the car. His close-cropped hair was such a pale shade of brown that it was almost as if he were bald. He asked Shelley if he worked out. Shelley said no, he didn't work at all. Never had and never would. Mungari asked him if he was on holiday, or taking the day off sick.

Enjoying himself, and letting it show, Shelley said he kind of lived off the land. Got by. He mentioned how hot it was and re-peated his offer of a drink. Dent said no but Mungari seemed to be thinking it over. The cop turned on his heel so his broad back was to Shelley, stood quietly for a moment, and then turned around again and cannily asked him how he knew about the axe in the car, since it couldn't be seen from the porch. Shelley swal-lowed hard, a real big gulp that was audible to one and all.

"Maybe you better come inside."

Mungari nodded solemnly. He and Dent exchanged a furtive look.

Shelley led them into the living room, told them to sit down and make themselves comfortable. He said he was going to go into the kitchen and get himself a beer and he'd be right back. Smiling, he advised them not to steal anything.

Mungari said, "Maybe a beer would be a good idea after all. A Heinie, if you got it. Or anything imported would be fine." He gave Dent a look. "Hey, Barry. A beer ain't gonna hurt."

Dent nodded glumly.

Mungari held up two fingers. He had the hands of a piano player. "Two beers," he said to Shelley.

Shelley went into the kitchen. All he had was a six-pack of Bud Lite, but it was more than they deserved. He went back into the living room carrying a beer in each hand. As he offered the cans to the two cops he popped the tabs simultaneously, with his index fingers. It was a cute little trick, but nobody seemed to notice.

Mungari said, "How come you aren't drinking?"

"No particular reason. Maybe because I'm not working?"

"Could I have a glass?" said Dent.

Whistling cheerfully, Shelley trotted back into the kitchen and fetched a couple of glasses, which the cops poured full. The wall opposite the fireplace was covered in framed photographs. Thirty years of family history. Dent pointed at a black and white of a kid pretending to paddle a canoe tied to a small dock, he asked Shelley if that was him, when he was little.

Shelley said, "I don't know who the hell it is."

"You don't?"

"That's right. And I don't know who anybody else is either. You could ask me questions about those pictures all day long, and I wouldn't be able to answer a single one of them."

Dent and Mungari exchanged a look. Shelley could see they were pretty pleased with themselves, that they thought they were on to something.

Mungari put his empty can and the full glass of beer carefully down on a mahogany coffee table. He took out his notebook. "What's your name?"

"Don't do that."

"Do what?" said Dent, his mouth tight.

"Take your glass off that table," Shelley told Mungari. Firm, not angry. He said, "I just waxed it. You're gonna leave a mark. Here, let me get you a coaster."

Shelley got a couple of coasters from a drawer in the sideboard. He laid them down on the mahogany table for Mungari.

Mungari placed his glass on one coaster and the can on another. His face had gone empty.

Shelley said, "Thanks, I appreciate that." He smiled. "You got to be careful with furniture like this. It didn't come out of a box from Ikea, know what I mean?"

"Could we have your name, please?" said Mungari. His voice was a little tight. He was staring hard at Shelley's throat.

"Shelley Byron Cooper."

Mungari didn't flinch or smile. He wrote the name down very seriously in a spiral-bound cop notebook, as if the act of writing would make it true. "You live here, do you, Shelley?"

"Yeah, sure."

Mungari waggled his Bic. "This's your house?"

"For the time being."

Dent said, "What's that supposed to mean? You own it?"

"No, I don't. But it was me who paid for the beer, if that's of any concern to either of you."

The cops simultaneously asked who did own the house, if it wasn't him.

Shelley scratched his head and did his best to look confused, goofin', as if he didn't know which of them to answer. Finally he said, "I guess the easiest way for you to find out would be to drive over to city hall and look it up."

Mungari made a chopping motion. He said, "Barry, would you mind . . ."

"Be right back," said Dent.

Shelley heard the cop's heavy-soled shoes go down the porch steps and thump back up again. Dent hadn't shut the door behind him when he went out and he didn't shut it when he came back in again. He carried a wrinkled brown paper bag. At a nod from Mungari he reached into the bag and pulled out a much smaller plastic bag – an evidence bag – that contained the Home Hardware hatchet.

Mungari said, "You recognize that?"

"What is this, some kind of trick question? It's a hatchet."

"Yeah, right, it's a hatchet. Or axe. I should've put it more plainly. What I meant was, do you recognize this particular axe? Have you ever seen it before?"

"No, I don't think so." Shelley brightened. "But the bag's from Safeway, if that's any help."

"Any idea who the axe might belong to, Shelley?"

"I don't know, I'm not too sure." Shelley scratched his neck along the line of his jaw, checked his fake Rolex.

Dent said, "Why don't you go ahead and hazard a wild guess, see if you get lucky?"

Shelley took a deep breath. "Abe Lincoln? Lizzie Borden? Jack Nicholson?" Dent's fingers tightened on the axe handle. Shelley smiled at him. He'd had enough of being interrogated. Could they prove anything? No way.

"There's a hardware store on Dunbar just up from Forty-First Avenue," said Mungari. "If we went over there and asked the guy behind the counter if he sold an axe recently to a musclebound dimwit, somebody looked approximately just like you, would he say yes or would he say no?"

"Why don't you ask him?"

"There's another hardware store on Dunbar just below Seventeenth," said Mungari, "and a lumber yard on Sixteenth, or we could drop by the Early Bird over there on Arbutus."

Shelley nodded. "Yeah, you could do that. Or you could talk to the complainant's pimp boyfriend, the guy's always hanging around, cupping his crotch and sneering at passing schoolgirls. They're fighting all the time, always fighting. What a temper he's got. Latinos!"

Neither cop had tasted his beer. The full glasses sat there on the coffee table as Mungari told Shelley that they'd be checking out the hardware stores in the neighbourhood and if there was any more trouble they'd be back, count on it.

Shelley told Mungari and Dent to beat it. He told them to shake their fat, donut-fed asses right out the door. Dent's face clouded over. For a moment or two, Shelley believed Dent was going to take a swing at him – Dent probably believed it too. But then, finally, the moment passed.

Shelley stood on the porch with his hands on his hips. He watched the cops cut across his lawn, hold tight to the gear on their belts as they jumped down from the granite retaining wall that separated the two yards, trample some low-slung purple flowers, trot up his neighbour's front steps and enter the house. They were inside no more than five minutes and came out looking overheated and not very happy. Dent glanced over his shoulder at Shelley as he and Mungari strode down Miss Miata's sidewalk towards their white-with-seablue-and-mountain-green-trim patrol car. Shelley waved. Dent said something to Mungari, who shrugged him off. The cops got into the car and drove slowly away.

What had Miss Miata expected, trampling on his toes the way she did? Even so, Shelley had made a mistake and he knew it. He liked living in large expensive houses, had worked hard to gain his reputation as a dependable fellow. Throwing it all away on a parking space was not smart. Why had he acted in such a rash and foolish manner?

The porch was bathed in sunlight. Birds flirted in the trees. A silver-coloured squirrel bounced across the grass. The white resin lawn furniture gleamed like a set of brand-new teeth. From this distance the bees were too small to see or hear, but no doubt they were down there, busy busy busy. It was an idyllic scene, marred only by the burly gang of gardeners a couple of houses down, who were defoliating a neighbour's yard at an amazing clip. Not that Shelley had anything against gardeners, or any other visible or invisible minority. It was the unbelievable racket their gas-powered machinery made, that he objected to; the lawnmower's blue thunder, the clacking of the chainsaw-like hedge clipper, the high-pitched whine of portable leafblowers. That was the trouble with expensive neighbourhoods. They were so *noisy*.

Shelley locked the front door. The Birkenstocks made hearty slapping sounds as he walked down into the garden. He slumped onto a lawn chair in the shade of a birch tree, and considered his

irrational, self-destructive behaviour. What demons had motivat-
ed him to act the way he did? It wasn't an easy question, and he
was not by nature an introspective person. The birds and machinery distracted him. His mind wandered. But was it possible that
he was getting tired of short-term leases, vicariously living the
lives of others in their absence? Spinning his wheels. Was he
getting old? Was it time for him to get a life of his own? It made
his head ache just thinking about it.

He decided to let his subconscious deal with it, down at the
beach.

Crossing the boulevard he pointed the remote at the 300sx, dis-
engaged the alarm system, and unlocked the doors. He got into
the car, unclamped The Club from the steering wheel. The soft,
cream-coloured leather upholstery was pleasantly warm. He
started the engine, got the air-conditioner going, tossed his towel
and the selected-at-random paperback on the passenger seat. The
book was a real fatty. Michener. The guy sure could type.

Shelley turned on the CD player. Bon Jovi. Good enough. He
shifted into first gear, checked his mirrors. He gave it a little gas,
eased out the clutch, drove sedately down to Forty-First, made a
right and drove north on Dunbar all the way to Fourth Avenue,
headed more or less due west for a mile or so, until he hit the loop
that led to Spanish Banks. By the time he caught sight of the beach
it was quarter to one by the dashboard clock; late enough so the
parking lots were crowded and there were lineups at the concession stands, people in shorts and Ts or swimsuits lined up for
greasy fish and chips, outsized hotdogs, soft drinks. Shelley
counted his calories like a miser counted the change in his pocket.
He wouldn't eat a hotdog if his life depended on it. What people
did to their bodies.

Shelley motored along in the sx at a steady thirty kilometres
per hour until he reached the westernmost parking lot, then
turned and cruised back again, until he was at that part of the beach
where the crowds were thickest. He pulled into the parking lot.

A red Mustang convertible was idling in a slot under a tree.

There were five kids in the car, all of them in their late teens, all of them wearing straw cowboy hats and identical mirror sunglasses, black cowboy-type shirts with shiny white buttons. The kids were just sitting there, not talking or even looking at each other. As if they didn't know each other at all, and it was sheer coincidence that had dumped them in the car. Shelley pulled up close. He stared hard at the driver. The kid fiddled with his radio, lit a cigarette and tossed the match out the window. The trio in the backseat lit up. The kid in the shotgun seat took off his hat. His blonde hair was slicked straight back. *He* lit up, blew smoke out his nose.

Shelley tapped the horn. They paid him no mind. Or, if you happened to be in a sour and unforgiving mood, you could say they ignored him. Shelley didn't appreciate being ignored, because it didn't suit his image of himself as a person who took up a whole lot of space, in all kinds of ways. He climbed out of the sx and walked up to the Mustang and leaned a muscular forearm on the strip of shiny chromed metal that ran along the curving sweep of the windshield.

All five cowpokes had noticed him by now. Yup, there he was, reflected in all ten lenses. He scratched his nose. Not because he itched, but for the simple pleasure of watching himself do it. Ten identical, perfectly synchronized hands. Ten identical noses. It was like being inside one of those discount appliance joints, with the wall of televisions all tuned to the same channel. He scratched himself some more, in slo-mo, and then smiled ten smiles, and said, "Any of you boys happen to know the definition of a cowboy?" He let it hang for a moment and then said, "A bovine flotation device."

The kid behind the wheel sucked his teeth.

Shelley said, "Nobody gets it? Okay, here's an easy one. There was a couple of cowboys riding down the side of the road, some cattle strung out in front of them. This guy driving by, he's a tourist, slows down to a crawl, takes some pictures, leans out the window. He's got a puzzled look on his face. Wants to know why the wranglers are all wearing baseball caps. What'd they tell him?"

No takers. Shelley said, "That they didn't want to be mistaken for truckers."

The kid behind the wheel sucked his teeth again. He said, "Is there something we can do for you?"

"Something *you* can do for me," said Shelley, singling him out, making him stand alone. "Move your car."

The bunch of them stared at him.

Shelley glanced around. Nobody was paying them any attention. He reached out very slowly, so as not to alarm the kid, and flicked the nearest lens with his fingernail.

"Glass, huh."

The kid nodded.

"Plastic's better. Somebody punches you in the face, you got a better chance of not losing an eye."

The kid in the shotgun seat sat up a little straighter. "Why would somebody punch him in the face?"

He'd seemed genuinely interested rather than concerned or frightened. Shelley smiled. "For not giving up his parking spot. See, I like to park in the shade, protect the paint and leather."

The driver said, "We're in your way? You want us to leave?"

"That's right, asshole."

"What'd you call me?"

"An asshole. You're *all* assholes. All five of you. See, this's how it works: whoever weighs the most is the biggest asshole, and so on down to the tiniest."

The driver glanced around. Empty blue sky and green trees and yellow, sun-bleached grass and sparkly ocean panned across his glasses. Whatever he was looking for, he apparently couldn't find it. He revved the Mustang's engine. "People like you oughtta be locked up."

"And throw away the key," said Shelley helpfully. He reached out with both hands and bounced his fingertips off the mirrored sunglasses, quick as Michener knocking off another epic. His nails, tap-dancing across the glass, made tiny scratching sounds.

The Mustang's tires squealed as the car shot out of the parking slot. The kid braked about twenty feet away, gave Shelley the finger. Shelley walked back to the sx. The Mustang's backup lights flashed white, and then the kid reversed hard, leaving two fat black stripes on the asphalt as he shot back into his slot.

Shelley climbed slowly out of the sx. The Mustang was a '67, prime, in showroom condition, rebuilt from the ground up. What he needed was blood, lots of it. If he reached across the driver, he could pin him against the seat with the weight of his body, while he decked the kid in the shotgun seat, broke his nose. The blood all over his brand-new upholstery would make the driver go nuts. He'd be wide open, and Shelley'd bust his nose too, one-punch him, bring his fist down like a hammer. Pow! Quarts of blood.

Then what? He'd have to find himself another beach, wouldn't he? Yeah, but it was worth it. Shelley moved in on the Mustang, adjusted his stride so he'd be leading with his left leg when he got in range and could, as he struck his first blow, put a little rotation into his body.

Or maybe he was acting irrationally again. Who was he kidding, with all this cast-iron chatter? Maybe he should just tuck his tail between his legs and vamoose . . .

As it happened, the kid in the backseat had his own agenda. The light under the tree was kind of tricky, but Shelley had the impression of a shiny black gun. He faltered, froze in mid-stride. The kid was all smiles as he swung the muzzle around, pointed it right at him.

Shelley wondered aloud where those dimwit donut-gobbling cops were, now that he needed them.

4

"Sorry we're late!"

"You're a few minutes early by my watch," said Parker. She gave Annie a hug and scooped up the big tartan bag that contained a couple of bottles of ice-cold Perrier, her wallet, sunscreen, makeup, paperback novel, off-duty gun, and the various other odds and ends required for a cop's day at the beach.

"Want some help?"

"No, I'm fine, thanks." Parker glanced quickly around the apartment. Nothing was on fire. She and Annie went out into the corridor. She shut the door and locked it, dropped her keyring into the bag and gave the bag a brisk shake, to encourage the keys to migrate to the bottom, where they couldn't be easily lost.

Annie said, "You look terrific."

"So do you, sweetheart."

"No, really. I mean, you look absolutely *amazingly* extra-terrific."

Parker double-checked the door. "Got a birthday coming up, do you?"

"I'm serious, Claire. You look really beautiful. Just watch dad's face when we come out the door. He's going to be absolutely knocked out."

Parker couldn't help smiling. Annie was thirteen years old, completely lacking in guile, and very pretty in her own right.

Parker was extremely fond of her, and Annie made it clear she felt the same way about Parker. But Detective Jack Willows wasn't a particularly demonstrative guy. At crime scenes, victim or witness interviews, or interrogations, you never had the foggiest idea what he was thinking unless he decided it was to his advantage to let you know. But there were times, when he and Parker were alone, that he could be so clear about his emotions and needs that there simply wasn't any room for error. And during those wonderful times Willows demanded the same from Parker. But that was one secret she doubted she'd ever share with Annie.

They took the stairs rather than the elevator down to the main floor. It was too nice a day for elevators, being boxed in. When they reached the lobby, Annie rushed ahead to push open the glass door. Willows had made a U-turn and parked directly in front of the apartment. He waved cheerfully at Parker as she and Annie came out of the building, and kept his eyes on her as he reached across to open the passenger-side door. He was still staring at her as she got into the car. Parker stuck her tongue out at him and twisted in her seat to pass her bag back to Annie, who'd climbed into the backseat. She buckled up, and was about to say something caustic to Willows about his uncharacteristically gaudy shirt when he leaned into her and kissed her lightly on the mouth. Parker was taken completely by surprise. Flustered, but making no attempt to disguise her pleasure, she said, "That was nice. What did I do to deserve it?" She frowned. "Wait a minute, that doesn't sound right. The feminists are going to be all over me."

Willows said, "One kiss, and you want an explanation? Tell me, Claire, are you familiar with the word *irresistible*?"

"Increasingly so," said Parker.

Willows glanced into the rearview mirror. Annie smiled angelically up at him, gave him a quick, vaguely conspiratorial wink.

Willows made a right on Burrard and drove two blocks, signalled a left turn onto Broadway and then changed his mind and kept on straight through the intersection. He hadn't been thinking. Was it Parker's perfume, or was he getting old? Whenever possible for the last four years, he'd avoided the 2100 block on Broadway, ever since an armoured-car robbery had gone all wrong in the supermarket parking lot. Two men had died. The gas station across the street had gone up in smoke. He still remembered the crime scene as vividly as if the holdup was going down right that minute; the crunch of snow underfoot as he and Parker had tracked the killer across the parking lot, found him crouched down low in a parked Volvo, his eyes big as the muzzle of the pump shotgun he clutched in his dirty little hands. The kid was wound so tight he couldn't move, but Willows had nearly shot him anyway, simply because he had it coming. It was the Volvo's owner who'd saved the kid's useless ass . . .

Parker said, "Jack?"

Willows was strangling the steering wheel. He made a conscious effort to relax, leaned back against the seat and started breathing again.

Parker said, "We better get into the other lane, Jack."

Willows nodded, made the lane change and then a quick left-hand turn onto Fourth Avenue, catching the light just as it changed from amber to red. Back in the sixties the street had been wall-to-wall pipe-and-leather shops and second-hand stores, low-level dope-dealers and vacant lots. Almost all the original buildings had been torn down and rebuilt. Now the street was all glass and steel; high-end clothing stores and coffee bars and ethnic restaurants . . .

Willows was wearing RayBans, but even so, he tilted his visor and swung it around against the sun beating down on him. Pedestrian and vehicular traffic was always thick on Fourth; a slow procession of cars and mountain bikes and motorcycles and trucks dancing spasmodically to the rhythm of out-of-sync traffic lights and death-defying jaywalkers.

As they continued north, the character of the street changed again, the trendy restaurants and boutiques replaced by a few older tenants. They crawled past the Comic Shop, and the dusty, larger-than-life poster of Spiderman that crowded the window, and then the big stainless-steel knife and spoon that flanked the doorway of Sophie's Cosmic Café. The restaurant was a favourite of Annie's, partly because of the food and good service but mostly because of the oddball sculptures glued to the walls. Directly across the street was the Speedy Muffler franchise where Willows had once taken his car for a new set of brakes only to discover that all he needed was a minor adjustment – no charge.

There was a Safeway a couple of blocks down the street. Parker said, "Annie, did you bring something to drink?"

"Six Cokes and two litres of lemonade."

Parker laughed. "That should do it."

"If we run out, there's always the concession stands."

Parker said, "We'll be fine, Annie." She reached behind her and patted Annie's blue-jeaned knee. "How's the new job?"

"Okay, I guess. I wish they'd give me more hours." Annie had applied for part- or full-time work all over the city's west side, and had been rewarded for her considerable efforts with a part-time job at a local pet-grooming business. She wore protective clothing on the job, but Willows still wasn't very happy about the nature of her work. Voluntary exposure to industrial-strength pesticides at minimum wage wasn't his idea of a wonderful summer holiday. But he'd made a few phone calls and satisfied himself that the business's safety standards were adequate and that as long as Annie wore her equipment she wasn't at risk. Of course, he still had Sean to worry about. Sean had landed his high-risk, low-wage job in early June, cleverly beating the stampede for menial summer work by quitting school three weeks before graduation.

At Alma, they had to stop for the light. There was a liquor store across the street that had a device capable of chilling a six-pack to drinkable levels in about five minutes. Willows toyed with the idea of suggesting a quick detour, reluctantly decided against it. Drinking in public was illegal, no matter how warm the weather or cold the beer. Besides, Annie would spend the rest of the day hurling insults at him and silently wondering if he was an alco-holic. Claire might arrest him. Best to stick with lemonade.

Willows cruised past the neatly tended grounds and trim, Lego-like brick houses of the soon-to-be-abandoned Jericho Armed Forces Base, and then, a little further down, the tall boxwood hedge that hid the Justice Institute's mock crashed airplane, and the complex of modest, white-painted buildings where he'd done his basic training. Less than a minute later he turned off Fourth and drove down towards the water, past the big old barracks that had been turned into a youth hostel.

A few minutes later he was driving parallel to the beach, cruising, taking it nice and slow. There was angle parking on the road and every so often a parking lot had been cut out of the wide strip of flat, grassy ground between the road and the beach. But the street was full and so were the lots. Willows drove west along the beach to the last of the parking lots. He turned in, searching in vain for an empty slot.

A red Ford Mustang convertible idled in the shade cast by the spreading branches of a beech tree. Willows slowed to a crawl. There were five men in the car, all of them in their late teens, wearing identical straw cowboy hats and big mirrored sunglasses. They were arguing about something, all of them talking at once, too loudly. Without warning, the driver made an angry, abrupt gesture of dismissal, and put the Mustang in gear and burned rubber out of the slot. Willows jabbed at the brakes, bringing his drab four-door sedan to a quick stop. The contents of the picnic basket clattered dangerously as the basket skidded across the seat. Annie swore, and promptly apologized. The Mustang's driver belatedly saw he'd almost caused an accident, and gave Willows the finger. There was a hoot of laughter, and in an instant all five men were giving him the finger. Five hats. Five pairs of sunglasses. Five fingers. Willows backed into the newly vacated parking space. He turned off the engine.

In the backseat, Annie said, "Nothing broke," in tones that indicated she couldn't understand why.

Willows unfastened his seatbelt, rolled up his window. He and

Parker and Annie climbed out of the car. Annie shut her door and checked to make sure it was locked. A cop's daughter. Willows looked across the parking lot and wide expanse of yellowed grass, towards the beach. A glossy black Datsun 300sx rolled slowly past, stereo throbbing. The side window came partway down. The driver stared morosely at Willows.

Willows, true to his nature, stared right back. The driver averted his gaze. The shiny black car accelerated, and was gone.

Annie said, "A Bon Jovi fan. Do you know him, daddy?"

Willows shrugged. "Hard to see through the glass. But no, I don't think so."

"Expensive car," said Parker.

Willows nodded. The 300sx was, indeed, a very expensive car.

"Expensive haircut, too," said Parker. "Maybe he's a male model. I'm pretty sure I've seen him somewhere. Not downtown. Maybe in an Eaton's catalogue . . ."

"The swimsuit issue," guessed Willows.

"Probably," admitted Parker, with a mischievous smile.

Annie said, "Hey, this's supposed to be a day at the beach, not a day at the parking lot. Let's go stake out some sand. I want to get in some swimming while the tide's still up."

Willows relieved her of the picnic basket. "Race you?"

Annie said, "You're on!" and started running. Willows shifted the picnic basket to his left hand, reached out and clasped Parker's hand with his right. He felt the heat of the sun on her flesh. She'd put on a wide-brimmed yellow straw hat, and the light filtering through the loose weave freckled her uptilted face.

Willows said, "You look like you just stepped out of a Norman Rockwell painting."

"What's that supposed to mean – cute but elderly?"

"No, I didn't mean that at all." Willows looked down at her, stared into her eyes. His voice had gone a little husky. He smiled.

Parker laughed. "Race you to the beach," she said, mimicking the tone of voice he'd used with Annie. Then she squeezed his

hand and pulled him close, leaned into him and kissed him lightly
on the mouth.

Behind them, about two hundred feet away, Shelley's sx crept
quietly into the parking lot. Shelley was keeping a low profile, for
now. He'd turned his good buddy Bon Jovi down to a muted
whisper. The cowboys had split, and the suburbanite had waltzed
in out of nowhere and grabbed his spot. Was that fair? Shelley
didn't think so. His sunny day had gone all cloudy and grey. He
was pissed, and likely to stay pissed until he'd power-flushed the
bilious cocktail of adrenalin and venom out of his veins. How to
do that without putting himself at risk was something he'd need
to think about.

5

When the black pistol had come up Shelley's thoughts had immediately turned to his bladder. Then he saw that what he'd believed was a gun was a cellular telephone. A Motorola, by the look of it. The cowpoke turned it in his hand so Shelley could see all the buttons, lit up pale green in the shadows. Cowpoke bit his lower lip as he stabbed at 9 and then 1 with his nicotine-stained finger. The Motorola made a remarkably pleasant sound, what you might expect to hear if an angel burped.

Cowpoke gave Shelley a big, fat, smirky, chickenshit smile. His finger hovered.

Shelley had spun on his heel and walked rapidly back to the sx, climbed in and slammed the door shut and cranked the air-conditioner down to sub-zero, punched up the stereo to drown the sound of all that nasty laughter. The music howled out of the speakers, so loud it made the 300sx vibrate like a tuning fork. People a hundred feet and more away swivelled towards him, their faces awash with gratification as they tried to identify the source of all that wonderful music. Shelley had powered out of there. A quarter-mile down the road he could still hear a kind of squealing noise, which he assumed was the cowboy quintet laughing at him. Until finally he realized he'd forgotten to disengage his emergency brake.

The clash with the Mustang full of cellular-ites had put him in a real foul mood, a *bona fide*, gold-plated tooth-grinder. He had driven down the road a mile or so, Bon Jovi swirling in his wake. His chrome-plated crowbar, the ideal precision instrument for trashing sheet metal and splintering glass, lay on the carpeted floor behind him. He'd turn around, wait until the cowpokes went for a stroll, and then turn their irreplaceable classic '67 Mustang into an untidy pile of scrap iron.

So now there he was, ready to rumble, and guess what happens next? The cowboys ride their Mustang into the sunset, and Mr. Happy snatches his parking spot. Unbelievable. Shelley glided past. One quick look and he was sure that the Happy family had just driven in from the suburbs, left the spaniel whining in the yard. He made himself a bet that Mr. Happy had mowed his lawn first thing that morning. That'd be the real deal Mrs. Happy made with her hubby. Mow the lawn or kiss the beach goodbye.

Mrs. Happy was fairly decent, he had to admit. In her thirties but still kind of chirpy-looking. Shelley told himself he wouldn't mind mowing *her* lawn first thing every Saturday morning. He waited until the Happy Family hit the beach, and then drove back and pulled the sx to a stop in front of their boring, chocolate-brown Chevrolet sedan.

It was a car from the suburbs if ever there was a car from the suburbs. A plain-brown-wrapper kind of vehicle. Shelley noted the blackwall tires. Way cool. He knew for a true fact that many people left their wallets and other valuables in the trunks of their cars when they hit the beach. Mr. Happy looked the cautious suburban type. Harmless enough, with his short hair and long shorts, trendy white no-sock sneakers.

Shelley eased out of the sx. He glanced around with a practised minimum of furtiveness, strolled casually over to the Chevy, crouched and unscrewed the little black plastic cap from the car's right rear tire. He used his thumbnail to depress the steel nipple. It took a long time, two or three minutes, for the tire to deflate. A switchblade knife or a bullet would've been quicker, but Shelley wasn't into deadly weapons. The tools of his trade – in rapidly decreasing order of importance – were unvarnished charm, sculptured good looks, moderately quick wits. Chuckles and muscles. But nobody but nobody could charm the air out of a fucking tire.

When the snake had run out of hiss, Shelley screwed the black plastic cap back on the nipple. He stood up, took another look around. Satisfied that his little caper had gone down unobserved, he climbed back in the sx, drove to the far end of the lot, and parked in the handicapped zone. There was a black nylon gym bag in the sx's trunk. He slipped his chrome-plated crowbar into the bag and walked back to the Chevy.

The tire was still flat. He tossed the gym bag on the grass, wedged the crowbar beneath the lip of the trunk directly below the lock and pushed down hard. Flakes of brown paint jumped at him. Metal buckled. He pushed harder, gave it everything he had. The crowbar skidded away from him. He sucked a knuckle, tasted fresh blood. His perfect body had been breached. He minutely examined his wound. A couple of kids on bicycles wheeled past. No helmets, no hands. No brains either, if they did a header. Shelley waited until they were gone and then went back to work.

The trunk popped wide open. The first item that caught his eye was a matt-black pump-action Remington shotgun. A box of shotgun shells lay nestled in the concave rim of the spare tire. There was a roadside emergency kit; a reflector and flares. A black metal flashlight that must've been eighteen inches long, plus the usual stuff – a steel jack for changing flats, the spare tire. He tugged at the shotgun, but it was padlocked into a clamp bolted directly to the car's body. There was nothing else of value in the trunk – no purse or wallet or expensive watch. He straightened, glanced around. An old dude in a floppy canvas hat, sharply pressed cotton pants, and a tie-dyed T-shirt was watching him in a kind of politely disinterested way, as his pooch watered a small beech tree. The guy had a portable metal detector slung over his shoulder. The dog emptied its bladder and vigorously sniffed the tree. What was the mutt thinking? I piss, therefore I am. Shelley shoved the

box of shotgun shells aside, grabbed the spare tire and hoisted it
out of the trunk and leaned it against the car. The geezer was still
watching him. Shelley made eye contact. The guy turned and
limped rapidly towards the beach, his dog trailing along behind.

Shelley stuffed the shotgun shells and roadside safety kit and
big, mean-looking black flashlight into the bag. Mr. Happy must
be a hunter or gun nut or, like the guy who owned the house he
was taking care of, a leftover survivalist. He tossed the Chevy's
jack handle into the gym bag so Mr. Happy wouldn't have anything handy to beat his wife and kid with, when he found out he'd
been robbed.

He grabbed the gym bag and pushed down the trunk lid. As he
did this, he noticed the stubby radio antenna clamped to the
trunk.

Shelley mulled over this new discovery. Brown Chevrolet.
Blackwall tires. Four doors. No hubcaps. Short-wave antenna.
Shotgun in the trunk. Put it all together, could it spell law en-
forcement? Shelley's heart went bumpety-bump. Lots of civilians
owned CB radios, right? He crouched and peeked inside the car
and saw nothing unusual. Even so, he stripped off his T-shirt and
wiped down the Remington and everything else he might have
left his fingerprints on, then hotfooted it back to the sx with as
much speed as common sense allowed.

He'd planned to spend a pleasant day at Spanish Banks, stealing wallets and watches, but now he couldn't. Now he had to leave.
Flee the crime scene.

The city was littered with beaches. There was a nude co-ed
beach where you could buy cold beer and smoke dope, check out
naked Mounties doing that sneaky undercover thing. A beach for
guys who preferred the company of guys. Beaches for families with
kids. There was even a beach, English Bay, that was used by all
kinds of people but that was a particular favourite of old men with
dark, leathery skin, who'd been soaking up the rays since before
the ozone scare, and would never stop no matter what. Was there

a lesbian beach? He conjured up a stretch of sand crowded with grim-looking women with military haircuts who wore cheap no-name sneakers, baggy pants and black leather jackets . . .

The sx, which was a lease vehicle, was costing him, when you toted up the astronomical insurance fees and at least two tanks of premium gasoline per week, almost a thousand dollars every thirty days. Even though his gasoline bills were usually paid for with somebody else's credit card, the net bite was close to ten grand a year. On top of the car, he had to cover the hydro bills for the house, food, toothpaste and razorblades, soap, get his hair cut every two weeks at thirty dollars a pop . . .

Shelley had looked at the old geezer with the metal detector and the dog, and it had been like looking into the mirror of the future. Movies and television had lied to him. Being a freelance thief was not the life of glamour and ease that it was cut out to be. If he was reincarnated, he wanted to be a diesel mechanic or a computer repairman or, best of all, some kind of artist. A famous painter . . .

Determined to keep his down time to a minimum, Shelley drove over to Kitsilano beach. The beach was a dogleg shape, facing west and north. His favourite part, from a purely recreational point of view, was on the north-facing side. The crowds were thinner. At night there was a spectacular picture-postcard view of the West End highrises across the water, dozens of buildings crammed in next to each other and lit up like chandeliers, stuffed with tens of thousands of invisible, anonymous drones.

The problem was that Shelley could hang out at that end of the beach all day long, and never get a chance to steal, because the people who frequented the area went down there to make out or smoke dope. Swimming was too risky, because of the heavy marine traffic and an ebb tide that swept all kinds of junk, even bullet-riddled human bodies, out of False Creek.

So, Shelley would work the long part of the leg, the beach's west-facing side. He bought fifty cents worth of parking tickets from the dispenser in the lot next to the tennis courts, grabbed his towel and sunglasses and the fat Michener paperback with the back cover that was starting to fall off, and struck out for what he hoped would be a reasonably profitable afternoon of stealing what he liked to think of as the 3 W's.

Wallets. Watches. Whatever.

As he walked towards the beach there was an open, grassy area on his left, populated by the usual mix of cute, Frisbee-chasing dogs with red bandannas tied around their necks, hackey-sackers and hundreds of sizzlers in the prone position, all of them turned towards the sun as if it were a magnetic force that controlled them utterly. A little farther along the beach, the big outdoor swimming pool was jammed to capacity and frothed under the windmill assault of almost two thousand swimmers. Nobody had ever drowned in that sparkling cauldron of chlorine and urine, but how the lifeguards kept track of everybody who wasn't a good-looking female, Shelley couldn't imagine. Dead ahead of him there was another, much-smaller grassy area, which was unoccupied except for a trio of beefy-type guys who didn't seem to be doing much of anything, other than watering the lawn with their sweat. Parks Board employees, perhaps. He kept walking until he reached the wide concrete strip that ran parallel to the beach for half a mile or so that was a favourite haunt of lawbreaking skate-boarders and cyclists. A woman smiled demurely at him, and was ignored. On Shelley's right was the pale blue-painted cinderblock lifeguard HQ, changing rooms, a take-out fish 'n' chips joint, and then lots more grass and an asphalt basketball court, a bunch of chunky guys firing the ball around, playing bumper cars with their bodies. Shelley had been told most of them were pimps or drug-dealers, but he thought this was probably bullshit, like his idea of a dyke beach full of heavyweight leather. What he did know was that some of the guys were on the court every day, all summer long, played from early afternoon until dark. So it must be that they worked the midnight shift, for how else would they pay for those saucy new Porsches and Jaguars and BMWs parked back there on the curb . . .

Shelley went over to the concession stand, got in line for a Diet Coke. It was gusty out on the water, windsurfers taking advantage. But in the lee of the building there was no breeze and the air was hot and dry. He yanked the gold-coloured silk shirt out of his pants and unfastened the buttons so it hung loose, and his lightly tanned washboard belly was on display.

A girl joined the lineup behind him, a redhead with more freckles than Kellogg had corn flakes. She was wearing a green bikini with white polka-dots, a pair of Foster Grants that kept slipping down her nose. She'd rolled the bottom of the bikini up, and Shelley couldn't help himself, when she turned to take a look at something behind her, he pulled back a little for a better angle. The lineup shuffled forward, and the redhead turned back to face him. What a terrific smile she had! Shelley smiled back, and apologized, said he wasn't an ogling kind of guy, but he'd wondered about her freckles. Not that it was any of his business but were they just on her face and shoulders, or, uh, all over? She cocked her hip, pushed the glasses back up on her nose. "Life's full of little mysteries, isn't it?" She had a nice voice, soft, feminine.

Shelley said, "Yeah, I guess so." Not exactly a brilliant response, but at least it was a step up from "Duh?"

The Foster Grants slipped down again. The redhead looked him over, up one side and down the next, those fabulous green eyes lingering here and there, taking in all the details. Shelley was relaxed, confident. Okay, so he forgot to brush his teeth from time to time. But what he *never* forgot was his slantboard situps, four sets of fifty, day in and day out. The line shuffled forward. He indicated the concession stand with a wave of his hand. "Lunch time?"

She gave him a quizzical look and said, "I don't mean to be rude, but would *you* eat here?"

Shelley nodded. "I usually skip lunch. Breakfast, too, as a matter of fact." He spread his arms wide. "It's part of what keeps me looking so . . ." He smiled down at her, waiting for her to fill in the blank.

"Skinny? Wimpy? Anorexic?"

Shelley laughed. Putting her on notice that he wasn't all bulk and brains. Letting her know there was something up there in the penthouse suite. That he had a sense of humour. Could take a joke. Mr. Lighthearted, that was Shelley.

The redhead ran her fingers through her hair, pushing it back. Shaved armpits. He wasn't sure how he felt about that. Legs, sure. But armpits? On the other hand, what difference did it make? He wanted to steal her cash and charge cards, not marry her.

He introduced himself. Shelley. Like the poet. She nodded. The line shuffled forward a few more inches. The asphalt was greasy with spilled food, so hot he could feel the heat rising up through the soles of his ill-fitting Birkenstocks. Smiling, he asked her what her name was.

"Bonnie."

Shelley tried to remember the lyrics to the song. *My bonnie lies . . .*

Her head tilted at a cute angle, the sun lighting up her hair. Looking up at him through her lashes, she said, "But my friends call me Bo."

"Right, like the baseball player."

Bo smiled, ducked her head, gently bit her lower lip. She squeezed his biceps with a pink-nailed, freckled hand. "No, like the constrictor."

Bo ordered a Diet Pepsi. Shelley, a large coffee. The concession guy acted as if he thought they were a unit. Shelley saw Bo didn't mind at all. He cracked his trick wallet and thumbed the wheel, showering the small, tightly woven, lighter-fluid-soaked cotton pad with sparks. The wallet burst into flames. Shelley gasped, and managed a fairly decent double-take. He waved the wallet in the air and then dramatically slammed it shut, so the flames shot out sideways and were extinguished. Very quickly and smoothly, he slipped the wallet into his back pocket, exchanging it for his *other* wallet, the one he kept his cash in, when he had any.

Bo stood there, wide-eyed, lips slightly parted, breathless. Absolutely amazed. The concession guy leaned against the counter, his face red as the chemical fire extinguisher he held cradled in his arms. Shelley resisted an urge to point and laugh. He flipped open his wallet. Bo said, "Let me see that!" and snatched it out of his hand. The concession guy, still looking more stupid than embarrassed, had migrated back to the cash register, and adopted, as he waited impatiently for the dollar ninety-five that Shelley owed him, the blank look of an amateur stoic. "Spontaneous combustion," said Shelley. "In my opinion it's one of the unsung dangers of this global-warming thing."

Bo gave up trying to figure out what made his wallet turn into a three-alarm inferno. She handed it back to him, and he flipped it open and, much to his apparent embarrassment, discovered the smallest denomination bill he had was a hundred. What gangsters called a c-note.

So, as anticipated, Bo paid for his coffee, which gave him a chance to take a quick peek into her purse. She had a reasonable amount of cash, fifty or sixty bucks, but what made Shelley's eyes light up was her collection of credit cards. He put his arm around her waist. Very casual, not making a big deal about it. Her skin was smooth and firm and warmed from within, silky from all the sunscreen she'd slathered on.

She felt very, very good. A strange, thread-thin shiver of guilt pierced his heart. If he shut his eyes, she could be anybody. But for now at least, she was just what he needed. And could either of them ask for more? He said, "Bo, are you alone?"

"Yeah, sure. Except there's a couple of creeps sitting just down the beach, who've been hitting on me. You up for that?"

Shelley struck a pose, playful but serious.

He walked her down to the beach, took pleasure in all the attention she received, the guys who stared at her and then gave him a careful look, as if wondering what he had and how they could get their share. If the scumballs were out there, they were lying low. He asked Bo to hold his coffee for him for a minute, leaned against a sun-bleached log and pulled off his Birkenstocks.

Bo said, "Know something?"

"What's that?"

"You don't exactly look like a sandals kind of person."

"Yeah? Why is that?"

She shrugged. The bikini held, but just. She said, "I don't know. It's just a feeling. Are you a vegetarian?"

Shelley slapped the Birkenstocks together, knocking the loose sand out of the treads. He said, "No, I'm a Scorpio" and gave her a just-kidding smile. He stared down the heat-rippled length of the beach. During the fierce winter storms, hundreds or even thousands of logs broke free from booms that were being towed across the open water beyond the harbour, and many of them washed up on Vancouver's beaches. Over the years the Parks Board had laid some of the bigger logs out on the sand in orderly rows for people to sit on or lean against, use as a windbreak. Along much of the length of Kits beach there were three parallel rows of logs. At summer's end, the abandoned beaches were groomed by bulldozers. If a log had been scorched by fire or otherwise needed replacing, it was done. When the bulldozers were finished, other machines went to work filtering cigarette butts and squashed beer cans and Rolex watches and diamond rings, gold chains and car keys, melted tubes of lipstick and foreign and domestic coins, steak knives and scorched spoons and hypodermic needles out of tons of sand. Nine months of rain leached away the blood and various other body fluids that had been spilled. By the time June rolled around again, the beaches were almost as neat and orderly as nature had made them.

Shelley, a vegetarian? When it didn't matter, it was better to be honest. He said, "I like a nice slab of beef now and then."

Bo nodded, licked her chops. They started walking again. The sand was pocked with ten zillion footprints. Every spot on every log was taken, the beach filled to capacity despite all the ozone warnings and cancer scares. Shelley lagged half a step behind, the better to admire Bo's walk. She had longer-than-average legs and a longer-than-average stride, a real nice roll to her hips.

She was still carrying his paper cup of coffee, hadn't given it back to him when he'd finished taking off the stupid, slightly-too-small Birkenstocks. He smiled. It was almost as if the coffee was a hostage.

If only he'd known.

6

Despite the weight and cumbersome bulk of the picnic basket, Annie had soon outstripped Willows and Parker, leaving them far behind as she hurried towards the beach. Parker reached out and took Willows' hand, squeezed and let go.

Parker said, "She's a lovely girl, Jack."

Willows nodded. Sometimes he thought Annie was a little too perfect, a bit too serious and responsible for her age. But this wasn't the time to talk about it. The sun beat down on them out of a flawless, pale blue sky that darkened imperceptibly towards the horizons. The mountains on the far side of the harbour were a soft greyish green, the ocean down by the beach a darker and more solid green. A long way out the sandy shallows fell suddenly away, the abrupt change in depth marked by a wavering line of foam and the transition from green to sparkling, deepwater blue. In Vancouver, summer often meant that the rain was warmer. But not today, not today.

Willows heard Annie's cry, looked up and saw that she had staked out an end section of a strategically positioned log several hundred feet down the beach. He'd kicked off his sneakers and the sand was painfully hot beneath his feet as he trudged towards her. Parker effortlessly matched him stride for stride, using her long legs to advantage. It seemed to him that he had to push himself forward, while Parker glided effortlessly across the sand. But this was typical. One of the many things he loved about her was the way she walked, as rapidly as a man, but with such effortless grace, never compromising her femininity.

Annie had every reason to be pleased with herself. She'd found a prime spot on the beach where, by this late time of the day, there were usually none to be had. And this particular log, a large, solid one in the front rank, with nothing between it and the water but a short stretch of beach, was a very good find. As far as Willows knew, logged beaches were pretty much a Vancouver phenomenon. It was easy to understand why. You needed a sheltered beach, so the logs wouldn't be washed away in the winter storms, and, even more unlikely, a steady supply of free logs. There weren't many cities in the world that Willows knew of that had those two crucial ingredients, and it was too bad, because the logs offered protection from the wind, and a semblance of privacy, a degree of seclusion in the middle of a wide-open space.

As they drew near, Parker smiled and said, "A five-star piece of real estate, Annie. Nice work!"

"Did you see those people heading towards the parking lot, the couple with the big yellow beach umbrella and the red-haired twins?"

"Yeah," said Willows, "but I heard them first."

Annie grinned. "It looked to me as if the twins'd had enough and their parents had decided to pack it in and go home. So I kept an eye open for a vacant spot near the water, figuring them for early risers, and that they'd want to be able to keep an eye on the kids when they went for a paddle."

Willows said, "You *deduced* there'd be a spot for us down here."

"A detective's daughter," said Parker.

Annie laughed, delighted at the thought. "Miss Marple, watch out!"

Willows shook the folds out of the tartan beach blanket. "Will somebody give me a hand with this, please?" He flicked the blanket towards Parker, who caught one corner and then another. Willows said, "Up," and raised his arms. Parker followed his lead. He said,

"Down," and the blanket billowed like a parachute as, working in unison, they lowered it carefully to the sand.

Annie popped open the lid of the picnic basket. "Anybody hungry?"

Willows shook his head. Parker said, "Not yet, honey."

"Want to go for a swim?" Annie pulled the T-shirt over her head and tossed it on the sand, kicked off her thongs. Her jeans were so loose she hardly needed to unfasten the top button, much less bother with the zipper. They puddled at her feet and she stepped out of them. Willows felt a pang. Annie was very much her own person, but physically, he could see a lot of her mother in the blossoming shape of her body, her colouring, and even the way she held herself – although he noticed she'd picked up a few of Parker's favourite phrases, "bullshit" being her current favourite.

Parker said, "Not for a while – maybe in half an hour or so, okay?"

"Daddy?"

"Don't wait for me, honey." Annie was wearing a two-piece bikini in a soft canary-yellow fabric. New, wasn't it? He said, "Stay inside the buoys, though, okay?"

"Buoys spelled with a *u*," said Parker.

Was it Willows' imagination, or had Annie looked a bit startled, and more than a little bit guilty? She was blushing, a lovely shade of pink. It hadn't been his imagination after all.

Annie gave Willows and Parker a friendly wave that kind of fell in between them, and strode off down the beach, long-legged and slim.

Willows said, "Have I seen that bathing suit before?"

"What do you think?" said Parker.

"I think I'd remember it if I had."

Parker smiled. "She bought it last weekend, when we went shopping at Oakridge. There was a sale."

Willows nodded, remembering.

Parker said, "I told her you might find it a little daring. She said that if you wanted a fight, that was fine with her."

"You're kidding." But he could see she wasn't. The idea of Annie calmly deciding to risk an argument over a borderline-skimpy bathing suit was a little daunting. Or, more accurately, downright terrifying.

He sat down on the blanket, looked out at the water. His daughter had swum out to the big wooden raft the Parks Board put out every summer. She sat on the raft, facing away from the beach, her legs dangling in the water. She wasn't alone. He wondered if the half-dozen boys crowded around her were friends, or just hoping.

"Jack?"

He glanced up.

Parker stood very close to him. She said, "The skirt first, or the blouse?"

Willows swallowed. "The skirt."

Parker wore a lightweight cotton skirt decorated with tiny pink flowers. She hooked her thumbs under the elasticized waistband, and pushed down. Under the skirt she wore the black one-piece Willows found so alluring. She bent a knee, posing. "Like what you see?"

"So far."

"I thought so." Parker crossed her arms and pulled her sleeveless blouse over her head. In the moment when she was blind, Willows took a good, long look at her, and then kept looking, as she let the blouse drift down to the sand.

Parker said, "Go ahead, make yourself at home."

"I wish I could, but there's a law against it."

Parker sat down next to him, rested a cool hand on his sun-warmed thigh, slid her finger under the leg of his khaki shorts, dug in her nail. "What law is that, Jack?"

Willows kissed her, and then kissed her again. "I can think of several, at the moment."

Parker made a small sound of desire. Her nails left pale marks on his skin as she let her hand fall away. "I think I want something to drink."

"*Drink to me only . . .*"

Parker turned her back to him. He admired the curve of her hip. She pushed back her jetblack hair as she glanced over her shoulder at him. "Don't stop now, Mr. Poet."

"*Drink to me only with thine eyes . . .*"

"Want some lemonade?"

Willows rubbed his hands together. "I'd *love* a glass of nice cold lemonade," he said with mock-enthusiasm.

Parker poured from the big two-litre thermos into two plastic tumblers decorated with a ring of stylized tulips; red on one glass, white on the other. She screwed the lid back on the thermos and handed the red-tulip tumbler to Willows. "Cheers."

"Here's looking at you, Claire."

Lowering her voice to a sultry whisper, Parker said, "I want you to recite some more poetry to me later, okay?"

"As long as I can use cue cards."

Parker gave him a bold look. "You're going to need a lot more than cue cards, big fella."

Willows drank his lemonade, set the empty tumbler into the sand, and unbuttoned his shirt. He tossed the shirt on the blanket, unzipped his shorts. Beneath the shorts he wore a boxer-type bathing suit in faded pink. He offered her his hand. "Last one in the water's an idiot."

"You're on, sport!" Parker accepted Willows' hand, and he pulled her lightly to her feet. She said, "Ready, set . . ." and gave him a brisk push in the wrong direction as she sprinted towards the water.

They swam a long way out, much farther than Willows would have gone had he been alone. He hadn't enjoyed ocean swimming since, while innocently dial-surfing his Sony many years ago, he'd happened upon Robert Shaw being eaten by a great white shark. The fact that there hadn't been a shark attack in all of Canada during the entire course of recorded history helped a little, but not much.

He rolled over on his back, sluiced saltwater out of his eyes and concentrated on keeping his toes out of the water. All he could see was sky. The carnival sounds of the beach came to him faintly. A gull passed high overhead. He glanced around. Where was Claire? He let himself drift into an upright position. The water was clouded with silt. His feet couldn't find the bottom. He had just begun to feel vulnerable when Claire clamped her teeth lightly down on his forearm. He repressed a scream of sheer terror. His arms windmilled as she pulled him under, rolled over on him and held on tight with her arms and legs. Her hands were all over him. Before he could react, she was gone.

He kicked hard towards the surface, shook water from his face, ran his fingers through his hair. He'd never thought of himself as vain, but neither did he want Claire to see him looking as if he'd just stuck his ear in a light socket. His vanity was kind of ridiculous, really. He and Claire had been partners a lot of years. They'd seen each other at their very best and awful worst. Neither of them had many secrets that the other didn't know about. But where was she?

Treading water, he used his arms and legs to churn his way through a complete circle. Parker came up behind him. She slipped her arms around his waist and gave him a slippery hug.

Willows let her take his weight, and she immediately released him. He flailed wildly, thrashing as he struggled to keep his head above water.

Parker said, "I can see why you were so eager to go for a swim, Jack. You're really in your element, aren't you?"

Willows got himself turned around. He spat out a mouthful of ocean and said, "I better check on Annie."

"Right," said Parker, laughing.

Willows struck out for shore with more enthusiasm than skill. Parker rolled over on her back and swam alongside; a five-foot-seven-inch, pale and shapely sprite.

Annie was still on the raft. It didn't look as if she'd moved a muscle during the time her father had been gone. But then, why would she bother, since the world had come to her? Chest-deep in the water, both feet firmly planted in the sand, Willows watched half a dozen tanned boys a year or two older than Annie take turns risking a broken neck in the faint hope of impressing his hope- fully unimpressionable daughter.

Willows checked his watch. Twenty past ten. He'd had nothing to eat since the previous evening. The fresh salt air and his brief swim had given him a healthy appetite. He tilted his body into the water and swam slowly but steadily towards Parker, who was loi- tering at the shoreline, waiting for him.

They walked up the beach hand in hand, past skittish seagulls, young lovers, mothers with children. The smell of hotdogs mingled with the sweet scent of sunscreen. It was surprising how deeply tanned some people were. Weren't they aware of the ragged holes in the ozone layer, or the very real risk of carcinoma? The toddler next door had tracked sand all over their blanket. Mom had dozed off. Willows tossed Parker a towel. He gave the blanket a shake, and then rooted around in the picnic basket until he found the sunscreen. He offered to take care of Parker's back. She sat cross-legged on the towel in front of him, and leaned back into his arms.

"You can take care of my front, too," she said playfully.

Mom had been playing possum. She cocked an eyebrow, smiled.

The morning drifted by. Frequent jaunts to the water to cool off were interspersed with leisurely dips into the picnic basket. The chicken was dismembered and consumed. Willows drank his share of lemonade.

By mid-afternoon, when the sun was at its worst, they decided they'd had more than enough sun 'n' surf, and that it was time to go home. Annie told Willows she'd meet them at the car, and then raced back towards the raft for one last dip, and to say goodbye to her new friends. Willows and Parker tidied up, taking care to leave the beach at least as clean as they'd found it. On the way back to the car, Parker made a short detour to the outside shower to rinse off her feet. Willows slowed, waiting for her to catch up. They walked across the baking asphalt towards the car.

Willows was unlocking the passenger-side door when he

noticed the flat. He said, "You might as well find some shade and make yourself comfortable, Claire. I've got a flat."

"A flat tire?" There was no denying it. The left rear tire was about as flat as it could get.

Willows fiddled with his keyring. He separated the trunk key and was about to insert it in the lock when he saw that the trunk lid wasn't quite shut. He experienced a moment of stunned disbelief. Flecks of brown paint speckled the rear bumper. The distinctive marks of a crowbar jumped out at him. He hadn't forgotten to lock the trunk; somebody had pried it open. He glanced around. His was the only car that had been broken into. He hooked a finger under the trunk lid and swung it up.

The shotgun was still there. A box of 12-gauge shells was missing. So was his roadside emergency kit. The MagLite. The jack.

Annie said, "There's never a cop around when you need one."

Willows gave her a sour look.

Parker said, "What'd he take?"

"Who?"

"The thief."

"What makes you think it was a guy?"

Parker smiled. "What's missing, Jack?"

"A box of shotgun shells. My flashlight and a few other odds and ends. The jack."

"The jack for jacking up the car, and changing the tire? That jack, Jack?"

Annie giggled. Willows nodded. He winked at his daughter, and felt a sense of loss as he realized that, a summer ago, in these circumstances, he'd have been required to give her a great big reassuring hug.

Parker said, "Are you going to call it in?"

"I doubt it." The lock had popped half out of the sheet metal. He was insured, but it wouldn't cost him much more than his deductible to buy and install a used lock from a wrecker's. If he dialled 911, he'd spend the next couple of hours answering questions. Plus there was always the chance some cop would snitch him to one of the local channels or a crime reporter. He could see the tabloid headlines, hear the chuckles. Being victimized was rarely a judicious career move. He surveyed the ranks of parked cars. There were a dozen or more older, full-size domestics parked in the lot. Any one of them would have a jack he could use. Or he could phone a tow truck, but that would probably cost him forty dollars or more.

He turned to ask Parker if she had an opinion on the subject and saw somebody's grandfather huffing down on him at full speed. The old man wore no-name sneakers, tan slacks, a tie-dyed T-shirt, oversized sunglasses and a floppy canvas hat. A fluffy white pooch not much bigger than a cat trailed along behind on a short leash. As they drew near the dog snarled at Parker.

"Don't pay no attention to Betsy," said the old man. He smiled, and Parker saw he'd taken care of his teeth. "She's the jealous type. Can't stand the thought of another woman in my life."

"I'm flattered," said Parker. She gave Annie a wry grin.

The old man introduced himself. His name was Alex Findley. He jerked a thumb at the beach. "Saw the guy busted into your car."

Annie knelt and offered Betsy the back of her hand. The dog sniffed. Annie scratched her behind the ears. Betsy jumped into her lap.

"Got a metal detector," said Alex, frowning. "I'm here most days, or over at Kits beach more likely, or even Third Beach, sometimes. Anyways, me 'n' Betsy was looking for Rolex watches down on the dunes. Got us a few beer-bottle caps and a dollar or two in change, and then the damn battery went and died on us. We was on our way home when I seen this fella mixin' it up with a buncha kids in a red car." He smiled at his dog. "Stopped to watch the show, didn't we Bets?"

"You saw the man who broke into our car?" said Parker.

"Twice. He drove off, and then he came back. He had a bag, a black zip-bag fulla tools. Used a big crowbar, musta been a yard long. Yeah, a yard-long chrome-plated crowbar."

"Chrome-plated?" said Willows.

"What I said."

"What did he look like?" said Parker.

"Big. Muscular. Kinda movie-star good looks. Who's that Australian guy, plays the psycho cop?"

"Mel Gibson?" said Parker. Willows gave her a look. She ignored him.

"Yeah, that's the one. Don't look *exactly* like him, mind you. But close enough, side on. Frontwise, I couldn't say."

"Hair colour?" said Parker hopefully.

"Didn't notice, really." Alex twisted his head down and away as he shucked the sunglasses. His pale blue eyes were small, rheumy, flecked with pockets of cloudy grey. He slipped the glasses back on. "Saw the guy drive off after he busted open your trunk. Had one of them low-slung sports jobs. Black. Went *Vroom, Vroom!* when he gunned the motor." His shoulder sagged. "Not much help, am I?"

"You're all we've got," said Parker. "There must be five thousand people on this beach, and you're the only person who noticed anything wrong."

Alex brightened. "Maybe I should quit lookin' for Rolexes," he said. "Maybe I should start lookin' for a damn *medal*!"

7

They lay around on the beach for a couple of hours, making small talk, rotating. Bo worked for a real-estate company. She mentioned the name, but it cut no ice with Shelley. Some small company. He thought at first she meant she was an agent, spent her working days flogging houses or condos or whatever. It turned out she was more of a specialist, sort of a private secretary type, who also acted, from time to time, as a "closer." Now there was a word to perk up a guy's ears. Shelley pressed for details. If there was an awkward client, she'd take him out to dinner. Wine and dine him. Limo him to someplace flashy but conservative. The Four Seasons, Bayshore. Make him feel important, for an hour or two.

Shelley had some questions he knew he had no business asking. Yet the questions lurked in the corners of his eyes.

Bo said, "You want to know if I have *sex* with them, don't you?" She'd spoken in kind of a loud voice, as if she were twenty feet or more away instead of sitting practically in his lap. People were watching them, sunglasses flashing as heads turned. Beach theatre. The price was right. Every seat was a front-row seat. Bo's sharp red nails raked Shelley's ribs. He screeched quietly, and lifted his arm so he could see the thin white lines she'd left on his flesh. Bo's mouth touched his ear. Very quietly, for him only, she said, "Well, I don't. I never did and I never will."

"None of my business," confessed Shelley, whispering.

"It is if you're interested."

"In what?" said Shelley, idly watching the windsurfers skip like gaudy demented moths across the glittery bay.

"In me." Bo rested her hand on his thigh. Her red-nailed fingers tap-danced a little higher. "Look at me."

Shelley was quick to do as he'd been told.

"Do you find me attractive?"

"Yeah. Sure. Of course I do."

Bonnie stared into his eyes, diving deep. "I mean as a person, a human being. I'm not speaking sexually, although of course I'm not ruling that aspect of the relationship out, either. I guess maybe what I'm trying to say is that I find you extremely attractive and I want very much to get to know you. To see if you're as nice on the inside as you are on the outside. And I want to know if you feel the same way about me." She smiled up at him. "These are dangerous times, Shelley. We have to be careful with each other. I understand that. If I'm going too fast for you . . ."

Shelley swallowed hard. He said, "No, wait. I do feel the same way you do." Even though he was pretty sure he meant it, he felt as if he were lying. Why was that? He'd have to get back to himself, think it over at some later date. Things were moving right along. He was breathing hard from trying to keep up.

Bonnie reached out, cupped his chin in her hand and turned his head so he was facing her. She said, "I don't know anything about you, Shell. Maybe you're the kind of guy, there's plenty of them around, who's looking for anything but a serious relationship."

"No, I can be serious." By way of evidence, Shelley rearranged his face.

Bonnie fluttered her lashes. Her nails dug deeper. "Serious enough to take me back to your place and cook me a nice dinner?"

"Uh, yeah. Sure."

"Got a car?"

Shelley squinted into the sunlight that turned her hair into a dazzling explosion. This was firm ground and he stepped down hard. "I look like the kinda guy'd ride the bus?"

"You look like the kind of guy who'd *drive* a bus," said Bo.

She was smiling, kind of. That delicious mouth turned up at the corners, a cool smile. She was kidding, he was almost certain she was kidding. Hadn't somebody told him that redheads were kidders? And wasn't that a twinkle in her seagreen eye? He said, "Yeah, I got a car. A real nice car, a 300sx. Black."

"Really?"

"Yeah," said Shelley, very casual. As a kidder she was okay, but he had to admit he liked her an awful lot more when she was all wide-eyed and amazed.

Bonnie stretched, stood up, and then bent in front of him and snapped up her "Peanuts" beach towel, shook away the sand. She folded the towel, dropped her paperback – *The Collected Dylan Thomas* – and a plastic bottle of sunscreen into her bag. "A 300sx. That's a pretty expensive car, isn't it?"

Shelley nodded. Modest, now that he'd gained some ground. He got his feet under him, stood up. He glanced idly around. He was pleased to see that his new girlfriend was being covertly stared at. Discreetly admired. He checked to make sure he hadn't left anything valuable lying behind, collected his gym bag and trotted after her, in a hurry to catch up.

As they trudged across the sand he swung his arm wide, a finger grazing her silky hip. She turned and smiled at him, her eyes dark green against the green of the grassy park beyond. It was nice being with her. It wasn't anything complicated, just a good feeling that her clean-but-spectacular good looks lent him. A gift of presence. He was a little surprised when she reached out and took his hand. They smiled at each other. He tried to analyse his feelings. It wasn't anything he was good at, introspection. But there was something about Bo that made him feel as if he were really there, rather than just kind of standing by. He felt involved. Part of the action. But it was more than that. She made him feel . . .

What did she make him feel, exactly? His mind wrestled with the problem, as he tried to put shape to his inner feelings. There was a special word but he couldn't find it, though he racked his brains all the way to the parking lot.

A ticket lay on the sharply slanted windshield. He used the remote to unlock the doors, walked around to the passenger side and opened the door for Bo. She made no effort to keep her knees together as she slid into the cockpit. He shut the door and walked around the sleek nose of the car, got in, unlocked The Club and stowed it away, tossed his gym bag in the backseat. He started the engine, cranked the air-conditioner to frozen alive. The Alpine clicked in. ZZ Top. He turned it down, a little. The leatherclad bucket seat enfolded him as he leaned back. He fastened his seatbelt. A rush of cool air turned beads of sweat into tiny balls of ice. He turned on the wipers. The ticket whizzed back and forth across the windshield and then fluttered away. He turned off the wipers. The air-conditioner had already blasted most of the hot air out of the car. He shut the door.

Bonnie said, "What a nice car."

"Yeah," said Shelley. From his tone of voice she might have pointed out to him that the sky was blue or the sun was hot or that McDonald's sold death in a bun. He reversed out of the slot and pointed the nose at the exit. The sx's twin exhausts burbled contentedly as they cruised slowly towards the street.

Shelley was in no hurry. He had three-quarters of a tank of gas. A ten-on-the-Richter-scale babe. Speaking for himself, no place he had to be unless he felt like being there. Though he drove a hot car, he usually kept to the speed limit. What was the big rush? Power was nice to have, in case you needed it. And the time almost always eventually came when you needed it. But until you needed it you didn't use it, because that was a waste of power.

Shelley braked. Bonnie leaned towards him and he thought for a minute she was going to grope or kiss him, but it was the Alpine's volume control she was interested in. Her carmine-nailed thumb and finger tweaked the dial in a clockwise direction, squeezed a few more watts through the speakers. The sx, low-slung and aggressive, straddled the sidewalk. Behind him and to his left crazy people whacked tennis balls beneath the killer sun. Shelley checked to make sure the road was clear. He goosed it, and they shot into a gap in the traffic not much bigger than the car.

Behind them, a horn blared. Bonnie powered down the window and tilted a finger to the sky.

There was an IGA only a couple of blocks from the house, but Shelley pulled a left on Arbutus so he could hit the Safeway, which was a lot bigger than the IGA, and better stocked, with a better selection of magazines and an in-store bakery. Not to mention better-looking and friendlier checkout girls. Plus the Safeway had a much wider selection of meat, which was why he believed it was less likely a couple of T-bones would be missed if they fell into his pocket.

He parked in a handicapped zone, hung the blue-and-white handicapped tag on the mirror.

Bonnie said, "Where'd you get that?"

"Found it." They sat there, looking at each other. Shelley unhooked the tag from the mirror and tossed it in the glove box. He backed out of the slot and soon found another.

Inside the store, it was cool and bright and inhumanly clean. Shelley scooped up a red plastic basket off a stack of identical baskets. He chose a couple of T-bones that must've come off a monster cow, handpicked a brace of Idaho potatoes from a bin, added a head of iceberg lettuce, an onion, celery, a green and a red pepper, handful of mushrooms, cluster of radishes and a bunch of green onions.

Bonnie said, "You don't need green onions. You've already got an onion."

"Onions are good for you."

"Unless you've got an allergy." She reached into the basket, plucked out the green onions and tossed them onto a heap of broccoli. The broccoli was piled on a mound of chunk ice. She popped a piece of ice into her mouth. He hoped she didn't cool herself off too much.

"What about this one?" Shelley hefted the big Spanish onion.

"Doesn't bother me."

"You're sure?"

"Hey, don't patronize me, okay?" On the far side of the store, Bonnie chose a pink toothbrush and dispenser of unwaxed floss.

"What kind of toothpaste you use?"

"Colgate," said Shelley.

Bonnie tossed a tube of mint-flavoured Crest into the basket.

"What about rubbers?"

"Uh . . ."

"You got any?"

Shelley said, "Well, uh . . ."

Bo took him by the hand and led him down the aisle. "I guess, when you're having sex with the mirror, there's no need to worry. Or do you both slip into one, simultaneously?" In the family-planning section, aisle E, Bo rigorously cross-examined Shelley about his preferred brand. He claimed to have no firm opinions on the matter. She plucked down one and then another shiny silver box containing a dozen lubricated Ramses. "This ought to do us," she said with a farmgirl's smile that distorted the freckles ranged along the bridge of her pert, slightly upturned nose.

Until what, wondered Shelley, aghast. Midnight? Sometime to-morrow morning? The end of the relationship?

The tab came to sixty-one dollars and thirty-eight cents. He pulled out his lonely hundred and paid cash.

It was a ten-minute drive from the Safeway to the house. Shelley parked out front. Bonnie went crazy.

"You *live* here?" Amazed again, just the way Shelley liked her. She loved the shiny green leaves of the rhodos, the quarter-century-old wisteria that a couple of months earlier had bloomed waterfalls of mauve in a failed attempt to disguise its sneaky intention to strangle the porch. Inside, she marvelled at the entrance hall, the oak staircase and gateleg balusters, the foot-square oak newel post topped off with an imitation-grape-cluster light fixture. "Show me around?" she said. Shelley stuffed the plastic Safeway bag into the fridge. She took his hand and he followed her from room to room, all around the house.

In the huge master bedroom she said, "This is where you sleep?"

"Or toss and turn," said Shelley with a grin.

He followed her down the hall. In and out of each and every one of the bathrooms and bedrooms. There was no detail that went unappreciated, from the quality of the baseboard moulding to the patterns of the goosedown duvets that lay upon the antique beds.

Shelley had thought Bo might offer to cook dinner, especially since he'd sprung for the meal, her toothbrush, toothpaste and floss. Plus the rubbers, which weren't cheap. But Bo was in no mood to slave over a hot stove. She helped herself to a beer from the fridge, gave Shelley a quick peck on the cheek and went out on the back deck and watched the robins plunder the cherry tree, her back to her hardworking host.

Shelley washed the two potatoes with warm water and soap, pierced them with a fork and stuck them in a four-hundred-degree oven. He slapped together the salad, set the table, and joined Bonnie on the deck. She'd finished her beer and dozed off. Disappointed but unwilling to disturb her, Shelley went inside and watched TV awhile. When the spuds were just about done he turned the gas up under a big stainless-steel frying pan, cut a chunk of fat off one of the steaks, greased the hot pan with the fat and dropped in the steaks. The world was full of wonderful sounds and one of the most wonderful sounds of all was the sound of sizzling meat. He had to push the steaks around to fit them both inside the pan. He cooked them the way he'd always liked them, charred on the outside and juicy pink in the middle.

By the time he had the meal on the table, Bonnie was up and

running. At the sink she splashed cold water on her face and told Shelley she'd had a dream in which they'd both been swimming naked at the foot of a waterfall – in the West Edmonton Mall. The sound of the steaks cooking had pulled her from her dreams. She'd confused the sound of scorched meat with the roar of the mall's waterfall.

It was just past five. That was a little early for most people, but Shelley liked that extra-long run of evening, an hour or two extra to digest the meal and burn away the calories. He watched Bo eat. She was quick, efficient, and very feminine. Dexterous. There was no wine but she was content to share a beer. When she'd finished eating she wiped her mouth with a linen napkin, told Shelley to sit and take it easy while she cleaned the table. All by herself, she figured out how to work the eleven-button dishwasher.

Shelley wandered into the kitchen. Maybe the red meat had given him courage, or maybe it was just that he wanted to be honest with her, or at least start out that way. He said, "This isn't my house, actually. I'm kind of renting."

"Yeah?"

"House-sitting, really." He chuckled inanely, and plucked at his shirt. "Half the time I don't even wear my own clothes, just help myself to whatever's in the closet."

"Sounds like a nice life."

"Help yourself," he said a little too quickly.

The two silver boxes of rubbers lay there on the counter, collecting light. Shelley felt vaguely embarrassed, but wasn't sure why. Enforced intimacy? It was something else to think about, wasn't it? As if his brain wasn't already overworked.

Bo opened and slammed shut drawers and cabinet doors until she found what she needed to make coffee. She asked him if she could use the phone. He pointed to the wall-mounted cordless. Discreet to a fault, he wandered into the living room, sprawled out on the couch, and sipped at his too-strong coffee as he wondered who in hell she was talking to. The possibilities seemed limitless but the call didn't take long. In only a minute or so Bonnie was kneeling beside him, resting her head on his thigh. Her voice was muffled as she said, "That was a lovely dinner."

"Glad you liked it," said Shelley, a bit gruff.

Outside, a robin chirped.

Bo raised her head. She looked him in the eye. "I have to go out for a while but I'll be back as soon as I can, okay?"

"Yeah, sure." Did Shelley sound nonchalant? He hoped so, but doubted it. What he'd do, he'd round up the bucket and Turtlewax and his sponge, run the hose down to the street, and wash and wax his car. Keep busy. Occupy his mind. He'd heard about guys who went to the beach and fell in love with a bikini and spent the rest of the summer in deep pain. Not necessarily bleeding, but slashed wide open.

Bo went upstairs. He heard the toilet flush. Bo trotted back downstairs, stopped his heart with a killer kiss, and was gone.

Shelley peeked out the window. Bo climbed into the backseat of an idling Blacktop cab. She leaned forward and rested her hand on the driver's shoulder as she spoke briefly to him. She leaned back. The cab pulled away.

Heartsick dope that he was, Shelley waved goodbye.

8

Willows turned on the bedside lamp. The big red numbers on the digital clock rolled over from 2:04 to 2:05. He picked up the phone before it could ring a second time.

"Willows."

"Jack, it's Homer."

"Morning, Inspector."

Parker slipped her arm around Willows. Her hand slid down his stomach, trailed across his thigh.

Bradley said, "BeachView Towers. Apartment 2327."

Willows rubbed the sleep from his eyes. He said, "Yeah, okay." He coughed. Still waking up. "Twenty minutes."

Parker sighed quietly. She pushed aside the sheets and slid out of bed. Willows watched her cross the room. She was very light on her feet, especially for a cop.

Bradley said, "You there, Jack?"

Willows grunted. There was no need to ask Bradley why he'd called, not at this time of the night. Someone neither of them knew had murdered someone neither of them had ever met.

"I called Parker. Mozart on the machine. Want me to call Eddy Orwell or is there a chance you can track her down?" This was Bradley at his most tactful. At two in the morning. Amazing.

Parker slipped into a white terrycloth robe. She blew Willows a kiss and padded down the hall towards the bathroom.

"Eddy's a good man," said Willows, "but he's kind of cranky if he doesn't get a full night's sleep."

"How would you know? Drive carefully, Jack." Cackling, Bradley disconnected.

Willows hung up. He rolled out of bed and followed Parker into the bathroom. Parker waved at him through the clear glass shower door. The bar of soap jumped out of her hand. She gave him a mock-coy look and bent to pick it up. Willows slid open the door and stepped into the spray of steamy water.

"Hot enough for you?" said Parker.

Willows waggled his eyebrows comically. He gave Parker a quick but thorough up-and-down look.

She said, "Want me to soap you down?"

"If you're in the mood."

Parker said, "Of *course* I'm in the mood. Let's do your mouth first." She moved in on him. "Open wide!"

BeachView Towers was on Beach Avenue, naturally enough. The building overlooked False Creek but was three long blocks from the closest actual beach, and was a little too close to the noise and dirt of the Granville Street bridge to command top dollar. The building was less than a year old. A uniform loitered at the double glass doors. Willows badged him. He'd kind of hoped the cop would open the door for them, but all he did was step aside. The lobby was bigger than Parker's apartment, the oversized sofas considerably more expensive than anything she could hope to afford. A bank of three elevators stood passively waiting, doors open. Willows stepped inside the closest of the three. Parker knuckled 23. Top floor. The penthouse. Bronzed doors slid shut, and they ascended, smooth and silent as angels.

The door to 2327 was wide open. The apartment was on the south side of the building, facing the water. A cloudy smear of black fingerprint powder lay on and around the shiny brass doorknob and deadbolt lock. There were no prints that Willows could see. He flashed his tin at the constable lounging against the far wall. The cop unfolded his index finger from his fist, pointed inside. He popped his gum.

Willows, a teasing upward lilt to his voice, said, "Juicy Fruit?" Parker smiled.

"Spearmint," said the cop. He blinked, catching the implication and resenting it immensely. Pissed, but what could he do?

The entrance hall hinted at the apartment's size. There was ample room for a gracious host and half a dozen departing guests. The floor was dark oak, the walls dark green with taupe trim. To Willows' left there was a closet with a tinted mirrored sliding door. Inside the closet a trio of full-length fur coats hung next to a man's leather trenchcoat and several other coats and jackets. Parker touched the nearest fur. Mink. She turned aside the lapel so she could see the label. Papas. Why did she suddenly crave a fur coat when she'd never wanted one before? Latex snapped as Willows wriggled into a pair of gloves.

They followed the run of oak planks into the living room. A wall of plate glass drew the eye to the glittering view.

"Jack?"

Inspector Homer Bradley was down at the far end of the generously proportioned through-hall, leaning against a peach-coloured wall. The overhead light bounced off his skull and too-prominent cheekbones. His fringe of white hair looked a little like a misplaced halo. He looked tired. Probably, given his age, and the time of night, he *was* tired. Willows followed Parker down the hall, past open doors leading to a den, a spacious bedroom, a bathroom with triple sinks in black marble. The apartment was all on one level and it was huge; he still hadn't seen the kitchen or dining room.

Bradley had disappeared into another room. The master bedroom, by the look of it. The view of False Creek was stunning. Willows could hear a tap running.

"Ensuite bathroom," said Bradley. "Looks like the killer washed up before he vacated the premises."

"Where is everybody?"

Bradley jerked his unlit cigar in the general direction of the far end of the apartment. "ME's come and gone. The CSU guys're tucked away in the media room. That's what you'd call it, right? There's a TV in there big as a movie screen." He smiled at Parker. "The crew's watching a movie, until we get done."

Willows studied the body. The victim lay on the bed. He was in his late fifties or early sixties. Stocky, broad-chested and muscular, maybe fifteen pounds overweight. His naked body was hairless, and gleamed pale yellow, the colour of lard. Except for a horse-shoe of hair above his close-set ears, he was bald. His eyebrows were black and bushy and needed trimming. His eyes were dull as the dullest boy's in a class of dullards. But a gold tooth shone bright. He'd been shot once, in the sternum, at point-blank range. There wasn't much blood.

"Who called it in?" said Parker.

"Miss Anonymous, from a payphone on Granville."

Parker indicated the corpse with a shiny silver pen. "He got a name?"

"Zagros Galee. He's a real-estate agent. *Was* a real-estate agent. Was a *live* real-estate agent. Worked for a company called Far West Realty. Offices in Calgary and Vancouver."

Parker shrugged.

"He had a deck of business cards with his picture on them in his jacket pocket. Far West Realty. Zagros Galee, Licensed Agent. Phone and fax. Pager. Cellphone." Bradley swept his arms wide in an expansive gesture. "The dump's for sale. Fact sheets on the counter in the kitchen. One point two million. Care to make an offer?"

"Who's the owner?"

"Tommy Lee. An expatriate Hong Konger. The super tells me Tommy's holidaying in the south of France. Or maybe the Caribbean, or the Italian Riviera. Nobody knows for sure. Tommy's hardly ever around, even when he's in town, which is usually only a few weeks out of the year. Tommy owns a log house in Whistler. Summer place on Whaler Bay. What'd they call people like that? Jet-setters. Sounds like a modern breed of dog. Some kind of speedster retriever." Bradley chewed on his cigar. He looked out the window. "Great view, huh?"

"Terrific," said Parker. She'd been prowling the room and now she was down on her knees, peering under the bed, the bright beam of her penlight skittering across the waxed floor. She said, "There's a spent casing under the bed."

"Yeah?" Bradley knelt down. He reached under the bed. His tired face distorted, he pressed against the frame, extending himself. "Can't reach it." He stood up. His knees creaked. He said, "I sound like a goddamn barn door."

The cartridge was small, a .22 or a .25 or maybe a .32 Magnum. Parker glanced at Zagros Galee's chest. The hole looked small, but it was always difficult to tell, with entrance wounds. Especially point-blank entrance wounds.

A few minutes later, in the bathroom, Parker stood by the sink, her head tilted, listening to the music of running water. She called Willows over and asked him if he heard anything unusual. He wasn't sure. Unusual in what way? She told him she thought there might be something down there, caught in the trap. A ring, maybe. Willows gave her a look. He turned off the tap.

From the bedroom, Bradley said, "Thankyou."

Mel Dutton tipped his hat to Parker as he eased into the bathroom. The room was large, but it was starting to feel a little crowded. Dutton was a big man and he was carrying a lot of bulky camera equipment; a Polaroid, a couple of Nikons, various accessories, a black nylon bag containing spare filters, lenses and film. Slope-shouldered, pushing fifty, he'd embarked on a successful weight-gain program a few years before and had never looked back. Day by day, his body had swelled in silence. Because he kept buying new clothes his slowly increasing bulk passed unnoticed for twenty pounds or so, despite the fact that he was surrounded by highly trained police officers – people who liked to think of themselves as observant. It was Parker who finally noticed that Dutton had graduated to a size-seventeen collar. Dutton explained that bulking up had many benefits. For example he had a reserved table at his neighbourhood Tim Horton's. On escalators, he never had to stand next to a stranger. Women stopped propositioning him. When he fell down, it didn't hurt as much. And on and on. He was, in short, unrepentant.

Dutton liked to think of himself as an artist. For years, he'd been pushing a proposal for a coffee-table book consisting of lurid crime-scene photographs culled from two decades behind the lens. The book was called *Sudden Death*, and during the past few years he'd sent an outline and sample pics to more than fifty publishers. Nobody was interested. To the average human being, the book was morbid almost beyond belief. Dutton became embittered. Photography was his life. He took the rejection slips personally; they diminished him in his own eyes, and he reacted quite naturally, by chowing down, gaining weight. The entire squadroom, even unusually insensitive cops like Eddy Orwell and Ralph Kearns, began to see obese people in a different light. No longer were they summarily dismissed as pigs at the trough; they were frustrated *artistes*.

There was nothing much in the bathroom that caught Dutton's eye, other than Parker, who'd pistol-whip him if he even thought about taking her picture. He backed into the bedroom, shot a dozen Polaroids, and switched to his Nikon. His beloved Nikon. The powerwinder whirred as he clicked through frame after frame of bulkloaded film. Zagros Galee jumped and twitched in the bursts of white light from the electronic flash. Dutton changed lenses, and the corpse fell still. Dutton began to compose his photographs with more care. He crouched and stagger-stepped across the room. His eye and brain, everything, every ounce of the two hundred and twenty pounds of him, had been squeezed into the camera. His plump index finger stroked the shutter release. The corpse was flailed by the light. Black shadows leapt across the bed. Zagros Galee rose up as if shaken from a deep sleep, then sank back onto the sheets.

Bradley said, "There's a spent cartridge under the bed, Mel."

Dutton nodded, kept shooting film. He changed lenses again and took an extreme close-up of Zagros' bullet head, his gaping mouth and the dark, wide-set eyes that seemed to have been encased in plastic.

When he got down to peek beneath the bed, his suit pants split down the seam from beltloop to crotch. Parker had looked before she could stop herself. Dutton wore canary-yellow underpants decorated with bright red hearts pierced by a stylized arrow. Still on his hands and knees, he fingered the tear, and gave her a rueful look. "I told the salesman I wanted a forty-eight, but oh no, he had to squeeze me into a forty-six. Me, a forty-six?" Dutton laughed bitterly. He took three quick shots of the spent cartridge under the bed, and clambered awkwardly to his feet. "Okay, I'm done." He glanced around. "Any special requests, before I head back downtown?"

"Lend me your camera," said Bradley, "and turn around. And bend over."

Dutton waggled a remonstrative finger. "For now, it's the nineties. Sexual harassment is strictly *verboten*, Inspector."

Willows used the tip of his pen to fish the cartridge out from under the bed. It was a .44 Magnum, manufactured in the U.S.A. by Sierra Bullets. He dropped the cartridge into a plastic evidence bag, sealed the bag tight.

As he strolled jauntily out of the room, cigar uptilted at a rakish angle and his hands in his jacket pockets, Bradley said, "Take your time, kids."

In the walk-in closet, Willows found fifteen suits, most of them grey or black and all of them double-breasted Armanis in shiny fabrics. The suits were a little long in the leg for Dutton, but the waist size was close enough, in an emergency. Fifty thousand dollars' worth of suits. Jeez.

Parker was working her way through the black-lacquered tallboy. There was a jewellery box on top of the bureau, box and lid both cut from a solid chunk of wood. She took a peek inside. Gold chain. Anchor-weight gold chain, and plenty of it. A man's diamond ring. Several diamond stud earrings. A gold Rolex ringed with diamonds.

Parker said, "Tommy likes diamonds."

"I don't think so, or he wouldn't have left them lying around like that." Willows gestured towards the entrance hall. "A hundred grand worth of dead animals, the same or more in diamonds. And he's trying to sell his apartment, letting strangers wander around as if they owned the place? This stuff should be in a vault."

"Or hidden at the back of my closet," said Parker.

Willows stood over the corpse. Zagros Galee wore a gold-coloured Seiko, a thick gold bracelet with links shaped like miniature horseshoes, and a plain gold wedding band. In the top drawer of the night table, he found an unopened package of contraceptives and an initialled solid-gold money clip containing a slim wad of crisp new hundreds. His gloves made counting the money difficult, but there was a thousand bucks in the clip. Consecutive serial numbers.

"The way I see it," said Parker, "he was shot to death by an altruistic burglar, following an episode of hot sex."

Willows drew her attention to the unopened pack of contraceptives.

"Okay," said Parker, "*before* they had sex. Or after they had unprotected sex – which could make an excellent motive."

Willows bent to the sheets. His nostrils flared at the scent of cologne. Calvin Klein, one of those.

They had a victim. There he was, close enough to touch. Now all they needed was a motive, and the perp or perps. He yawned widely. A motive, the perp, and a cup of coffee sweetened with a dollop of Scotch.

They found Inspector Bradley in the kitchen, surrounded by freeloading crime-scene-unit cops dressed in baggy white coveralls. The cops looked like modern-day Klansmen, but were probably, on average, more conservative in their politics. Bradley gave the appearance of being calm, but had chewed an inch or two off his unlit cigar. He raised an eyebrow.

Willows shrugged.

Parker didn't have much to add to that, but didn't want to leave Bradley hanging in front of the troops. She said, "Robbery doesn't appear to have been a motive. There's a ton of expensive jewellery in there. No bruises or contusions on the victim's body."

"And I bet you looked real hard," said one of the Klansmen.

"No signs of a struggle," added Parker. "The door was locked?" Bradley nodded.

She said, "Whoever shot him knew him pretty well, was on intimate terms with him." She turned and stared the jokester cop straight in the eye, until he faltered, and looked away.

"Chickenshit," said Parker.

The cop bristled. He thrust out his chin. "You say somethin'?"

"No, wait," said Bradley.

"I said you were a chickenshit." Parker effortlessly stared the cop down again. Two for two. Willows smiled and smiled.

The csu leader pushed forward. "You finished in there?" He had spoken to Willows, but Jack ignored him.

Parker let the question lie there for a moment, gathering dust. Finally she said, "Yeah, we're finished. Go ahead, make yourselves at home."

Bradley waited until the csu cops had filed down the hall and then said, "My dad used to tell me, 'A friend is a friend forever, but an enemy is an enemy for life.' "

"I let that jerk step on me, I'm done," said Parker with conviction. She took a hard line, but she had good reason; she'd seen first-hand what happened to female officers who didn't stand tall. The pressure kept on getting worse, until they quit. And the minute they were gone, they were gone.

Bradley said, "Let's step outside, get some fresh air." He gave Parker a reassuring smile, and she saw that his left front bottom tooth was dying, turning black. He pushed open a sliding glass door on a duckboard patio, lots of potted shrubbery and a few small trees, a patio table and half a dozen chairs, a small fishpond made out of interlocked four-by-fours with a black plastic liner. A mosquito buzzed her. Bradley rotated his cigar as he lit up with a big wooden kitchen match. The match had burned down to his fingers by the time he'd gotten the cigar going to his satisfaction. He exhaled a cloud of aromatic Cuban smoke, spread his arms wide. "Isn't that an absolutely *wonderful* view!"

Willows slapped at a mosquito. Had Bradley dragged them outside so he could enjoy his cigar, or lit his cigar to keep away the mosquitos?

One point two million, thought Parker. From where she happened to be standing she could see the lights of two bridges, city hall, a working cement factory, most of False Creek and a couple of billion dollars' worth of sailboats. There was hardly any traffic on either of the bridges. When she turned to look behind her she had a view of the downtown core as well as several bits and pieces of the North Shore mountains. She was downwind of Bradley, moved away as he exhaled another cloud of smoke. The pond was empty but for a few dark fish. Carp? She bent over the still water. The muzzle of a short-barrelled revolver peeped out at her from the bottom of the pool. The water was clear and the light was good. The gun was a big-bore revolver, stainless. The water was so clear that she could see the four hollowpoints in the chambers. The gun was almost certainly a .44.

"Jack . . ."

Parker slipped out of her jacket. She rolled up the sleeve of her blouse. The fish scattered in panic as she slid her hand into the water. The pond was only about two feet deep. She hooked a finger inside the revolver's trigger guard.

The gun was a Smith & Wesson model 624. A .44 Magnum. Four-inch barrel. No signs of rust. Pondwater dripped from the muzzle.

Bradley said, "Assuming that's the murder weapon, why would the killer toss it in the pond instead of off the side of the building into False Creek, where it'd be a hell of a lot less likely to be found?"

"We'll ask him, when we catch him," said Willows. There were powder smudges and stippling on Zagros Galee's chest; the shot had been fired at close range but wasn't a contact wound. The highrise was built of solid concrete and the soundproofing would be state of the art. If the .44 was the murder weapon, it would've made a hell of a racket. *Somebody* should have heard the shot. Who was Miss Anonymous? Hookers carried cheap knives, not expensive handguns. And a hooker would've taken the cash and jewellery. Or was there a whole bunch of stuff that had disappeared and they didn't know about? It was kind of late to be doing business, but could she have been a prospective client? Or – and Willows kind of liked this one – a competing agent? There'd be a tape at 312 Main of Miss Anonymous' call. Maybe he'd get lucky and recognize her voice. Dream on. He made a mental note to check the local cab companies as soon as the time of death was established, to see if there'd been any calls from the building for a pickup, during the right time frame.

Parker said, "Why is the floor number in the elevator twenty-three, instead of "P" for penthouse?"

"It was changed at the request of the owner," said Bradley. He smiled. "Mr. Lee didn't want people thinking he might be in some way involved with the magazine."

Parker almost said, "What magazine?" She caught herself in the nick of time.

Bradley flicked ash over the railing. A kayak slipped silently over black water, turned in towards the powerboats moored at the south end of the bridge. The kayak was painted black or dark blue. The paddler was dressed in dark clothing. Bradley made a mental note to tell the uniform stationed at the apartment door to call the harbour patrol. He pointed into the night sky, far off to the north. "Look, there's the Big Dipper."

Parker followed the line of his arm.

"See it?" said Bradley.

Parker nodded. Yeah, there it was, all right.

9

Shelley was awakened by the sound of somebody doing their best to kick in his front door. He snapped upright, his sleepy eyes struggling to claw light out of the darkness. Man, what a *racket*. Where was he? On the sofa. He'd fallen asleep watching a Woody Allen movie. Woody and Mia, before the fall. So funny! He checked his watch. It was a little after three. Who'd pound on his door at three o'clock in the morning? The two beer-guzzling cops? Miss Miata's boyfriend? Nobody he could think of that he wanted to know.

Or was it, could it be . . . *Bo*?

His heart leapt. He ran his fingers through his hair and trotted over to the door, snapped on the porch light.

Bo had her freckled nose pressed against the bevelled glass. She gave him a great big smile, even though he doubted she could see him. What a lovely woman. Gorgeous. She could make a fortune, selling encyclopedias. Or a dose of rat poison and a glass of water, if she was in the mood. He slipped the deadbolt, unhooked the safety chain and swung wide the door. Bo said, "Glad to see me?" She bent at the knees to pick up her battered suitcase.

"Anybody would be," said Shelley. He reached out to take the suitcase but she brushed right past him.

Shelley looked out at the street. Nothing.

The suitcase thumped on the oak floor. What'd she have in there

– her anvil collection? Bo put her arms around him. He turned into her. She kicked shut the door.

In the den, Mia Farrow said something that sounded like, "I wish I knew . . ."

Bo stroked Shelley's biceps. She adjusted a lock of his hair, and then reached up and grabbed his ears, pulled him down where she could get at him, and kissed him like she really meant it.

"Where've you been?" said Shelley when she'd finally finished pulping his lips. Was he whining? Maybe a little.

"Believe me, you don't want to know."

She smelled like she'd been working out. Running, maybe. The roots of her hair were damp, and there was a glow to her skin. She was wearing white leather Nikes, pink socks, silk shorts in a shiny mock-tartan, a low-cut, skintight, fluorescent-green-with-pink-polka-dots tanktop. No lipstick.

Shelley thought she looked great.

He looked her up and down and up and down again, as she led him into the kitchen, opened the refrigerator door, and helped herself to a Diet Coke.

He said, "I was worried about you."

She poked him in the ribs. "Don't make a habit of it."

"Not exactly *worried*," amended Shelley. "Not worried you could take care of yourself, or anything like that. What I mean is, I was worried that you weren't coming back."

Bo scrunched up her forehead. Thinking. She shrugged. "Well, I *am* here. For now, anyway. So stop worrying. Worry never got anybody anything except a migraine." She pried the can's metal tab back enough to let the gas escape with a low hiss, but not so much that you could tell the can had been opened by looking at it.

Shelley watched, fascinated, as she tilted back her head to drink. He watched her throat move, silky and smooth. She looked at him and said, "Where else would I go?"

"Somewhere else." A twisted grin. "There must be a million places you could be if you wanted to."

Bo drank some Coke. She made a face. "What've you been doing since I left, Shell?"

"Nothing much. I washed the dishes and put them away. Walked around the block a few times. Watched some TV."

"Yeah, what'd you watch?"

"Uh, all kinds of stuff. Whatever was on. *Hard Copy*, part of a Woody Allen movie, one of the old ones . . ."

Bo moved up against him, wriggled her body. She said, "I need a shower, and so do you."

"I do?"

Bo laughed. "Don't look so *worried*. You don't smell bad, if that's what you're thinking." She giggled. "Kind of musty, maybe. It isn't that you *need* a shower, it's just that you should *take* a shower." The shape of her face changed as she drank some more Coke. "You go first, so I can use all the water I want without *worrying* about there being enough left for you."

Shelley hesitated.

Bo reached behind him and friskily slapped his butt. "Move it, handsome. I want you kissin' clean all over, and I mean now."

It wasn't that he was shy. Hell, no. But . . .

She handed him the Coke, said, "Don't blame me if you run out of water," and turned and walked away. He heard her footsteps on the stairs, imagined he heard the slippery sound of her clothes hitting the floor. And then, for sure, he did hear the thunder of the shower. He put the unfinished Coke back in the fridge and went back into the den and sat down on the sofa, the cushions still warm from the heat of his body. Woody sure was a lovable shmuck. Smart, too. And rich. Sophisticated. But kind of a messed-up dude, if Mia could be believed.

He was watching a commercial for Saturn automobiles when Bo came back downstairs. He'd taken a look at a Saturn when he was in the market for a new car. Not that he expected to get one, just that it was always a good idea to comparison shop. The cars were a lot smaller than he'd expected. Not quite tiny, but getting there. The models they hired to stand alongside the car in the magazine ads must be about four feet tall.

Bo was wearing one of his silk shirts. Or actually it belonged to the owner of the house. The shirt was unbuttoned, but artfully arranged. She'd washed her flaming red hair and towelled it dry, fluffed it up so it had that devil-may-care curly look that was so popular, in certain circles. She smelled of expensive perfume, and had put on fresh lipstick in a retro-pink that he found, uh, alluring. When she leaned into him, the shirt went south. Her smooth damp skin radiated heat, felt like it was about one hundred and twenty degrees. She said, "Your turn."

Shelley's eyes flicked from her breasts to the screen and back again. The movie started. Woody and Mia were in the kitchen, yakking. His memory totted up at least a hundred freckles . . .

Bo said, "Isn't this the one with a happy ending, kind of?"

Shelley nodded. He said, "Yeah, I think so." He snuck another look down her neckline.

She said, "I left it running."

"Yeah?" What was she talking about?

"The shower," said Bo. "Hurry up, okay?" She kissed him on the mouth. He imagined his mouth turning pink. He reached for her but she turned and walked away from him, the shirt billowing, then falling back. Bo oblivious or not caring. Or very much aware, and caring a great deal.

Shelley fumbled with the buttons of his shirt as he trotted up the stairs. Sometimes you had to take a chance in life. Hadn't he fallen in love with her already, on a certain level? Not that he was sure he'd recognize the symptoms, whatever they were. He had no urge to sneak an apple on her desk, so it was different than last time, back in grade seven. How could he love her if he wasn't willing to take a chance?

There was a puddle of water on the bathroom floor. Her lipstick and perfume lay on the counter. He picked them up. Touch, touch. Smell, smell. The water was a little too hot. He turned down the temperature and stepped beneath the spray. She must've used his soap. He turned the bar in his hands, working up a lather, and then sudsed his groin. He imagined what she must look like, cleaning herself. He washed his legs, his buttocks, his belly. He washed his arms and his armpits. His hair was damp. The bathroom was thick with steam. He washed his hair twice, turned the temperature up a notch or two and stood there, sluicing himself off beneath the spray.

The phone rang. He wondered who could be calling him at that time of night. Nobody. The phone rang again. He turned off the shower and grabbed a towel. The phone kept ringing. He stepped out of the shower. Drops of water splattered on the marble floor. Cones of steam swirled in the lights. He yelled, "Bo, could you get that for me, please?" The phone kept ringing. He wrapped the towel around his waist and went into the bedroom and picked up and said hello.

Someone close enough to touch breathed heavily into his ear. He said, "Who is this?"

Whoever'd called slammed down the phone. The air was suddenly chill. Goosebumps blossomed.

The front door slammed shut.

He yelled, "Bonnie? Bo!"

Down on the street, a car started with a roar, then settled down. The exhausts burbled steadily. Shelley knew that sound as he knew the beating of his heart. He ran to the window. The sx's headlights illuminated an empty street, a strip of well-mowed boulevard.

Bo leaned across the passenger seat to look up at him. Her face was a pale oval. She waved at him.

Shelley lost the towel as he hit the front porch steps. The scent of flowers hung heavy in the air.

By the time he reached the street she was gone, vanished. He stood there in the middle of the road under the streetlight, naked as a man could be, risking arrest and incarceration. Lights blinked in the sky. A big jet thundered down towards the airport, was lost in the glitter. Shockwaves pounded him.

Back in the house, he discovered that she'd taken his wallet and his watch. The fridge door was open. She'd taken the can of Coke, too.

He kicked the scuffed suitcase over on its side. Unlatched and opened it. He couldn't have been more wrong. It wasn't anvils she collected, it was bricks.

10

The sun was flirting with the horizon and Bradley was long gone by the time the surly CSU thugs left. Parker kept Willows waiting while she went back out on the patio to find out if she could see as far as the white-clad peak of Mt. Baker, deep into Washington State and more than one hundred miles away.

Easy.

They took a last quick look around the apartment and then sealed the door with wire and a lead tag, yellow crime-scene tape.

Zagros Galee lived on East Nineteenth, just the wrong side of Main. The house was only a few years old and was typical of houses that were being built all around the city. Design without imagination, architecture without merit. The stucco was such a bland colour that it was hardly a colour at all, the windows were framed in aluminum; the roof clad in heavy, dull black tiles. The front steps were concrete and the railing was made of twisted wrought-iron. An aluminum rail fence with a baked-on brown-enamel finish defined the property. Concrete-block posts at the front gate supported placid miniature lions cast in cement. Willows unlatched the gate. The King of Beasts' eyes had been sloppily spraypainted fluorescent orange. Willows was generally opposed to vandalism, but in this case sympathized with the artist's sentiment.

There were lights on inside the house even though the sun was well clear of the horizon and it was a bright and sunny day. A cloud of starlings whirred out of a maple tree and descended on the neighbour's gravelled front yard. A pot-bellied little boy made of white-painted concrete urinated endlessly into a tiny pool. Parker and Willows climbed the steps without much enthusiasm. They were about to inflict bottomless grief on a fellow human being. Some essentially innocent soul. Willows thumbed the buzzer.

The starlings swaggered *en masse* towards the pool of mock urine. They capered about in the water, jockeying for position, rubbing shoulders, jostling, chattering brainlessly, gargling with relish.

The door opened a crack.

Willows held up his badge. He identified himself, and then Parker. The door swung wide. A small child, a girl no more than three or four years old, stared solemnly up at them. She wore a fluffy pale-pink sleeper. A stuffed crocodile dragged its toothy face on the carpet. There was something about the set of the child's eyes that reminded Parker of Zagros Galee.

Parker said, "Is your mommy home?" The girl nodded. She scratched her nose and offered Parker her hand. Parker said, "Maybe you better call her, sweetheart."

Mrs. Galee was about five-two, a little overweight. She had toffee-coloured skin and unruly bleached-blond hair. She was in her late thirties. Her given name was Moira. She wore a loose-fitting pale-blue short-sleeved cotton blouse, baggy white tennis shorts, worn Nikes, gold hoop earrings and more makeup than Parker used in a week. She led them into the kitchen, at the back of the house. She'd cooked herself a breakfast of scrambled eggs, sausages and hash browns, whole-wheat toast. A sprig of parsley paid token obeyance to the gods of good health. There was something that was odd about the meal, but Parker couldn't think what it was.

The kitchen table was made of hundreds of small blocks of maple that had been glued together and then finished with a high-gloss sheen. It looked like a jigsaw puzzle for simpletons. The chairs had maple-block seats and maple-veneer plywood backs that had been ergonomically designed to please the eye and vex the spine. Mrs. Galee invited the two detectives to sit down. Parker sat directly across from her. Willows took the chair on Mrs. Galee's right, at the far end of the table. The little girl sat on her mother's lap and from time to time picked at her congealing breakfast.

Parker said, "Do you know why we're here, Mrs. Galee?"

"Zagros did something, eh? What'd he do?"

Parker glanced at Willows. She said, "Could we speak to you alone for a moment? Is there someone – a neighbour – your child could spend some time with, while we're talking to you?"

"Nothing you could say about Zagros would shock her." Moira Galee speared a sausage. She chewed and swallowed. Her voice was bitter as she said, "Michelle knows very well what kind of fool her father has become."

Whew! thought Parker.

Willows discreetly took out his spiral-bound notebook and the silver Cross pen Annie had given him on his last birthday.

Parker said, "Well, I don't want to argue with you, Mrs. Galee. I have to tell you that you should prepare yourself for a terrible shock."

The woman's head came up. She nodded.

Parker showed her the most discreet of Mel Dutton's Polaroids. "Is this your husband?"

"Yes, that is Zagros."

Parker returned the photograph to her purse.

Mrs. Galee quartered a sausage. She used her fork to shove a piece of meat through a mound of ketchup, brought the fork up to her mouth. Her cheek bulged. She stared thoughtfully across the table at Parker. "Would you like some coffee?"

"Please," said Parker.

Mrs. Galee put her daughter aside. She went over to the counter and poured two cups of coffee. She put the coffee down in front of the detectives and fetched a four-litre plastic jug of milk from the fridge. She thumped the jug of milk down on the table between them, and then gave her daughter a sausage and a piece of toast and told her to go into her room, shut the door and play quietly until she was called for. The child left without a word.

"Now, tell me what happened."

"We have some very bad news," said Parker.

"Yes, what is it?"

Experience had taught Parker what a disaster it could be to beat about the bush. Without further preamble, she said, "Mrs. Galee, I'm sorry to have to tell you that your husband is dead."

"He's dead?"

"Yes, I'm sorry, but it's true. He's dead."

"Murdered," said Willows.

The widow scooped a forkful of scrambled egg from her plate. She lifted the fork to her lips, held it rock steady, and then lowered it to the plate. She looked out the back window at a loop of power line.

"Murdered, you say. Someone killed him?"

Parker nodded.

"Where did this happen?"

"Downtown," said Parker vaguely.

"No, I mean what part of his body." The woman reached across the table. She grasped Parker's arm and held her tight. "Tell me, was he wounded in the penis?"

Willows drank some coffee. It was better than Inspector Bradley's. It was better than the coffee he made at home, in fact.

"Why do you think that might be the case?" said Parker.

"What do you imagine? It was the part of him that was always getting him into trouble. I don't know what it was about him. Such an ugly man, don't you think?" She glanced keenly at Parker. "He was so sure of himself, so certain of his charms."

Parker said, "How long had you been married, Mrs. Galee?"

"Eleven years. We have only the one child. Michelle. My sweet baby."

"Do you know anyone who would want to harm your husband?"

"Everyone he met. Anyone who happened to pass him on the street. He cared for no one but himself." The tines of Moira Galee's fork clanged violently against her plate. "His penis was like an overcooked sausage, all wrinkled and black. He was the worst kind of pig."

"How do you know he was involved with other women?" said Parker.

"He told me. He bragged about it. He thought he was so wonderful. He couldn't stop talking about himself, the idiot." She glared at Parker. Her eyes were wet with grief. But who was she grieving for, her husband or herself?

Parker reached across the table and took her hand. If ever there was a time, now was the time. "Did you kill him?" she said quietly.

"Over and over again. Why not? He deserved it." She wiped her face with the back of her hand. "No, I didn't kill him. I couldn't afford to kill him. If I killed him, how would I live? Who would pay the bills?"

Parker settled back. She poured a dollop of milk into her coffee and screwed the orange plastic cap back on the jug. "Who were his friends?"

"He didn't have any friends. Not real friends. He had women. All his friends were women. Men didn't like him. He had a reputation; he was a man who took other men's women. So men stayed away from him."

"There must've been somebody . . ." Parker faltered. "Did he have any relatives?"

"He has a brother in Iran. His father and mother have been dead a long time, many years." She scraped the blade of her knife across the tines of her fork. "That's it, there's no one else." She ate another segment of sausage. No ketchup, this time. She said, "I knew someone would kill him, that it was only a matter of time. He couldn't stop himself, with the women. It was a sickness but he wouldn't admit it. And there was something else. He was not a very good salesman. He would try to sell a house and end up seducing the woman. Or more often he offended her, and there would be a complaint. He was fired many, many times. But he kept making money. More and more money. Always more money."

"But not from selling houses, is that what you're telling me?"

"He told me it was houses, but I didn't believe him. I never believed him. He was always lying. To me, Michelle, whoever would listen. He did it out of habit or maybe just for practice, to improve his skills."

The child, Michelle, padded silently into the kitchen. She stole the last sausage from her mother's plate, offered it to the crocodile, and left as quietly as she had come.

"Isn't she beautiful?"

"Very beautiful," said Parker.

Mrs. Galee turned to Willows. "Tell me what you think, what is truly in your mind."

"She's a very beautiful child," said Willows. "Exceptionally beautiful."

"She has her father's eyes. Such beautiful eyes, so large and dark. It was Zagros' eyes that I fell in love with. Not the eyes of your picture but the eyes of his life. So lovely. Not like a man's eyes at all, in some ways. Eyes that were soft, and could be wounded. He had such long lashes. When we were younger, his eyes were full of laughter and sometimes I wept with joy just to look at him, if you can believe such a thing."

Willows flexed his wrist. He was getting writer's cramp. Moira Galee seemed to have forgotten that he was there, and he was glad of it, because he was very sure that his presence was an impediment to the investigation. He scratched his nose with the end of his pen. Some women got the men they deserved, but most didn't. Probably it was the same with men.

Parker said, "Did he have any enemies – that you knew of?"

"Many. But I don't know who they were. He has a phone in his office, for business, that has a separate number."

Parker said, "He had an office here, in the house?"

"Yes."

"What about his social life?"

"I told you, he had no friends. His job was everything to him. Whatever job he had that made him so happy. Something to do with real estate, because that was all he knew."

Parker's chair creaked as she leaned forward. She made a vague gesture that encompassed the house and everything in it. "You don't know where the money came from?"

"How could I know when he would never tell me? He sold only three or four houses or apartments in a year. In the past year, two small sales. But he always had plenty of money."

"What kind of financial arrangement did you have?"

Moira Galee chased the last of the scrambled egg across her plate. "He gave me money every week, for food. He paid the telephone and electric and gas and all the other bills. He gave me money for clothing and other things as I needed it. For example if Michelle needed a new winter coat I had to tell him exactly how much it would cost. Then he would give me the money and I would buy the coat and show him the receipt."

Parker said, "You mentioned that he had a business telephone in his room. Would you mind showing us his office now, please?"

For the first time, Mrs. Galee showed signs of discomfort. "Why do you want to see it?"

"Your husband has been murdered," said Parker. "Our job is to find out who murdered him."

"How could the room help you?"

"We won't know," said Parker, "until we look." She offered Mrs. Galee a sympathetic smile. "Despite any problems you may have had, surely you want your husband's murderer brought to justice."

"Yes, of course." Moira Galee cleared the table. Willows put away his pen and notebook as she put the dirty dishes in the dishwasher, added soap, turned the machine on, and led them up a steep flight of narrow, enclosed stairs to the finished attic. Bright scraps of red, blue, purple, and green carpet had been cut to size and tacked to the treads.

At the landing, larger pieces of carpet had been strewn haphazardly about. The ceiling sloped so sharply that Willows had to duck his head. There were two doors, one at either end of the landing. Mrs. Galee led them around a brick chimney. The door to the dead man's office was deadbolted, but Willows had brought Zagros Galee's keyring from the BeachView apartment. He and Parker pulled on latex gloves. Willows unlocked the door. Parker told Mrs. Galee she'd call her if she needed her. She and Willows entered the room. Parker firmly shut the door.

The room ran right across the width of the house; the steeply pitched ceiling came down to within a few feet of the floor. The drywall had been taped, but not sanded or painted. A small window overlooked the backyard, unpaved alley, a collapsed Ford Pinto. The only pieces of furniture in the room were a camp cot and a small wooden packing crate. A crumpled down sleeping bag lay on the cot. A lamp from Ikea had been clamped to the bed's metal frame. On the crate was a Panasonic fax machine and a glass ashtray overflowing with cigarette butts. The cigarettes were all the same brand. No lipstick. The fax had an integral telephone and answering machine. The red message light flashed in sequences of three.

Willows pressed the rewind and playback buttons.

Three hangups. He turned the volume up, until the machine hissed like a mildly perturbed snake. The tape continue to unwind.

Parker checked out the bed. She turned the sleeping bag inside out, and then flipped over the thin mattress, pulled the bed away from the wall, examined the Ikea lamp. Finally, she kept the fax machine securely in place with a splayed hand as she tilted the crate and looked beneath it.

Beneath the scraps of carpet there was nothing but fir boards. The tape rolled on.

Parker said, "Turn it down, Jack. It's giving me the creeps."

Willows turned down the volume. The window was held closed by a hook and nail. He swung it open and stuck his head outside and looked around. A squirrel bounced across a neighbour's lawn.

Zagros Galee had not taped or stapled or otherwise fastened any clues to the skin of his house. Willows left the window open. It was stuffy inside the little room. Downstairs, a child shrieked.

They'd looked everywhere, found nothing.

He flipped open the Panasonic's trapdoor of black plastic, turned over the tape, and pressed the playback button.

A woman said, "Zagros? Come and see me."

Willows perked up. He let the tape spool right through to the end, but the woman didn't call back. She sounded young, in her twenties or even younger. No accent that he could detect. Willows ejected the tape, dropped it in the pocket of his sports jacket.

Parker picked up the fax machine and put it on the bed. She placed the ashtray on the floor and turned the packing crate upside down. A buff legal-size envelope had been push-pinned to an inside wall. The envelope was bulky with its contents.

Willows smiled. "What made you do that?"

Parker shrugged. The envelope was held in place with four pins. She pulled the pins out one by one, ripped open the envelope and shook fat wads of American cash onto the bed. The top and bottom bills of each tight-packed stack of money were hundreds, and so were all the bills in between.

Willows sat down on the bed and started counting. The bundles of cash were all of identical thickness. It took him only a few minutes to calculate that the dead real-estate agent had socked away a cool thirty thousand dollars, in U.S. funds.

He briefly checked his written notes. Mrs. Galee had given them all the ammunition a judge would need to allow them to confiscate the money.

In the meantime, it was probably best to leave things pretty much as they'd found them. He suggested as much to Parker. She stuffed the cash back in the envelope and push-pinned the envelope to the inside of the packing crate. Willows placed the fax machine and ashtray back on the crate. He pulled the window shut and fastened the latch.

Parker suddenly realized that what was odd about Moira Galee's breakfast was that she had arranged the food on her plate in exactly the same way it was done at Denny's restaurants, right down to that small sprig of parsley.

They found Mrs. Galee in Michelle's bedroom, tidying up. Parker asked her if there was anyone who could take care of the child for an hour or two.

"You want me to look at Zagros?"

"Just for a moment." Parker glanced at the little girl. She had her alligator tucked beneath her arm and seemed deeply involved in a picture book. But you never could tell.

"Do I have to do it?"

Parker nodded.

"He's gone. Good! Or you could say it was too bad, a terrible thing. I don't want to see him again. Do you understand?"

"Sure," said Parker. Because after all, what was one more lie.

11

The door slammed shut. Shelley heard her footsteps on the stairs and then, all of a sudden, there she was. He rubbed sleep from his eyes. Birdsong drifted in through the open window. He'd been wide awake all night, past sunrise. The newspaper had thumped against the front door at ten past seven. The delivery guy whistling a tune from *Showboat* as he'd approached the house. Shelley glanced at the bedside clock. It was a few minutes past ten; he'd slept an hour or two at most.

Bo had a big paper bag full of croissants, a hotel-size jar of marmalade, lattes from *Bean Around The World*, a copy of the *Province*. She was also carrying a large tartan suitcase, big brother to the bag that had contained the bricks. She plunked herself down on the kingsize bed and worked the cardboard lid off a latte, asked Shelley if marmalade was okay.

He nodded.

Her pink tongue dipped into cinnamon-laced foam. "You call the cops?"

"About what?"

"Me stealing your overpowered sports car. Which I got washed and hot-waxed at that Esso station, Forty-First and Granville." She squeezed his thigh through the blankets. "I like that unshaven, hair all messed up, casual kind of gonna-brush-my-teeth-in-a-minute look. Real cute."

"So I've been told." To his way of thinking, Bo didn't look too cute herself, with that big mouse under her eye. Maybe she'd walked into a door, but he had a feeling somebody'd slugged her, and slugged her hard. His brain was awhirl, buzzing with anger and questions. But, for the moment at least, he was going to keep quiet. Bo seemed a little high-strung. The last thing she needed was him nagging at her. Or was that all wrong, would she think he was apathetic and disinterested, if he didn't speak up?

Bo squeezed him again, a little higher up. She smiled into his eyes.

Shelley drank some coffee. It was pretty good. He glanced at the *Province* headline. TOT MURDERED! It was the paper's all-time favourite phrase. Bo unscrewed the lid from the marmalade jar. She dipped the point of a croissant into the jar and passed the croissant to Shelley. Their fingers touched.

He said, "Nah, I didn't phone the cops. What would I tell them? That my new girlfriend borrowed my car?"

Bo smiled. "You knew I was coming back, did you?"

"Yeah, sure. I figured, as long as I had your suitcase full of bricks, what choice did you have?"

"Good point." A scattering of crumbs lay across Bo's delicious tanned thighs. She industriously licked marmalade from her fingers, brushed the crumbs away.

Shelley drank some more coffee, to give himself an excuse to swallow.

Bo said, "Isn't it a wonderful day!"

He nodded. Bo took his croissant. She squished it up until she could dip it partway into the marmalade, passed it back to him. "I forgot the knife. Want me to read to you?"

"Sure," said Shelley. He felt oddly happy. He wolfed down the last of the croissant, cradled the latte to his chest and snuggled a little deeper into bed.

Bo read him those few nuggets of good news she was able to cull from the tabloid-style pages of the newspaper. It was an unhappy world. Sudden death, all the way from age-old personal vendettas to massive armed conflicts, raged all across the globe. Bo read the dialogue and then leaned into him and showed him the "Calvin and Hobbes" strip. He chuckled manfully.

"You don't think it's funny?"

Shelley said, "No, I do. I think it's *very* funny. The guy's a genius." He held her hand. "I like your tiger voice."

"Really?" Bo seemed enormously pleased. She rattled the newspaper. "You didn't exactly split a gut."

"I'm sorry. I'm tired. I was up all night."

She smiled. "Worrying? About me? Now *that's* funny!" She grasped the duvet and gave it a good shake. Bits and pieces of croissant rained down upon the hardwood floor. The duvet settled over him. She said, "You've got a terrific body, handsome." Lightly brushed a stray lock of hair from his forehead. "Why don't you get some sleep. We can make love later, okay?"

"Okay," said Shelley. The coffee should've perked him up but hadn't. On the other hand, he'd only slept an hour or two all night. Bo closed his eyes with her fingers, kissed his eyelids, kissed him gently on the mouth. She tasted of ripe fruit, oranges and strawberries . . .

He heard her footsteps moving away from him, and then the roar of the shower across the hall. She was a very clean young lady. But what was she was so eager to wash away? He fell asleep dreaming of her standing in the shower, the shower washing away her freckles, washing the red out of her hair. She turned and turned. The water beat down upon her, gradually eroded her features, washed her down the drain. The dream seemed to last a very long time. When it finally ended, Bo could have been anyone . . .

Shelley slept all through the morning and into the afternoon. When he finally awoke, the journey from deep sleep to a state of full alert was virtually instantaneous.

The house was quiet. A few birds twittered out in the garden. The curtains had been pulled to shield him from the sun. A gentle breeze made faint shadows dance along the wall. Bo had cleared away the breakfast leftovers and the newspaper. His three shirts had been freshly ironed; they hung from coat hangers hooked over the doorknob.

He sat up, eased out of bed, and padded naked into the bathroom. He stood at the toilet, urinating. The twin sinks, countertop and bathtub gleamed unnaturally. He shook himself and flushed. A fresh roll of toilet paper had been put on the dispenser, loose end out the way he liked it. The toothpaste spray had been wiped from the mirrors. The faucets sparkled, and he'd have bet his two front teeth there wasn't a goddamn germ in sight.

He turned on the shower.

As an afterthought, he lowered the toilet seat.

He showered, dried himself off, dressed in clean Levi's and a freshly ironed shirt, went downstairs.

The TV was playing to an audience of zero. Bo had been watching the Home Shopping Network. What he liked to think of as the Crystal Elephant Channel. She'd hit the mute button, bless her. He called her name.

No answer.

He turned off the TV and then thought better of it and turned it back on again. But in doing this he eliminated the mute feature. A guy with a whispery gangster's voice advised him to buy an autographed baseball. Yeah, okay. The remote control had slipped down between the sofa's cushions. He rooted it out, hit the mute. The word "MUTE" appeared in soft green letters in the bottom left corner of the screen. Shelley would like to see a programmable TV that let you choose your own word, a synonym. Something along the lines of "SHADDUP!" He began in a not-particularly-organized way to traverse the main floor of the house.

He couldn't find Bo anywhere, though there were small signs of her almost everywhere he looked. Drawers that had been opened but not closed. Things that had been picked up and put down in not quite the right place. Not to put too fine a point on it, but the girl was a snoop.

It occurred to Shelley that she might have taken his car for another test-drive. He jogged to the window. The sx squatted placidly in the shadows by the boulevard, freshly waxed paint gleaming in the speckled shade.

He heard the suck of rubber as the refrigerator door was yanked open. The door thumped shut. A bottle cap spun on the counter.

Bo was wearing a shiny silk suit with a little too much drape at the cuffs. A black silk shirt, yellow silk tie. Black lace-up shoes with three-inch heels and pointy, steel-capped toes. She'd dyed her hair blue-black and cut it short, in a kind of free-spirit buzz-cut. She had one plain gold and two diamond studs in her left ear and two plain gold studs in her right ear. Shelley wished he knew the code. He wished he knew if there *was* a code. The freckles had vanished. Bo's eyes were shiny brown, the pupils swollen and black. She'd plucked or shaved away her eyebrows. Her steel-rimmed glasses were wwii style, with circular, oversized lenses too large for her face. Bo had metamorphosed into a skinny Chinese kid in his early twenties, who was suffering from prema-ture male-pattern baldness.

But no. There she was, out on the deck. So who was the kid? Shelley asked him, point-blank. He added, "And what the hell are you doing in my house?"

The Chinese guy stared blandly at him. The suit was gunmetal grey, a double-breasted three-button model with stylish high lapels. His neck was about a size twelve. He held a bottle of beer in each hand, very loosely, and seemed completely at ease. Shelley doubted if the kid weighed more than one-thirty, but the way he held himself, every ounce of him must've been packed full of self-esteem. That or the unlikely bulge beneath his left armpit meant he was packing a gun in a shoulder rig.

Shelley said, "Are you a friend of Bo's?"

"Who?"

The kid was already moving away from him, towards the open door that led to the deck. He was a little too light on his feet to make it as a logger. Shelley's nose twitched at the scent of his cologne.

Bo waved at him through the open door. She lay on her stomach on a mauve-cushioned white-resin chaise longue, naked but for a fluffy white towel that inadequately covered her bum. There might be certain aspects of her life about which he was not fully informed, but one thing he knew for sure was that she wasn't unduly modest.

The kid had gone outside. Shelley followed him as far as the doorway. There was an older guy sitting bolt upright in one of the chairs. He could've been eighty or a hundred. The kid handed him a bottle of beer. The old guy's suit was silk, gunmetal grey, the same high-style model worn by the kid. Ditto his black silk shirt and yellow silk tie. Shelley didn't like the look of either of them. In a movie, they'd be the really bad guys, torturers and that ilk. Unredeemables. He had a strong feeling that in real life they were much worse. The kind of guys who punched women, for example. But it was always best to assume the best. He smiled a welcoming smile and stepped boldly onto the deck, bare feet padding on the boards.

Bo said, "Shell, I'd like you to meet some friends of mine."

Shelley waited. He was careful not to put his hands in his pockets. The kid had slumped into a chair, was sucking on his beer. His father continued to practise being implacable. Neither of them offered a friendly hand. Shelley wondered if it was possible to design a pocket-size collapsible crowbar.

Bo said, "This is Mr. Sticks and his son, Andrew."

"Sticks?" said Shelley, leaning forward a little, not quite believing that he'd got it right.

"Sticks," said Bo. She spelled it out for him.

Shelley unbuttoned his shirt, the pale blue Bass denim he'd bought at a factory outlet in Blaine and defiantly smuggled across the border a year or two earlier, when he was tending a condo in Delta. He stripped off the shirt and tossed it to Bo, turned and glared hard at his uninvited guests. In the face of his apparent eagerness to kick ass, Mr. Sticks and young Andrew searched the sky for interesting cloud formations. Bo struggled into the shirt. She fine-tuned the towel as she rolled over on her back.

"C'mere and gimme a kiss, baby."

Shelley wasn't at all sure who was supposed to volunteer, until he saw that she was crooking a finger at him. He kept an eye on the crowd as he went over and bent down and was given a noisy smack on the lips. He pulled up a chair and sat on the edge of it, tense, ready to go. Bo rested a hand on his thigh. Mr. Sticks looked pretty good for an old guy – probably it was all that monosodium glutamate in his diet – but the excessively cautious way he held himself in the chair gave away his antiquity. Still, if you trowelled on the makeup and lit him carefully enough, he and Andrew would be just about perfect for an Ivory Soap commercial . . .

If one of them had slugged Bo in the eye, it had to be the kid. Andrew. Shelley's stomach muscles tightened involuntarily. He glanced at Bo, and then turned his attention on the old man. "Were you invited, or just happen to be in the neighbourhood and thought you'd drop by?"

The old man's hair was a little on the long side, slicked straight back. No grey in it, not a trace. He was cooler than a cucumber though his son – if that's who he was – was sweating buckets. Shelley checked out the old man's ears. Kind of floppy, but unadorned.

The sun was on the move. Bo's feet were in shadow. He became aware of the musky scent of her sunscreen. Somewhere not far off somebody's lawn was being mowed.

Shelley cleared his throat. He clasped his hands. "Well, if we're all done talking . . ."

Andrew said, "I think you should know that Bonnie is my wife."

"Bullshit," said Bo, jumping to her feet. The towel puddled on the deck. The shirt had half an inch to spare, unless she took a deep breath.

"My beloved wife."

Mr. Sticks muttered something Shelley couldn't make out. Time to take a brush-up course in Mandarin. Or muttering.

"Common-law," Andrew amended. But that still wasn't good enough. He glared at his father, who responded by sipping delicately at his beer and then venting a loud belch and grinning broadly.

"Okay," said Andrew, "but she's my girlfriend and we're engaged."

Bo's raucous laughter was tinged with despair.

"We're redhot lovers," Andrew said, and seemed to mean it. He swilled the last of his beer and glanced twistedly towards the kitchen, as if willing the refrigerator to frog-march through the open door. His beady eyes lighted on Shelley, veered away. The lawnmower droned unmusically. Bo shook her head, as if mortally embarrassed. Mr. Sticks had dozed off.

Andrew stood up. He started towards the kitchen. Shelley said, "You've been cut off, kid."

"I was gonna take a leak."

"Use the toilet." Andrew disappeared into the house. "Put the seat back down when you're finished!" Shelley yelled after him. He glanced across the lane at the fisherman's house, then remembered that the fisherman had gone fishing, wasn't due back for a week or more. Wasn't that always the way? There was never a fisherman around when you needed one.

Bo said, "Get *rid* of them!"

"Yeah, okay." Shelley frowned, as he tried to formulate a plan. What worried him was that both Mr. Sticks and Andrew were wearing suits, and it wasn't suit weather. Mr. Sticks' eyes were open. He unbuttoned his suit. It came as no great surprise when Andrew stepped out on the deck with *his* suit unbuttoned. He went right at Shelley, no preliminaries, charged him as if he were a tank, but stopped short and snatched up Bo's towel. He snapped the towel at Bo's legs.

Shelley said, "Hey!"

"Hey what?" Andrew snapped the towel again, missing his redhot babe by scant inches. The little finger of his left hand was curled up like a McCain's French fry. He made a move towards his jacket. Yes, he had a gun. So did Mr. Sticks. Except for the

rhythmic flaring of Andrew's nostrils, father and son were absolutely motionless.

Shelley tried to think of something clever to say. When that
didn't work, he tried to think of something stupid to say. Under
the circumstances, any kind of thinking at all was an almost impossible chore.

Andrew said, "Put her clothing in a bag and bring it to me."

"What kind of bag?" said Shelley, eyeing the gun. It was weird.
His emotions were all mixed up. He was terrified, but ready to
die. Sort of. It was a fine line but he had to walk it. The thing
to remember was that agreeable was smart and obsequious was
chickenshit, and that all present knew the difference between the
two.

12

No surprises at the morgue. Mrs. Galee readily identified her husband's mortal remains. That was Zagros, all right. She enquired as to the whereabouts of his gold bracelet, the gold-plated Seiko. She signed everything out. Willows arranged for a unit to drive her home. He advised the cop behind the wheel not to worry if his fare wanted to be dropped off at a pawnshop.

It was Parker's turn to drive. As she unlocked the car she said, "I wonder if she's got a key to the upstairs room."

"Probably. She didn't ask us for her husband's."

Parker got into the Ford. She reached across to unlock Willows' door. He climbed in and rolled down his window. Parker started the engine and drove slowly towards the exit. She said, "No she didn't, and she didn't seem all that interested in hanging around to find out what was in there, either."

Willows said, "I doubt if she knows about the thirty grand. She was too calm. She'd have stopped us from making the search."

Parker made a right. "What d'you want to do about the money?"

"Talk to Bradley, but leave it where it is, for now."

"You shouldn't have pinched the tape, Jack."

"What tape?" said Willows, deadpan.

It was a Sunday, and the third floor of 312 Main was quiet and still. Grey enamelled-steel desks and legal-size file cabinets glowed dully under the strip fluorescent ceiling lights. The utilitarian carpet had been recently vacuumed, wastepaper baskets emptied. The pebbled glass door to Bradley's office was open a crack, but there was no movement within. Willows glanced inside. The office was empty, but Bradley's dark-blue uniform jacket was hung over the back of his chair, silver pips glowing softly. The entire Public Safety Building was a no-smoking area. An unlit cigar leaned into his spotless ashtray.

Willows went back to his desk. His desk and Parker's butted up against each other, so close that his paperwork often avalanched into her work area. She was on the phone. It took him a moment to realize she was talking to his daughter.

Parker said, "So where is he now?" She frowned. "No, it's okay. Tell her not to worry about it." She paused. "I know, I know. It's just terrible, but the main thing is, he's going to survive."

Parker saw the look on Willows' face. She cupped her hand over the mouthpiece and said, "It's Barney."

The family cat. Willows let go a deep breath. He said, "What about him? What's happened?"

Parker held up a restraining hand. She listened hard for a moment and then said, "No, don't worry about a thing. We'll take care of it." She said, "He's right here, honey. Do you want to talk to him?"

She handed Willows the phone.

Willows said, "Hi, Annie. What's the problem?"

Barney had darted in front of a car. His left foreleg was broken. There was a good chance the vet at the emergency clinic would have to amputate. The bill was going to be very steep.

Willows said, "I can't come home, Annie. We're in the middle of a case. But I'll tell you what. I'll authorize the vet to do whatever she can, no matter what the cost. Have you talked to Sean? Is he home? Well, give him a call. Tell him what happened and ask him if he can come home as soon as possible, to keep you company. If you can't get in touch with him, phone Pauline's mother and tell her what happened." Willows' mind raced. "Have you got any money? Good. I know you aren't hungry, but it would probably be a good idea to eat something. Annie, there's no point in hanging around the vet's all by yourself. I'd really prefer you didn't do that, Annie. It's important to remember that whatever happens to Barney is out of your hands. Who took him to the vet's? The woman who lives in the new house at the end of the block? She . . . did you get her name? That's okay, Annie. Try to be calm, all right?"

Willows encouraged his daughter to keep talking until she finally ran out of steam. He spoke to the vet's secretary, assured her he wanted the vet to do whatever was necessary to save Barney's life. By way of authenticating his sincerity, he gave her his Visa number.

Annie came back on the line. She wanted to speak to Claire. He handed over the phone. A shadow moved inside Bradley's office. Willows pushed back his chair.

Bradley was at his battered cherrywood desk, engrossed in a two-inch-thick file. The cigar was clamped between his teeth. He used it to point at the varnished wooden chair in front of his desk. Willows made himself as comfortable as the chair allowed. Bradley hunched forward in his black leather recliner. His moving finger guided his eyes to the bottom of the page. He marked his spot with the cigar and shut the file folder.

"What's Claire up to?"

Willows jerked a thumb over his shoulder. "On the phone."

Bradley raised an enquiring eyebrow.

"A hit and run," said Willows. "The family cat."

Bradley made a small sound of sympathy and distress. He was not a cat-and-dog kind of guy. "So how's the Galee thing coming along? You talked to the wife – how'd she take it?"

"With remarkable calm," said Willows.

"She kill him?"

"Maybe, but I doubt it." Willows brought his inspector up to speed. He told him about Moira Galee's insistence that her husband was a much-loathed womanizer, that Galee had a healthy cash flow despite his moderate success as a real-estate agent. That Mrs. Galee had said her husband had no friends that she knew of. That they'd found the locked room in the attic, the bed and the fax machine, the message on the answering machine. He told Bradley that they'd had a minor breakthrough. As soon as they'd arrived at 312 Main they'd listened to the tape of the anonymous 911 phone-in on the murder. There hadn't been time for a voice analysis, but it sounded to him and Parker as if the same woman had made a phone call to Galee shortly before he'd died.

"Any idea who she might be?"

"She sounded young, educated. But that's about it, Inspector." Willows told Bradley about the thirty thousand American dollars push-pinned to the inside of the packing crate.

Bradley said, "Thirty grand, U.S. That's more than enough to buy a brand-new Jeep Grand Cherokee. You going after the money?"

"Not yet, Inspector." Willows tried to imagine Bradley hunched over the wheel of a sporty Cherokee, a big grin on his face as he ploughed through deep snow or across a high-mountain creek.

"Do you have any evidence at all," said Bradley, "that Galee was involved in illegal activities?"

"Nope."

"Well, if you should obtain such evidence, waste no time in obtaining a court order to confiscate the dough, understand?"

Willows nodded. It was time for some good news. He said, "We traced the Smith and Wesson Parker found in the fishpond."

"Yeah?"

"The gun belonged to Galee. He bought it a couple of months ago, got his registration back from Ottawa last week and picked it up from the dealer on Wednesday."

"He have a carry permit?"

"No, he didn't."

"So why was he packing a gun? Because he thought he might need it to defend himself? If so, from whom?" Bradley pointed at

Willows with the mangy end of his cigar. "Talk to the people he worked with, everybody. His supervisor, fellow real-estate agents . . ."

Willows said, "We're working on it, Inspector. It's Sunday. The office is closed. The secretarial staff has the day off, the agents are at open houses, trying to move product. We've got the office manager's name – it was printed on the victim's business cards. We're doing what we can to track him down, but we can only be in one place at a time, and we just finished with his wife."

"Tick tick tick," said Bradley. "Oikawa talk to you?"

"Not lately."

"Dan's in charge of organizing Ralph Kearns' retirement party. He tries to rope you in, tell him to see me." Bradley opened the file, found his place, and stuck the cigar back in his mouth.

Parker was still on the phone. She'd propped up Zagros Galee's business card against an ersatz frame made of a bent paper clip. As Willows approached she cupped her hand over the receiver. "I talked to Dr. Larkins. Annie hasn't seen Barney and I told her not to let her see him until we're with her. Barney's a mess. He's going to lose the leg, but he'll probably live. She said three-legged cats are a dime a dozen. I tried to get in touch with Sean, but . . ." She uncupped her hand from the phone and said, "Mr. Rothstein? Detective Claire Parker. Yes, that's right. I'd like to talk to you about one of your staff, Mr. Zagros Galee." Parker waited. She said, "I'd rather not discuss my reasons over the phone. Yes, of course. Half an hour? See you there."

She cradled the phone. "Grab your clubs, Jack."

Sidney Rothstein was a member in good standing of the Shaughnessy Golf & Country Club, on SouthWest Marine Drive. Shaughnessy is the most exclusive and expensive club in the city, but Sid Rothstein, at ease in the clubhouse restaurant, was at pains to make it clear that he was not an expensive or exclusive kind of guy. He'd been on the driving range, trying out his new Taylor

Made No. 1 wood when his Nokia vibrated against his thigh, alerting him to the fact that he had a call.

"I don't care if I'm on the eighteenth hole and there's a thousand bucks riding on the shot," he said, "my phone's always in my pocket and I'm *always* ready to answer a call." He reached across to give Parker's hand a friendly pat. Willows didn't mind. Rothstein was in his late sixties, overweight and not at all worried about it, balding, wearing a heavy gold wedding ring. Even better, he had puppy-dog eyes and a kindly smile, and came across as a genuinely nice guy.

Rothstein glanced at his menu, tossed it down. "You two look beyond hungry. What time did you say Zagros was killed?"

"We're not sure," said Parker. "Sometime last night."

"And you got the call at two, three in the morning, been humping it ever since. Cold coffee. No breakfast, no lunch. Am I right?"

"You're right," said Willows.

"And when I'm right, I'm right. Let me recommend the crab sandwiches." He eyed Parker and Willows in turn. "Either or both of you a homeowner, by any chance?" Willows nodded. Rothstein grinned. "Okay, there you go. My treat. It's a legitimate business expense. In a few years, maybe you'll gimme a call. You like crab?" He glanced up at the hovering waitress. "Jennifer, crab all around, a martini for yours truly. No wait, better make it a double." He smiled at Parker. "Wanna get smashed with me?"

"Coffee," said Parker.

"I'll have a Becks," said Willows. He smiled at Rothstein. "This is what I always imagined it'd be like, when I was at the Academy. Hanging out with rich people, and then arresting one of them."

"Yeah? When I was a kid I always imagined the worst. The very worst. Absolutely the very worst." He laughed harshly. "And for a long time, lemme tell you, all my dreams came true." He leaned back in his upholstered chair and spread his arms wide. "But hey, take a look at me now. I'm reasonably healthy, unreasonably wealthy. If I ain't exactly a fountain of wisdom, at least I got a rock-solid rep as a wiseass." The waitress brought their drinks. Rothstein tucked into his martini. He sighed, wiped his mouth with a linen napkin. "But we're not here to talk about yours truly, are we?" He touched Parker's arm. "So fire away, grill me like a steak."

"How long had you known Zagros Galee?"

"Not long. A year? Somewhere in there."

"That's how long he worked for your firm, a year?"

"Yeah, yeah. But listen. The way we work it, what we do is provide office space, telephones and faxes, office supplies, logistical support, and secretarial staff. And of course our rep as a reliable company, pillar of the community and all that stuff. The rest is up to the agents. How they do is up to them. What I'm getting at, not too quickly, is that they pay us a fixed rate for the basics and extra for extras. Want a paper clip? Fine. Pay here. What they get in return, they get to keep 100 percent of their commissions. So, Zagros, every so often he'd make a sale. But, speaking plainly, he was no fireball. I mean, he had a hard time finding commissions. You don't have to be a genius to figure out that it's tough to sell a property unless you've got a property to sell." Rothstein had finished his martini. Neither Parker nor Willows had seen him signal to the waitress but there she was, fresh drink in hand.

"Thankyou, Jennifer. You're an officer and a gentleman." Rothstein tasted his martini and found it entirely to his satisfaction.

Willows said, "But that wasn't a problem, I take it."

"Excuse me?"

"It wasn't a problem that Mr. Galee didn't move much property, as long as he paid his rent."

"Well, yes. That's true. To a certain extent. But on the other hand, we like to think of ourselves as a smallish-but-high-profile firm, which translates to lots of signs on lots of lawns."

The crab sandwiches arrived. Parker's coffee was topped up.

Willows allowed Rothstein to sweet-talk him into another beer. Rothstein told Jennifer that she very well knew he'd had more than enough to drink, but he'd better have another all the same.

The sandwiches had been quartered. The bread was fresh and so was the crab, the shredded lettuce flawlessly crisp.

Willows dug in. The beer had sharpened his appetite. He had to force himself not to eat too quickly.

Parker said, "I take it you weren't too happy with Mr. Galee's performance."

"I was very unhappy. *Very* unhappy. Very *unhappy*. As were the majority of people he dealt with. His secretary – she's part of a pool – was extremely unhappy with the things many of his customers had to say to her." Rothstein's sandwich was untouched. He sipped at his martini.

"Were you planning to let him go?"

"Yeah, fire him. See, the messages he'd been getting lately, they were kind of unusual."

Parker said, "Speak plainly, Mr. Rothstein."

"Sidney, please."

"What're you getting at, Sidney?"

"The bottom of my glass, I do believe." Rothstein ate an olive. He turned towards the bar, waved his empty glass above his head. "Jennifer, if you'd be so kind . . ."

Willows said, "Mr. Galee was running some kind of scam out of his office, wasn't he?"

"*Scam* might be too harsh a word. On the other hand, it might not do him justice. There was a young woman who called Zagros frequently during the past week or so, wouldn't leave a message. Rothstein smiled, pleased with his phrase-making. He added, "She dropped by the office on Thursday. Zagros was out. Nobody knew where he was. She hung around awhile, reading magazines. Stayed maybe half an hour, drove away in a black Jaguar convertible." He sipped. "Nice-looking woman, terrific car."

"Can you describe her for us?" said Parker.

"A model, movie star. Beautiful. A stunner. But a couple of centuries too young for an old coot like me."

"Come on, now," said Parker.

Willows said, "Could you try to be a little more specific, Sid?"

"She was tall, about five foot eight. Very slim, but, uh, *stacked*. Big green eyes, lots of red hair . . ."

Rothstein trailed off. He smiled at Parker, shrugged. That was it, all he knew. By way of apology, he added, "See, she wasn't just drop-dead gorgeous. She was also incredibly *sexy*. But young enough to be my daughter's daughter. It made me very uncomfortable, just looking at her. I didn't want to go home feeling like a sticky old man . . ."

"Did she leave her name?" said Parker.

"Nope. Never. Not then, or when she phoned. When Galee finally showed up at the office, I asked him who she was. He was shocked. Denied that he knew her. This was out of character, believe me. He claimed it must be a case of mistaken identity." Rothstein smiled. *A case of mistaken identity.* There was another good one. Jennifer approached the table with his third double martini. He waited until she was out of earshot and said, "There was a rumour flying around the office awhile that he was a *pimp*."

Parker said, "I'm sorry, I didn't catch that. People thought Mr. Galee was a what?"

"Pimp," said Sidney. He blushed. "It sounds ridiculous, now that he's dead. But, well, you know how people talk. He wasn't making any sales, but all of a sudden, starting a couple of months ago, he began doing very well, from a financial point of view."

"How did you know?" said Willows. "Did he confide in you?"

"Zagros? Hell no. What gave the game away was the expensive suits, his new Lexus. The fact that he had plenty of cash on him, stopped arguing about every penny he owed in office supplies . . . I suppose the thing about him that struck me most forcibly was the change in his attitude. Suddenly he was one happy fella, not a care in the world." Sidney stared down at his plate. His crab sandwich was untouched. The plastic swords, two green and one red, from his three double martinis lay in a tidy row alongside his plate. Aside from the fact that his eyes were a little loose in their sockets, he appeared to be stone-cold sober.

Willows sipped his beer. He and Parker exchanged a look. Willows said, "Was there anyone Mr. Galee worked with who was close to him in any way?"

"Close to Zagros? Not that I know of." Sidney peeked cautiously inside his sandwich, laid the wedge of bread back down as delicately as if it had been the lid of a vampire's coffin. "Well, actually . . . Can I tell you something in confidence? I mean, if I suggested there was someone it might benefit you to talk to, or interview, would it be possible for you to do so without informing her as to how you got her name?"

"No problem," said Parker without hesitation.

"There was a woman. Julia Delfino. Julia's an agent, works for a small company that does most of its business in Richmond. She's a swell girl. Had an affair, more of a brief fling really, with Zagros about six months ago. Or so I heard." Rothstein winked at Parker. "Are you by any chance in the market for a new home?"

"Not really," said Parker.

"Don't worry about it, she'll sell you one anyway."

Sidney had an electronic organizer. He dialled up Julia Delfino's office number, cellphone and pager numbers, her home telephone number. Wrote the four numbers down on a clean napkin and passed the napkin to Parker.

"There you go. That ought to do you."

Rothstein poked around in his sandwich. He ate a tiny morsel of crab. It was impossible to say if his appetite had improved or he was merely looking for a reason to hang around long enough to order another martini. His head came up. He said, "What I'll never forget about Zagros, I think I mentioned this already, but what's gonna stick with me was that he was so *happy*."

Outside, back in the real world, the parking lot baked in the sun. It was Willows' turn to drive. He unlocked his door and swung it wide open and then walked around to the far side of the car and unlocked and opened Parker's door. A gleaming white Cadillac pulled into the lot. The white-haired driver took a long time getting out of the car. His wife was even slower. They studied Willows and Parker as if assessing the risk of walking past them to the clubhouse. Willows eased into the unmarked Ford. The dashboard radiated heat. He cranked down his window and started the engine. Parker got in beside him. She rolled down her window, fastened her seatbelt and shut her door. Willows said, "Could we do our job more efficiently if our cars were equipped with air-conditioning?"

"No question," said Parker.

"Drove Cadillacs instead of Fords and Chevys?"

"Absolutely."

Willows waited for the traffic to clear and then turned onto Southwest Marine. He drove a four-year-old Honda Prelude. Parker had recently bought a second-hand Mazda. Neither of them would ever stroll into a showroom with a down payment on a shiny new Jaguar or Cadillac.

But here he was, investigating a murder. Pursuing a murderer. Hot on the trail of a drop-dead-gorgeous redhead.

Not a bad life, was it?

13

Shelley was no brain surgeon, but he had a hunch the black Jaguar ragtop parked up tight behind his sx belonged to Mr. Sticks. For sure, none of his immediate neighbours would stoop to owning such an indecently flashy set of wheels. On the other hand, wild card, he had to keep in mind that the guy two doors due east had dropped by when Shelley first moved in, to advise him that he specialized in entertainment law and was always on the browse for hot new talent. Was Shelley interested in a career in modelling? Not really. But anyhow, there was a slim chance the Jag belonged to one of the lawyer's clients. It was a chance Shelley was willing to take. The lawyer was a workaholic. One of those poor saps in his mid-forties who was pushing sixty. He was always at the office. Sunday or not, he was never home. The guy's Nordic-style wife had given Shelley a hot look a couple of times, when they'd happened to bump into each other at the local video store or whatever. She was probably ten years younger than hubby, but gaining fast. As if the two of them were in some kind of unspoken race to grow old and die. She was cute enough to pass muster, but not his type. Too worried. Too intense. Above all, too available.

Especially now that he had Bo. He hoped.

There was a BCAA sticker on the Jag's rear bumper, which Shelley found kind of puzzling. Why would a person buy or lease an expensive car and then advertise the fact that he was constantly worried about it breaking down? He opened and closed the wirecutters as he walked past the wisteria and rhododendrons towards the car. He'd only used the cutters once since he'd bought them; they were almost brand-new, still a little stiff.

The Jag's top was down, which he certainly appreciated. He went around to the driver's side and reached in and popped the hood. He dismantled the alarm first, and then the cellular telephone. In thirty seconds more, he'd popped the distributor cap and bent the points completely out of alignment. He stuck the wirecutters in his back pocket and slammed down the hood, spread his arms wide like a winning contestant in a car-busting contest. He was a long way from being a certified and licensed mechanic, but in two minutes flat he'd rendered the Jaguar totally useless except, debatably, as an art object. He went back into the house, stuffed Bo's sports bra and makeup kit and a few other odds and ends into a plastic Safeway bag, and carried everything downstairs and out onto the deck. He tossed the bag to Andrew. The kid poked around as if itemizing the contents. Shelley made a small noise indicating heartfelt disgust. Andrew sheepishly tucked the bag under his arm.

Bo had changed into clingy black silk shorts, a shimmery orange silk tanktop that looked as if it would set your fingers alight the moment you dared touch. Shelley was more than willing to take the risk.

But not right now.

Bo was staring at him. Looking as if she were waiting for him to blow a bugle and lead a thundering charge. Shelley spread his hands in a gesture of extra-meek supplication, as if to say, What can I do? What *can* I do?

Bo followed Mr. Sticks and Andrew out of the house. Nobody said so much as a single word.

Shelley stood on the porch. He noticed that his neighbours on either side were busily fooling around in the garden but not getting much done. Big ears. Mr. Sticks pressed a small plastic bag containing a couple of dozen weird-looking coins into Shelley's hand. He nodded inanely, turned away. Had Shelley been *tipped*? As the unlikely trio reached the end of the sidewalk Andrew spun on his heel and brought his arm up past his shoulder in a throwing motion. Something that might have been a bat out of hell twinkled darkly as it skimmed through sunlight, zipped past Shelley at eye level and buried itself in the side of the house. He turned and glanced curiously behind him. The kid had flung one of those nasty five-pointed Kung-Fu-type death stars at him, missed by not much more than a foot at a range of sixty feet or more.

Shelley waved, but not goodbye. He blew Bo a kiss and gave her the thumbs-up sign. Andrew slid behind the wheel of the Jag. Looking *très* cool in his wraparound oil-on-water sunglasses. Mr. Sticks and Bo climbed into the backseat. Mr. Sticks said something to her, waggled an admonishing finger. She fastened her seatbelt.

The Jag's starter motor chugged industriously. The chugging segued into a high whine. Silence. Andrew put his upper body into it as he turned the key again.

Shelley took a close look at the death star. It was dark grey, smooth to the touch. The points were very thin and very sharp. Teflon-coated. He used the wirecutters to pry the ugly damn thing out of the house. There was a mark in the shingle where the point had gone in, but you'd have to be looking to see it.

The Jaguar's starter whined petulantly.

Shelley went inside. Shut the door, but didn't lock it. In the kitchen, he looked up the BCAA in the Yellow Pages, made the call. He gave the woman at the other end of the line Mr. Sticks' unlikely name and the Jag's vanity licence-plate number. He admitted he didn't know Mr. Sticks' membership number but said he could get it for her if she wanted him to. The woman told him it was okay, that a vehicle would be there shortly. Shelley tried to pin her down, timewise, but she was a slippery fish indeed. He hung up, unlocked the basement door, and went downstairs.

The light in the workshop had burnt out. He made the trip upstairs for a fresh bulb, trotted back downstairs again. Changed bulbs all by himself. He hadn't been in the basement since he'd taken possession of the house, but had a good memory of where things were. In a drawer beneath the workbench he found a roll of stretchy black electrician's tape. The sports equipment was in a storage closet. Hockey stick or baseball bat? He chose a kid-size aluminum Louisville Slugger with a skintight black rubber grip. The bat hadn't been used much. Shelley stepped away from the wall. He took a few practice swings. Reminded himself to swing from the hips. He swung again, a lot harder. The bat made a thin whistling sound. It was all coming back to him now. Rotate the shoulders, turn the wrists. He powered through another swing. The bat cut the air like a machete.

He went back upstairs. The Jaguar was still grinding away. Making a noise like a frustrated giant gnashing his molars. By now Mr. Sticks would have done his math and come to the inescapable conclusion that one busted Jaguar plus one dead cellular telephone plus one dysfunctional car alarm added up to one extremely unlikely coincidence.

Shelley got set.

According to the information neatly printed in gold on the barrel, the Louisville Slugger was 29 inches long, had a maximum diameter of 7 inches and weighed 58 ounces. Baseball is a game of statistics. Shelley had worked out that 58 ounces amounted to more than three pounds but less than four when the Jag's starter motor suddenly fell silent.

Batter *up!*

He settled into his stance, adjusted his clothing. Was he ready? He was beyond ready. But then he remembered he hadn't checked the French doors that gave access to the deck at the back of the house, which meant he could easily be outflanked. He hurried to the rear of the house. Both doors were locked. Thankyou, Bo. He trotted back to his position.

A few moments later he heard footsteps on the stairs. Risking a quick peek through the lace-curtained bevelled-glass window he caught a glimpse of Andrew hurling himself across the porch. The door crashed open, knocked him against the oak-panelled wall. He slid to the floor, dazed. Unseen shutters popped open and snapped shut. The world turned black and white, black and white. Why had he believed that Andrew would knock? The kid was shouting Shelley's name but looking in entirely the wrong direction. From behind, posture-wise, he looked like a blind, pint-size sumo wrestler.

Shelley cleared his throat.

Andrew spun around, quick as a top. Shelley took his cut. The kid's skull was at least four times as big as a regulation softball. Whiffing was impossible. Andrew skittered away, crablike. His eyes were huge. The bat made a horrible sickening sound as it struck a corner of the oak newel post. His first at-bat in ten years, naturally his timing was a little off. He'd whiffed. The kid tried to come up under him as he pivoted on his heel, following the bat. Off-balance, Shelley kicked him in the shoulder. The tactic was graceless and the blow lacked power, but Andrew backed off. Shelley cocked the bat. Andrew dipped his hand into his pocket, came up with a butterfly knife. The perforated aluminum handles clacked sharply together. The sharply pointed, double-edged blade sucked up the light and spat it out.

Shelley waggled the bat. "Think you can pinch my babe? Pinch yourself, dimwit. Wake up and smell the coffee."

The knifeblade flashed. Figure-eights. Concentric circles. Mobius strips. Zig-zags.

Shelley swung the bat. Strike two. A line of blood sprang up across his knuckles.

Andrew mimed kissing his blade.

Shelley went for his kneecaps. Bad move. He jerked back his head and just managed to save his eye. Yikes. He had a thirty-pound weight advantage, three or four inches of extra reach. What he didn't have was blinding speed, or a killer instinct. Andrew, on the other hand, was 100 percent all-beef assassin.

The knife came at him. The kid had drawn first blood, gained confidence, and taken the initiative. His plan was to back Shelley into a corner, where the bat wouldn't do him much good. Shelley stood his ground. Andrew retreated. He reached into his jacket pocket and came up with a death star.

Shelley feinted, swung hard and released. The bat flashed across six feet of hallway, smacked the kid in the ribs and knocked him on his ass. The knife clattered on the floor. Andrew's lungs turned into whoopee cushions. Shelley scooped up the bat, used it as a battering ram, the fat end punching the kid in the middle of his narrow forehead twice, skidding off his temple as he fell.

Shelley leaned the bat against a wall, picked up the knife and folded the blade into the metal handles, dropped it in his pocket.

Andrew grabbed him by the ankles, yanked his feet out from under him. He bared his teeth and made as if to bite Shelley in the area of his genitals. Shelley grabbed one of Bo's bricks. He brought the brick forcibly down, hitting Andrew in the middle of the little whorl of hair at the back of his head.

Andrew sagged onto the floor, groaned, rolled over. He'd sat on his death star. It stuck out of his ass like a miniature UFO that had charted a tragic course. Shelley left it right where it was. He went through Andrew's pockets, found half a dozen death stars, a couple of metal sticks held together with a short length of chain, a tiny .25-calibre pistol in black and stainless steel, mother-of-pearl grips decorated with a red rose. Andrew was well-armed but carried no wallet. Shelley took care not to scratch the finish, as he dumped the hardware on the hall table.

Andrew's forehead had puffed up something fierce. He looked as if he was suffering from a sudden onslaught of encephalitis. He was limp as a dead jellyfish. Shelley tied his hands together with electrician's tape. He picked him up in a fireman's lift, turned so he could admire himself in the hall mirror. The death star sticking out of Andrew's skinny butt should have been hilarious, but wasn't. He shifted Andrew around until his paltry weight was evenly distributed, then carried him through the open door and

down the front-porch steps, past gawking neighbours, dark-leaved
rhododendrons, the rustling sword-like leaves of the bamboo.
Down at the edge of the lawn, in the shade of a patch of giant
daisies, a red-breasted robin violently wrenched a worm from
the soil.

Shelley trotted down the three wide granite steps to the sidewalk. He smiled at Bo and she smiled back. He saw that she'd un-
buckled her seatbelt. He offered her his hand, helped her out of
the car. Mr. Sticks yanked free the death star as Shelley lowered
Andrew carefully into the backseat. Andrew's complexion was
right off the colour chart.

Shelley looked Bo in the eye. "You okay?"

"Yeah, I'm fine." She tilted her head. "Why, is there something
wrong with the way I look?"

"You look great," said Shelley. He tenderly kissed her hand, then
turned his attention to the old man, Mr. Sticks. "I called BCAA
about ten minutes ago." Though it seemed like a lifetime. "They
should be here any minute."

"Thankyou," said Mr. Sticks. The flat of his hand touched his
son's boiled-egg forehead. His slim fingers unashamedly groped
Andrew's suit. He frowned. "Where is my Titan Tigress?"

Shelley grinned down at him. "Say what, pops?"

"My little gun," said Mr. Sticks with great dignity.

"I kept it. It's a keepsake. I kept the knife, too, and a few death
stars, to wish upon."

"I must have my little gun."

"You can't have your little gun," said Shelley. "Or anything else
I took away from your homicidal maniac halfwit son. What you
should focus on is that I could've just as easily kept him, too."

Bo said, "I'm thirsty."

Shelley took her hand. Backing away from the Jag he said, "You
should put the roof up, so you don't get too much sun. And roll
up the windows and lock the doors, because this is a dangerous
and violent neighbourhood."

Mr. Sticks stared at him. He didn't move an inch. Not a nostril twitched. Not an eyelash fluttered. The dude wasn't merely unruffled, he was downright imperturbable. Or at least that's what he wanted people to think. But Shelley had a hunch it was all hoax. He'd bet serious money that deep inside, Mr. Sticks was a veritable seething cauldron of emotions.

As soon as they'd entered the house, Shelley deadbolted the door. A certain amount of maintenance was in order. Plastic wood. A bit of paint. He slipped Mr. Sticks' Titan Tigress into the back pocket of his jeans, led Bo into the kitchen. He sat her down on a stool, got a lowball glass out of the cupboard and poured her two fingers of Glenfiddich single-malt whisky. He handed her the glass, got a waxed carton of orange juice out of the fridge. "Cheers."

"Cheers," said Bo. She knocked back her drink all of a piece, and almost coughed herself off her stool.

"Like another?"

"Hit me." She giggled, and touched her eye.

Shelley poured her a skimpy shot. He leaned against the counter beside her. He touched her hair. His finger came lightly down on a freckle. It was up to her, but he hoped she wouldn't drink too much. He was nobody's angel, but never in his life had he made love to a woman who wasn't, so to speak, entirely on top of the situation. And he wasn't about to change now, not when there was so much on the line.

Bo said, "I thought you were going to let them have me."

"Shame on you," said Shelley gently.

"I am ashamed. I'm *so* ashamed."

"Forget it. No big deal." Shelley could be gracious when he was a winner. He put his arm around her. What a nice fit. He said, "Did you lock the back doors?" She nodded.

Shelley drank some orange juice. Was it Bert Parks who'd been the Florida orange-juice spokesman all those years? He'd always liked Bert.

Bo said, "I hate those bastards. Both of them. They're both bastards, and I *hate* them. Bastards."

"Who are they?"

Bo shrugged, as if the whole mess was just entirely too complicated to explain. She said, "Do you *love* me?"

Shelley said, "Uh . . ."

"Prove it." She offered up her glass.

Shelley poured her another shot of Glenfiddich, and then added
a couple of ice cubes in the faint hope of watering down the
alcohol. As he put the glass down in front of her there was a tentative knock on the door.

Bo said, "Uh-oh. I think I heard a bogey-mans."

Shelley approached with caution. The guy standing nervously
on the porch wore a dark blue uniform, pale blue shirt with
BCAA flashers. He looked a little – but not much – like Bruce
Springsteen.

Shelley unlocked the door and swung it open just wide enough
to admit an anorexic snake.

Bruce smiled, tipped his cap. "Excuse me, do you own that black
sx out there?"

"Not that it's any of your business, but it's a lease." Shelley realized he was still a little tense.

"I gotta tow the Jag. Would you mind moving your car?"

Shelley heard a siren. He stepped out on the porch. An ambulance braked to a smooth stop behind the BCAA truck. Wilful Mr.
Sticks had ignored his advice to put up the Jag's roof. Andrew lay
awkwardly across the backseat, broiling in the sun. His lights were
out. His bulb needed changing. Shelley hoped he wasn't dead. He
said, "What happened to the kid?"

"Guess he slipped and fell trying to repair the car."

Shelley nodded. He said, "Gimme a minute to get my keys."

By the time he made it down to the boulevard, Andrew was
strapped to a gurney. Those paramedic types were all business,
weren't they? He got into the sx, unlocked The Club. The ambulance sped off as he started the car. He made a U-turn and parked
opposite the Jag.

"Where's the old guy?"

"What old guy?"

"The Chinese guy. The kid's father."

Bruce tied a short length of thick rope to the steering wheel. He held the rope tight as he slammed the Jag's door. *Thunk.* "Beats me."

"He was here a minute ago."

Bruce nodded, disinterested.

"Have a nice day, pard."

"Yeah, you too. Thanks for moving your car."

Shelley made his way past the phalanx of flowers and bees, back inside the house. Bo had plunked herself and the bottle of Glenfiddich down in front of the television. She was watching the Crystal Elephant Channel. Shelley went into the kitchen to get himself a lowball glass. Maybe if *he* got drunk, Bo would have no compunctions whatsoever about taking full advantage of *him.*

14

Earth dikes turned Richmond's tidal marshes into farmland. Rapacious developers and generations of incompetent or corrupt politicians have turned the farmland into square mile upon square mile of featureless tract housing. If you like flat and treeless, and don't mind breathing inferior-quality air, Richmond is the place to be. Until the big one hits, the earth dikes crumble, and the rich dark soil turns to jelly . . .

Much of the Lower Mainland's burgeoning Asian population has settled in Richmond. Land is still relatively inexpensive in the area, and developers, serving a perceived need, have built thousands upon thousands of enormous houses on tiny, low-maintenance lots. Another reason the area is so popular with Asians is that Richmond sounds remarkably like "rich man." A mall caters almost exclusively to the Chinese. Signs in Mandarin or Cantonese are everywhere. Despite the current government's attempt to preserve farmland, block-square housing developments seem to be popping up all over the place.

Richmond is on the prowl. An outsider driving through the "downtown core" might be forgiven for thinking the municipality's growth is whimsical and ill-planned, out of control.

The endless development was, of course, a real-estate agent's dream.

Parker called Julia Delfino from a payphone. The agent was en route to an open house she'd scheduled from one to three that afternoon. Delfino had a low, whisky-and-soda voice. From three to five, her presence was required at a cocktail party hosted by the developers of a new condominium complex. She had booked a meeting with a prospective client for five-fifteen, and had an important dinner date at seven. Parker asked her for the address of the open house. Delfino apologized but said she expected to be very busy and doubted she'd have time to speak to the police. Parker told her that she and Willows could be at the open house in about half an hour – a little after one. She strongly suggested that Delfino put herself in a receptive mood. The agent asked Parker what she wanted to see her about. Parker said that she looked forward to meeting her. Delfino reluctantly gave her the address of the open house, and hung up.

Parker's quarter clanged down into the coin-return slot. It was only a quarter, but it was free. Her instinct was to grab that quarter and run. But she held back. She was an honest person, a cop. But if she left the coin in the return slot, how would it benefit B.C. Tel? And if the machine had rejected her offering, who was she to judge?

Willows drove them east on SouthWest Marine. The airport was far away to their right, the view blocked by towering evergreen hedges that hid mile after mile of multi-million-dollar homes in a mix of architectural styles ranging from mock-Mediterranean to weirdly bloated fairy-tale-style cottage in the woods. But as they continued east, the situation rapidly changed. Soon the neighbourhood was middle-class at best. They bumped over a set of railway tracks. A condominium complex crowded the sidewalk. Outside the 7-Eleven at the corner of Granville and Marine, three grossly overweight men stood in the shade drinking enormous bucket-sized Slurpees. At Oak, the light was red. Willows said, "What'd she sound like?"

"Who?"

"Julia Delfino."

"Mid-twenties. Full of energy. Kind of sexy. Definitely on the make."

The light changed to flashing green. Willows turned right and joined the flow of traffic streaming over the bridge. Chrome and glass glittered in the sun. Who *were* all these people? Cops, victims, crooks.

"She wasn't terribly eager to see us," Parker added.

"No surprise," said Willows. Zagros Galee's identity had been withheld until Mrs. Galee had given permission to release his name to the media, which she'd done after viewing the body at the morgue. By now it was likely Julia Delfino was aware that her married ex-lover had been murdered. Willows had a happy thought. His fingers played a tune on the steering wheel. Maybe it wasn't her crowded schedule that had made Delfino reluctant to talk to the cops. Maybe, just maybe, it was the guilty conscience of a murderer. Zagros had been shot dead as he lay naked in bed, unarmed but for a pack of contraceptives. Wasn't it possible that there'd been a reconciliation, followed by a lover's spat? Female real-estate agents were vulnerable to attack as they held open houses. Some had bought large dogs. Had Julia Delfino used Galee's .44-calibre Smith & Wesson on him, spontaneously shot him dead during a lovers' quarrel as he lay in bed, naked and vulnerable? It was a pleasant thought. Handguns illegally imported from the States were usually cheap throwaways. If the Smith had been legally purchased, it would be easy to trace. The physical evidence collected at the crime scene was being collated. Had Julia dropped a fingerprint, fibres, or even a single hair? A confession would be a lovely thing. In a murder case the first twenty-four hours were crucial, and they were running out of time.

Willows' thoughts turned to his domestic problems. He said, "When we get there, remind me to phone Annie."

Parker nodded. If Barney survived, the bills were going to be very high. She wondered what an amputation and after-surgery care were worth. Probably a thousand dollars or more. There was going to be trouble when she insisted on paying half the bill. She thought about her own childhood, a childhood that she'd endured without the benefit of a household pet. Her father had been a welder at a North Shore shipyard; he'd died shortly before her third birthday, and her mother had never remarried. Life had been hard. They'd lost the house and never owned another. It was tough finding a landlord who approved of children, much less pets.

The car slowed as Willows took an off-ramp. A rusty van roared past in the inside lane. Burglars on their way to a fence? He took another off-ramp, made a left at the lights. They passed over Moray Bridge, across the middle arm of the Fraser River. It was windy, and the water had a restless, rumpled look. A family on bicycles rode towards them along the path that followed the top of the dike. Parker unfurled a map.

Following her directions, Willows drove along Sea Island Way, made a right on Garden City Road and then a left on Capstan Way. The street names were cute, but the terrain was unendingly flat and monotonous. The subdivision had been designed like a maze, but Julia Delfino's open-house signs, like a trail of crumbs in the forest, led them on. There was plenty of road, but no sidewalks. The landscaping was minimal – each front yard had a small patch of grass, a thin sprinkling of shrubs, a concrete driveway that led straight to the double garage. There were no mature trees to be seen anywhere. Parker wondered what it would be like to live here; to drive out of your house and down the carefully winding streets, past so many similar but not-quite-identical dwellings. You could live there a long time and never meet your neighbours. Maybe that was the attraction.

Willows parked on the street, behind a white Mercedes. He and Parker got out of the car and walked up the driveway towards the house. They were only a block or two from highway 99; the sound of traffic was a constant droning hum. The sky above them was a flawless blue. Not a single child cried or laughed. No television blared. No dogs barked. No cats meowed. No bird dared chirp.

A plastic sign to one side of the open double front door read

"Please remove your shoes." Fat chance. The house was brand-new and smelt of paint and chemicals. The wall-to-wall carpet was tinged with the faintest shade of pink. They found Julia Delfino in the kitchen, sitting at the built-in nook. The table was bare except for a matt-black cellular telephone. Delfino stared intently down at her cupped palms, as if hoping to divine her future. She was completely unaware of their presence. Willows moved a step closer. The agent was watching baseball on a tiny battery-powered portable television. Electronic images of human beings no bigger than fingernail cuttings capered on the black and white screen. The sound was like miniature crickets. Willows cleared his throat, and she glanced up, startled.

The television screen went blank. She managed to awkwardly extricate herself from the cramped nook.

Parker said, "Julia Delfino? I'm detective Claire Parker. This is my partner, detective Jack Willows."

Willows nodded, smiled.

Speaking to Parker, Delfino said, "I thought you were going to be alone."

Parker smiled.

Delfino shrugged. "Not that it matters," she said without conviction.

Parker had been conned by the agent's voice; Julia Delfino was not exactly as advertised. Parker had guessed her age at somewhere in the low or mid-twenties, but mid-fifties was closer to it. Delfino was of average height and at least thirty pounds overweight. She wore gold-coloured high heels, a loose, pleated black skirt, a canary-coloured blouse, a sleeveless vest in a hard, shiny, gold-coloured fabric, gold hoop earrings, several gold necklaces, a gold bracelet and gold wedding band, a gold engagement ring with a triple crown of full-carat diamonds. Delfino's appetite for jewellery was mirrored by her penchant for an excess of makeup; her wide mouth and tapered fingernails were Porsche-red, her dark eyes heavily shadowed, and her cheeks the colour of a sunset.

Parker eased into the nook. She took out her notebook. Willows lounged by the euro-sink. He opened and closed a cupboard. Delfino asked to see their badges. They obliged.

"Isn't this Mountie-land? Do you guys have any clout outside of the city?"

"Not much more clout than any other citizen," said Parker. She smiled. "We'd like to ask you some questions, that's all."

"A few harmless questions," said Delfino. She glanced at her gold watch. "I've been here almost three-quarters of an hour, and haven't seen a soul. This time last year, they'd have knocked down the doors. Nobody wants to admit it, but the market's dead. Absolutely dead."

"Why is that?"

"Interest rates. Economic uncertainty. An oversupply of product. Or maybe a shift in the wind. Who can say?" She adjusted the watch on her wrist. "This's about Zagros, isn't it?"

"What makes you think so?"

"My boss called me and told me he'd been killed."

Willows had his notebook out, pen poised.

"What's your boss's name?" said Parker.

"Dennis Grant."

"How'd he find out that Mr. Galee had died?"

"Somebody must've told him, I guess."

Willows turned on the tap. He watched the water splash into the basin, collect itself, find direction, swirl down the drain.

Parker said, "You didn't ask who that might have been?"

Willows turned off the water. He turned it back on again, then off. He slid open a drawer. He turned on the tap, fine-tuned it until it was dripping at about thirty beats a minute.

Julia Delfino looked out the window. "Sid Rothstein told him. Sid managed the office where Zagros worked."

"How did *he* find out Mr. Galee was dead?" asked Parker.

"Ask him. He hated Zagros' guts, so maybe he did it." Julia smacked her forehead. "Hey, just kidding!"

"About what?" said Parker. She gave Willows a sharp look. He turned off the tap.

"About Sid killing Zagros. He hated him, but he'd never have killed him."

"Why did he hate him?"

"Zagros had an affair with his wife, after they were divorced."

"After Mr. Rothstein and his wife were divorced, she and Zagros had an affair?"

Delfino nodded. Her mane of thick black hair had an inch-wide streak of grey in it that swept straight up from her forehead, and resembled a tombstone. She said, "Sid would never murder anybody. Not unless he could find a way to make a dollar from it. And Zagros was *always* broke. Anyway, if he had wanted to kill Zagros, he'd have had to go to the end of a very long line."

"Mr. Galee had a knack for annoying people, did he?"

"What he had was a knack for getting into bed with other people's wives and girlfriends. Or, even better, wives *and* girl-friends."

Parker said, "The two of you were fairly close at one point, I understand."

"Who told you that?"

"Is it true?"

Julia Delfino nodded. Her hoop earrings sent scimitars of yellow light dancing across the kitchen ceiling. "Unfairly close is more like it." She looked out the window. "It was a mutual-conve-nience sort of thing. The sort of thing that doesn't last."

Willows took a look inside the fridge. It was empty except for a bottle of Dom Perignon with a red-and-blue ribbon tied around the neck.

"A gift for the new owners," volunteered the agent.

Willows did some quick calculations. The asking price was $525,000. Julia Delfino's commission was probably somewhere in the region of fifteen grand. Subtract a hundred tax-deductible dollars for the champagne and it still added up to a healthy profit. And if she failed to make a sale, she had the wherewithal to drown her sorrows.

"What kind of person was Zagros?" said Parker, as Willows inspected the built-in microwave's controls.

"Selfish. Conceited. A long way from insatiable." Delfino toyed with the portable television. "Bald. After we split up, I must have asked myself a dozen times why I got involved with such a self-serving creep in the first place." She shrugged. "He was available, uncomplicated. Neither of us was much interested in small talk, if you know what I mean."

Maybe, thought Parker. But surely there were brief intervals when that was the only option available to them. She said, "Did Mr. Galee ever talk to you about his work?"

"That's *all* he talked about, when he was in the mood for talking. He was more interested in the art of the lecture than back-and-forth dialogue. What you might call a big-mouth-small-ears type of guy." For the first time since the interview had begun, Delfino looked directly at Willows. "Is he really dead?"

Willows said, "Yeah, he's really dead." He smiled. "Really, *really* dead. Did you kill him?"

"No. Absolutely not. I didn't have anything to do with it." Delfino turned her attention back to Parker. "Should I call a lawyer?"

"Not just yet. Did Mr. Galee have any enemies, that you knew of?"

"Thousands. He had the personality of a cheese grater. Look, in this business, people are always screwing each other around, doing everything they can to snag a listing, stay solvent. That's just the way it is."

"Was Mr. Galee good at his job?"

"He was terrible. Too intense, he never let up. A good agent needs to know when to turn it on and when to turn it off. Zagros didn't have those skills. He was about as lighthearted as a brick. He made people uncomfortable. If you ask me, he should've been a tax collector or a bailiff, something along those lines."

Willows swung open the door of the built-in dishwasher. He slid out the rack. Very nice.

Parker said, "Did you ever meet his wife?"

"Moira? No, never."

"Did he talk about her?"

"Not that I recall."

"His daughter?"

"What daughter, if you know what I mean."

Willows' head came up. He slid the rack into the washer and shut the door. "Could I borrow your phone?"

Delfino hesitated, and then said, "Yes, of course." She handed Willows her cellphone. He dialled his home number as he strolled out of the room.

"Did Zagros ever mention any other source of income?" said Parker.

"No, but he must've been up to something, especially recently."

"Why do you say that?"

"The past few months, he spent a lot more money than he earned, and he paid for everything with cash. So he wasn't running a tab on a fistful of credit cards, like some guys I've known."

"Did you ask him where the money came from?"

"You bet I did."

"What did he say?"

"That he didn't want to talk about it, and didn't want me talking about it either. End of conversation."

Parker said, "Where were you last night, Julia?"

"What time?"

"All night long." Parker smiled. "Dawn to dusk."

"I was with a friend. We went out for dinner and drinks, spent the night at my apartment. He left about seven this morning."

Parker waited.

"It was Sid," said Julia. "Can you believe it?" Her face became very serious. "How did Zagros die?"

"Quickly," said Parker.

15

Early on in life, Shelley came to the realization that he was a deeply flawed human being. Arrogant, self-centred. A poor listener. Kind of slothful. Cursed with a tendency to commit petty criminal acts. He was smart enough, but no genius. In truth, you could easily fill a shopping cart with his defects. He accepted as straight goods that if he hadn't been endowed with outstanding good looks, a surfeit of skin-deep charm and a certain amount of native cunning, he'd probably be delivering pizza for Mr. Domino and lucky to get the work.

But at the moment he was feeling pretty good, because he believed he'd strolled into a tricky situation and acquitted himself well.

As the towtruck hauled the Jaguar around the corner at the end of the block, he walked back into the house relishing the prospect of a friendly ambush. Hadn't he saved Bo's luscious ass? Wasn't it reasonable of him to expect her to demonstrate boundless gratitude via a thigh-crushing scissor grip and a great big sloppy wet kiss? Or at least a hug?

To his amazement and consternation, she was pissed. Flouncing down on the couch, she proceeded to give him verbal hell.

"Throwing them out was a great idea. But did you have to destroy that beautiful *car*?"

"I didn't destroy it, I dismantled it. Couple of hundred bucks

in parts and labour, they're back in business." Was he whining?
Only a little.

"Okay, forget the car. Why were you so violent? You hit Andy
with a *baseball* bat. What if you'd *killed* him?"

"Wait a minute," said Shelley, waving his arms as if for an
official time-out. He was starting to feel a little righteous himself,
fire in his belly from a slow burn of indignation. There was no
feeling on earth like the feeling that you were absolutely 100
percent right. He said, "Don't forget, that sweet little boy was
packing iron. He had a *gun*, and a pocketful of Teflon-coated death
stars, and those short metal sticks, I forget what they're called, a
chain holds them together, connects them. You whip them around,
tuck them under your armpit." All he could think of was Ninja
Turtles. He glanced helplessly about. How in the world did he get
into this mess? He said, "I didn't pick a fight with your two pals –
it was the other way around, remember?"

Shelley turned his back on Bo and bit his tongue. Stuck it
partway out of his mouth and bit down on it hard enough to hurt.
His career as a bouncer had ended a few months earlier, following
a spontaneous decision to heave an obnoxious drunk down a flight
of concrete stairs. Gratuitous violence, they'd called it. None of
the downtown clubs would hire him anymore, and he sure as hell
wasn't going to work those Burnaby or Yaletown dumps. But the
point was that he seemed to be charting an increasingly violent
course, and was worried about it. The incident with the Miata had
been terminally stupid. His willingness to take on the five cowboys
unbelievably dumb. He knew what was wrong with him because
he'd read about it in a magazine. He was unhappy with his life.
That's why he never formed a permanent relationship with
anyone, or settled down in any way. His aberrant behaviour was
self-destructive.

But now here was Bo, making his heart go pitter-patter. Making
him think, for the first time in probably his whole life, about
someone other than his own sweet self. And she was mad at him,
because he'd saved her. Now who was all screwed up?

And she wasn't finished yet.

"Shelley, don't you turn your back on me!"

He turned to face her, obedient as a beaten dog.

"What if Andy'd taken the bat away from you and used it to beat you to death? Did you think for even a moment about what would happen to *me*?"

She'd turned the television back on. Shelley lowered his head as if mortified by his behaviour. Now he got it. He hadn't saved her. Mr. Sticks and Andy would be back, and next time they'd be madder than hornets.

The crystal elephant hucksters were promoting autographed baseballs in domed glass jars, at sixty bucks a pop. Man, he'd rather have an autographed hernia. He conjured up an image of a generic-type baseball player hunched over a swiftly moving conveyor belt. Felt pen in hand, the player hastily scrawled his indecipherable signature on an endless stream of cheap Taiwanese baseballs. Shelley zoomed in for a closeup. The look on the player's face was the look of a man whose soul was deader than a doornail.

He blinked. A clock down at the bottom of the screen ticked off the seconds, as time ran out on this opportunity of a lifetime. Also prominently displayed was a running total of the number of baseballs sold. If the figure was accurate, there were hundreds of no-brainers out there who owned both a TV set and a credit card, who'd somehow learned how to dial a toll-free number.

Bo was yelling at him, so loud that he couldn't hear the huckster finish his pitch. She stepped in front of him, kept her smooth tanned legs straight, knees locked, as she bent to turn off the television.

She pointed at the couch. "Sit down."

Shelley did as he was told. He flung out his arm across the back of the couch, so he'd look more relaxed. Bo stood there, no more than three or four feet away, looking awfully good. His primeval side jockeyed for position. He had the presence of mind to cross his legs, the better to disguise his erection if he got one. Maybe sixty bucks wasn't such a bad price after all, especially if you considered that the player was risking writer's cramp, tendinitis, conceivably a premature end to his dazzling career . . .

Bonnie said, "Stop looking at me like that."

"Like what?"

Bo hesitated. "Romantically. We need to have a serious talk. There are things that have to be cleared up."

"Yeah, okay. If you say so." A dark cloud passed across Bo's eyes. Did she think he was being flippant? He said, "Let's have a serious talk about how you got the mouse."

"Andrew punched me." Bo seemed more resigned than annoyed. She added, "He hit me with a straight left."

"Why'd he do a thing like that?"

"Because Mr. Sticks told him to."

"Same question," said Shelley. He wondered if Bo had told him the truth about who'd bopped her. But why would she lie? But on the other hand, what did it profit her to tell him the truth? He wished he'd hit the kid with every brick in the suitcase, one brick at a time.

It was no more than a hop, skip and a jump to Shelley's lap. Bo curled up on him like a kitten; as if she had every moral right to be there and intended to make herself right at home. She said, "I'd rather not talk about it, if you don't mind." She kissed him chastely on the forehead.

Shelley wasn't giving up that easily. He said, "How'd you get to know a couple of guys like that?"

Bo pulled back from him a little. "What d'you mean, 'like that'? Like what, exactly?"

"Women-punchers. Death-star throwers. Guys that wear exactly the same suit. *That* kind of guy."

"I was out of work, looking for a job. Mr. Sticks was looking for someone with my particular talents. A mutual friend introduced us." She ran her slim fingers through the tousled conflagration of her hair. Her thumbnail was bitten to the quick. She was terrified, and he hadn't noticed until that very minute. Was he losing it? Had he ever had it?

He said, "You worked for them?"

She nodded.

"Doing what?"

"All sorts of stuff." Bo ran an explorative finger into his ear with the same oddly detached fascination employed by an infant as it industriously attempts to poke out its doting mother's eye.

"Could you be just a little more specific, please?"

"Secretarial work. You know. Typing letters. Answering the phone . . ."

Shelley waited.

She gestured vaguely. "If a client got difficult, balked at the last moment, Mr. Sticks expected me to do what I could to close the deal."

Shelley's unwieldy imagination sent his blood pressure sky-rocketing. His new babe had red-lined his pulse. His skull felt too tight. He had a sense of brain cells bursting like a bagful of microwave popcorn.

"The way Mr. Sticks put it," said Bo, "was that Andrew was the Beast and I was the Beauty."

"And who was Mr. Sticks?"

"The Brains," said Bo.

"What kind of deals did you close?"

"Big deals. Really big deals. Especially compared to stealing some poor girl's purse when all she ever did to you was go for a swim."

"What're you talking about?"

"As if you don't know."

The blood rushed to Shelley's cheeks. He was red as a brand-new fire engine, jolted. Bo was onto him, his little scams. Had he picked her up, back there on the beach? Or had it been the other way around? Alarm bells jangled. They both spent a lot of time at the beach. She must have seen him at work, one day. He hoped he didn't look anywhere near as shifty and furtive and cornered as he felt.

As if divining his thoughts, Bo said, "You're a handsome man, Shell, and you've got a nice personality." She paused, looking sad. "Until recently, you'd have been my dream date, everything I'd ever wanted in a guy. But suddenly I'm a little bit older and a whole lot wiser. My standards are higher than they were a week ago, Shell. They have to be, if I'm going to survive. See, I need a man who's ready to step up to the plate for me, and swing for the fences." She had held his eyes but now she looked away. "I'd hoped that truly special someone might be you, but . . ."

"But what? What did I do wrong?" Shelley was confused. Who wouldn't be? He had no idea what she was talking about. Who would? She'd given him hell for bopping the kid, and in the same breath told him she was looking for a guy who'd swing for the fences. Outside, in the lane, a car drove past a little too slowly. Shelley sat up straight so he could see out the window. Miss Miata. He rubbed his chin. "You and me, there's a spark, and we both know it, Bo. Don't we?" He hugged her. She was stiff and unresponsive as Barbie. "Don't we?" he said again, like the idiot he was.

Bo slid off his lap, went into the kitchen. Opened and slammed shut the refrigerator door. A moment or two later she came back into the room, carrying his last bottle of beer by the neck, between two fingers. She unscrewed the cap and tossed it in the fireplace. A sliver of gold foil spiralled swiftly down to the hardwood floor. She sipped, passed the bottle to Shelley.

"Mr. Sticks is Andrew's grandfather."

"What happened – they conspired to skip a generation?"

"Andrew's father was killed in a helicopter crash. Smuggling a stolen Mercedes-Benz to Beijing. He'd pinched a gangster's car, apparently. The point is that Mr. Sticks learned something from his son's death. To be ruthless. Andrew told me not long after I starting working for him about a business associate of Mr. Sticks', who did something that Mr. Sticks felt was unacceptable."

"Like what?"

Bo shrugged. She plunked herself back down on his lap, wriggled and squirmed, making herself comfortable. Drank some beer and passed the bottle to him and took it back. Her huge green eyes swallowed him all of a piece. She said, "You're right. There is a spark between us. But even the hottest fires have to be tended, Shell." She kissed him hard on the mouth. "What Mr. Sticks and Andrew did, they took the associate for a ride in his Cessna airplane. Do you know where Cultus Lake is?"

Shelley pointed. Bo swung his arm around ten or fifteen degrees. She said, "They flew over the lake, and Andrew tied one end of a two-hundred-foot length of rope around the associate's ankles and lowered him out the door. Mr. Sticks flew low enough to dunk him. Then they flew over some trees, and some mountains. Andrew said he was terrified the guy would get caught on a branch or something, and they'd crash. He told me Mr. Sticks flew all over the place, until they were almost out of fuel, and then charted a course for the deep woods, climbed up to an altitude of five thousand feet and . . ."

"Cut the rope," said Shelley.

Bo nodded. She rested her head against his chest. Now he knew why she was upset that he'd pounded Andrew. Gramps and the kid were killers. She said, "Don't give Mr. Sticks his gun back, okay?"

Shelley said, "Yeah, okay."

Bo wrapped her arms around his neck. "Kiss me, Shell."

Shelley kissed her awhile, to the best of his ability. Bo made small musical sounds of intense pleasure, sounding a lot like a creek he used to fish, when he was a kid and still had time for that kind of thing. She broke away from him. Her lipstick was smeared. She kissed him again, poured her soul into him. "Would you like to make some serious money, Shell?"

"Not really." He hadn't given it a moment's thought, just blurted it out. Who did he think he was, Richie Rich? No, but he was alive, and though it was undeniably a temporary situation, he had no desire to hurry things along. Dead was forever, after all.

He pictured himself lying flat on his back in a coffin with his arms folded across his chest and a death star sticking out of his forehead.

Bo said, "All you want out of life is to keep scraping wallets off the beach?"

Shelley moved his shoulders in a gesture that was partly careless shrug and partly a silent plea to stop picking on him.

Bo took his hand and placed it on her breast. How could soft and firm dwell together in such perfect harmony? Shelley's heart soared.

"Living in other people's houses," said Bo, "wearing other people's clothes, brushing your teeth with somebody else's toothbrush . . ."

He sat there, immobile. Refusing to be baited.

"Okay, *fine*. Be true to yourself and see where it gets you!" Bo jumped to her feet. "Sit there and vegetate forever, until the day you die."

Shelley's throat was dry.

Bo bent modestly at the knee as she turned on the television. A burst of insincere laughter choked the room. The screen was filled with a photograph of a gold ring. The ring was solid ten-karat gold and weighed a ton. A ton! Well no, chuckle chuckle, not quite that much! The tiny green jewel was an emerald, and the two diamonds that flanked it were certified zirconium. Or was the plural zirconia? Yuk yuk.

Bo flounced out onto the sundeck, taking what was left of the beer with her. The Cogswells, owners of the house, were due back in late December. How long would it take Mr. Sticks and his prematurely balding grandson to get around to taking him for a ride in their Cessna? Not that long. The TV huckster told him the ring would make a perfect engagement ring for those considering marriage. Shelley sat up a little straighter. The ring was $240.19, plus $9.81 for shipping and handling. He was duly warned that limited quantities of this very special and unique item were available, and that if he wanted to get in on the deal he'd better speed-dial that special toll-free number real pronto. In other words, quick.

A sequence of jerky still photographs displayed the ring from all points of the compass. The ring would look terrific on Bo. Complement her lovely green eyes. But two hundred and fifty bucks was a lot of dough.

The digital clock at the bottom corner of the screen said 1:24 LEFT. In a moment it said 1:23 LEFT. Shelley could see how this was going to turn out, in about 1:22. He had no money, no prospects. Time – his life – was running out at an unfair rate of speed and he couldn't afford to do anything about it.

His hand cupped the memory of Bo's perfect breast. She had turned to him in quiet desperation and asked him point-blank no promises or bullshit if he had the balls to earn a barrel full of money. And he'd looked her straight in her fist-blackened eye and turned her down flat.

But then, he was a deeply flawed human being, wasn't he? Self-centred. A poor listener. Kind of slothful and kind of a wimp. He stared morosely at the television.

0:57 LEFT.

16

Parker drove them back to the city. Willows had kicked off his brogues and put his stockinged feet up on the dash. He wriggled his toes. A warm breeze flowed in through the open window. He closed his eyes.

Parker said, "Off-duty, are we?"

Willows ignored her. Parker slipped on a pair of sunglasses, repressed a yawn, checked her watch. On less than two hours' sleep, she and Willows had already worked a shift and a half. No wonder she was tired.

"Jack?"

Willows stirred.

Parker said, "Nobody knew him because nobody liked him. His social life was a constant round of totally unemotional affairs." Parker corrected herself. "Unemotional in the sense that the only needs he met were his own. He made no attempt to disguise the fact that he wasn't making it as a real-estate agent, yet openly drove an expensive car, let it be known that he had plenty of cash."

Willows rubbed his eyes. "Maybe that's why he was killed, because people were bound to start asking questions, and someone was afraid that Galee was likely to provide answers."

Parker nodded. She braked as a mail truck cut in front of her, blocking her view of the North Shore mountains, the twin peaks of the Lions. Smog had turned the mountains from a lush emerald green to a paler, almost-olive colour.

Had some unseen presence or unsuspected factor altered the way she viewed the Zagros Galee murder?

The mail truck swerved into the curb lane and turned left off a side street. Granville all the way down to Broadway was in gridlock. She should've turned off two blocks back, at Sixteenth. It was a mistake that was easily rectified. She pulled over to the curb, parked in a loading zone and dropped the visor so the faded cardboard POLICE VEHICLE sign was in plain view.

Willows took his feet off the dashboard. He sat up, glanced around. He yawned.

Parker killed the engine.

Willows said, "What's up?"

"We're half a block from Szaz's," said Parker. "It's time for lunch. Protein. Carbohydrates. Hot coffee, and plenty of it."

Willows fumbled with his brogues. Left foot. Right foot. He remembered the first time he'd managed to tie his laces, that big breakthrough. Give him another thirty years, and he'd be back to square one. Depressing thought. He pushed open the car door and got out. The air was hot and still. A bright-eyed mannikin wearing a leather bra and panties stared haughtily down at him from a shop window. Parker waited for him at the intersection. There was a marked crosswalk, but no light. They crossed the street together, side by side. All around them the city hummed and throbbed.

Parker pushed open the restaurant's glass door, held it for Willows as he followed her inside. The air-conditioning washed over them. They were led to a window booth. The waitress was in her early forties, her hair tied in a tight nest-coloured bun and her glasses sliding partway down her nose. She gave Parker a nice smile as she put menus and glasses of ice-water down on the table.

"Claire, isn't it? Where've you been?"

"Here and there. How're you doing, Susan?"

"Getting by." The waitress smiled at Willows. "You two know what you want, or d'you need a few minutes to decide?"

"Side salad and a bowl of chowder for me," said Parker. "Light dressing on the salad. And a cup of coffee, please."

Willows looked up from his menu, ordered coffee and a Denver omelette.

"Comes with a salad or fries."

"Fries," said Willows, "and don't spare the cholesterol."

"I'll see what I can do."

Willows drank some water. "How do you two know each other?"

"I used to eat here fairly often, when I first moved into my apartment. It's only about a ten-minute walk." Parker shrugged. "It's a nice restaurant, part of the neighbourhood."

Willows reached across the table and squeezed Parker's hand. She was touched by this uncharacteristic display of affection. On the job he tended to be restrained, even aloof. Parker was pretty much the same way herself. It was habit. It was training. It was the job. You held yourself in at all times, or risked losing it all at the worst possible time. She bent her head and brushed Willows' fingers with her lips. He drank some more water.

Parker said, "I always thought being a cop was kind of a weird job, but now I'm not so sure."

"Compared to selling houses?"

"Who are you working for, when it comes right down to it? The guy who's selling the house or the guy who's buying it. Or nobody but yourself?"

Their waitress arrived with coffee, and Parker's salad.

Parker said, "It's a question of ethics. You're walking a tightrope every minute of the day." She ate some salad. "Rothstein's typical. Just a little too easy to get to know."

"And that makes him suspect, doesn't it?"

"It does to me."

"Me too," said Willows. He looked up as the waitress arrived with their order. His omelette had been cooked just the way he liked it; perfectly formed and golden brown, a little crisp around the edges. A mountain of French fries crowded the plate. What pleased him most of all was that the cook had not burdened him with a gratuitous sprig of parsley.

The waitress dipped into her apron pocket and came up with several extra packets of crackers. "Unsalted, right?"

"Absolutely right," said Parker. She slid her spoon deep into the steaming chowder, lifted it carefully to her mouth, sipped and swallowed.

"Good?" said Willows.

"These clams did not die in vain. How's the omelette?"

Willows' mouth was full. He chewed and swallowed. "I doubt you'd find a better one in Denver." He drank some coffee, separated another forkful of omelette from the mass, reached for the ketchup.

"What'd you think of Julia Delfino?"

"Too large and too loud. Too much makeup. Too much jewellery. What more could a man ask?" He gave her a sharp look. "You experiencing pangs of jealousy?"

Parker laughed. "Sorry, Jack."

Willows' beeper chirped as he was getting back into the car. He went inside the shop with the scantily clad mannikin in the window. The woman behind the cash register was in her early twenties, tall and dangerously slim, sceptical by design. She wore a black leather vest fastened with chain links, a tight mini in black leather. Her hair was cropped short, dyed in a checkerboard pattern of silver and black. Willows glanced around. An exaggeratedly voluptuous mannikin wearing a see-through skirt and black leather gloves posed in the harsh white headlight of a fifties-era Harley.

"Is there something I can do for you?"

Willows flashed his tin. He asked her if he could use the phone.

"Yeah, sure. Help yourself."

The telephone was encased in thin black leather. Willows dialled the number displayed on his pager.

Eddy Orwell picked up on the third ring. He told Willows he was hereby delegated to bring two cases of cold beer to Ralph Kearns' retirement party, and mentioned off-handedly that he had a lead in the Zagros Galee killing.

"Nice work, Eddy."

Orwell gave him two names. Howard Pincott and his wife, Rose, lived in apartment 2225, located directly beneath the penthouse in which Zagros Galee had died. Orwell began to describe Rose Pincott in graphic and borderline-tasteless detail.

Willows hung up, thanked the clerk. He left the shop, crossed the sidewalk and got into the car.

"BeachView Towers, and step on it!"

Parker smiled, started the motor.

She checked the traffic and pulled away from the curb.

Howard Pincott was large, well-preserved, in his mid-sixties. He had the look of a man who took good care of himself, exercised regularly, and watched what he ate. Pincott was a wealthy fellow, and he was quick to say so. He volunteered that a hotel in downtown Toronto had been in the family for three generations. It was one of the very few large, privately owned hotels in the country, worth a fortune. He also owned a beach house in Maui and a ranch not far from Auckland. His wife, Rose, was a New Zealander. She got homesick at least once a year, usually during the ski season. Did Willows ski?

"Not usually, during August."

"That's the middle of winter, down there. You can ski all day, chopper down into the valleys and fish for monster trout in the evening. Do you fish?"

"From time to time," said Willows. His split-cane and graphite rods and Hardy reels were gathering dust in the basement. Maybe in the fall, if he asked nicely, Sean would deign to spend a weekend with him. They could drive up to Kamloops, tie on some feathery

black leeches, and flail the lakes . . . "Is your wife home, Mr.
Pincott?"

"She'll be with us in a moment. Would you like a drink?"
Pincott peered anxiously at Parker. "Glass of white wine, some-
thing a little stronger, a martini?" He fixed his pale blue eyes on
Willows. "Or maybe a beer?"

"A glass of water would be nice," said Parker.

"Perrier? Evian?"

"Tap," said Parker, "would be just fine."

"You sure? Ice? Would you like some ice?"

"If you've got it."

Pincott let that one slide. "Jack," he said, "what'll you have?"

"I'm fine, for now."

"You're not thirsty? In this heat. Amazing. You should visit the
Kalahari, give lectures to camels." Pincott rubbed his hands briskly
together. "Make yourselves at home. I'll be right back."

Willows went over to the window and looked out. The view was
minutely less spectacular than from the penthouse, directly above.
He glanced around, taking in the apartment as he tried to divine
the nature of the people who lived in it. The furniture was dark,
heavy, seemingly brand-new. The art that hung on the pastel walls
was lavishly framed but uninvolving. He had the same disquieting
sense of lifelessness that he'd experienced upstairs. There was
nothing in the room that drew you in or risked offence. From what
he had seen, the apartment was as comfortable and as soullessly
impersonal as a suite in an upscale hotel; a convenient place to
pause for a moment, between more-exotic destinations.

The musical chiming of ice preceded Pincott into the room. He
walked with the precarious balance of a neophyte choirboy. A slice
of lime clung to the rim of Parker's glass. He'd apparently decided
that, if no one else wanted a martini, he'd better have one himself.
Smiling brightly, he said, "Sorry I took so long. Rose'll be in any
moment now." To Willows he said, "Are you sure you won't have
something to drink?"

Willows ignored him.

Parker said, "Where is your wife, Mr. Pincott?"

"She's, uh, taking a shower." He drank some martini. "I don't mean to be rude, but we weren't expecting you quite so soon."

"While we're waiting," said Willows, "why don't you tell us what happened last night."

"Well, as I said to the other detective, Rose and I got into Seattle about seven-thirty that night, picked up the car, and drove home." He allowed himself a small, self-congratulatory smile. "We made pretty good time. There was the usual lineup at the border but we have a Pace Lane sticker, so we breezed right through. Traffic from the border into the city was fairly light. It was three minutes to eleven when I pulled into our parking slot and killed the engine."

Parker said, "That was the exact time, three minutes to eleven?"

"I had a fifty-dollar bet with Rose that we'd be home by eleven." Pincott buried his self-congratulatory grin in his martini as he toasted his success.

"He promised not to speed, but I fell asleep on the I-5 and I'd bet a million he cheated," said Rose Pincott from the open living-room doorway. She smiled at the two detectives as she made her entrance. She was lightly tanned, in her early thirties. Her honey-coloured hair was still damp from the shower. A flesh-coloured silk robe was tied tightly at her narrow waist. Her legs were long and shapely, breasts by Wonderbra. Parker noted that, although Rose hadn't bothered to dress, she'd at least had the decency to make herself up and splash on some perfume. Rose offered her hand. Parker briefly shook. Willows was as quick.

Howard Pincott handled the introductions and then said, "So anyway, all I've told them so far was how long it took us to get home, and how much dough you lost. But that's it, honey. I swear I haven't said a word about what actually *happened*."

Rose smiled. "Is that a martini, darling?"

Pincott nodded. As if to prove his point, he drained his glass. "Did you mix a pitcher?"

"I certainly did, my sweet. Would you care for a drink?"

"I'd love a drink."

"Be right back," said Pincott.

Willows had never heard an adult male referred to as "darling," except in colourized movies. As Pincott left, he said, "Why don't you just go ahead and tell us what happened, Mrs. Pincott."

"Rose."

Willows nodded. "Rose it is."

"Well, let me think." She went over to the sofa by the window and sat down. Parker moved a few steps to her left, so the light wasn't in her eyes. Willows stayed put. In the kitchen, Pincott was singing softly. An ode to the dead real-estate agent, perhaps.

"We came upstairs to the apartment together. Howard unlocked the door and let me in, and then he went back down to the basement for the rest of the luggage. I checked the answering machine and fax machine in the den, for messages. The apartment was hot and stuffy, because we'd been away for several weeks, and Howard had turned down the air-conditioning. Anyway, I'd opened the sliding door in the bedroom, and I could hear someone yelling. In this building, that's rather unusual." She smiled. "Quality soundproofing, I suppose. Anyway, whoever was yelling sounded very angry, enraged. I was curious, so I went outside, onto the balcony. The yelling was coming from the penthouse, from the outside garden."

Pincott came back into the room, doing his choirboy walk. His lips were shiny and wet. Was he drunk? His hand was steady as he offered a martini to his wife.

Rose said, "Thankyou, darling."

"You're extremely welcome, my pet."

Rose drank an inch of martini. "So anyway, there's all this yelling going on, two men shouting at each other, cursing and swearing. Suddenly it stopped. Like somebody had flipped a switch. One second there was all this screaming and shouting, and the next moment it was absolutely silent. Kind of spooky . . ."

Willows said, "You say you heard two voices?"

"Yes, that's right. There were two of them. One sounded quite young. The other wasn't so loud."

"No women?"

"Not unless they were baritones, or mute."

"Were any names mentioned?"

"Yes they were, but they weren't the kind of names I'd care to repeat in mixed company." Rose crossed her legs. She ran the palm of her hand along her silken calf.   .

"Then what?" said Parker.

"Howard arrived with the rest of the luggage. By then the shouting had started again. He listened in for a moment, and then shut the door and turned up the stereo, and we took a shower."

"Shut the door and locked it and reset the alarm," said Pincott. "I don't mind telling you, I had visions of those two hotheads rappelling down onto the balcony, pillaging and looting . . ."

"Pillaging and raping," said Rose.

"That too," agreed Pincott. He cast Willows a look that was furtive and defensive. "In hindsight," he added, "I don't think any reasonable person could fault my precautions."

"You didn't hear a gunshot?"

"No, absolutely not. We certainly didn't. But as I said, I'd turned up the stereo to drown out the shouting. It was very unpleasant. Nasty. But listen to this: about midnight, just as we went to bed, it started up all over again. More yelling. But this time it was coming from *inside* the building."

"Rose got up and went out in the hall to see if she could find out what the hell was going on," Pincott said. "I told her she was crazy, but she ignored me."

"I could hear them, but I couldn't see them, so I knew they must be in the stairwell."

"The stairs go all the way down to the basement," said Pincott. "Fire regulations, in case the elevators break down."

"That's where they were, in the stairwell. I opened the door and I could hear them as clearly as if they were standing right next to me."

"Did you *see* them?" asked Parker.

"Not exactly." A gold star had been painted on a deep blue background on all ten of Rose's toenails. She caught Willows looking, and wiggled her toes. Looking straight at him, she held out her glass to her husband and said, "Would you mind freshening my drink, darling?"

Howard excused himself, solemnly walked a fairly straight line to the kitchen.

"What do you mean by 'not exactly'?" asked Parker.

"I could see their shadows. On the walls. They were kind of deformed, but I could make out their general shape."

From the kitchen came the high-pitched whine of a blender, rattle of ice. Pincott was singing a tune from *West Side Story*.

"They were both wearing suits," said Rose. One of them had his jacket off."

"How do you know that?" said Willows.

"Because he was swinging it around his head, like a bullfighter."

"Ever seen a bullfight?" said Pincott, back already, drinks in hand. "We've seen 'em in Spain *and* Mexico. Absolutely disgusting." His martini spilled over his wrist as he bobbed and weaved. "But so *exciting!*"

"Careful with the drinks, darling."

"Right, sorry." The mild criticism had slapped Pincott into a state of near-sobriety. He gingerly handed his wife her martini.

Rose said, "They were both real skinny, and not too tall. They both had short hair. One of them, his ears stuck out. The other was very excitable."

"You followed them down the stairs?"

"All the way to the basement," said Rose. She smiled. "Bet you didn't think I had the guts."

"By the time she got back I was in dreamland," said Pincott. "She woke me up, pounding on the door. It'd swung shut. She was locked out. My God, I thought I was in the middle of an earthquake. I'd been dreaming about sheep. Stylishly dressed sheep, wearing clothing from Descente, North Face, Schoffel. Gloves by

Kombi and Seirus. Bolle and Smith goggles. There were dozens of them, some on snowboards, some on skis. You should've seen the fuzzy little buggers tear down that mountain. Zooooom! And I'd look up, and they'd be on the lifts, stubby little legs dangling way up there in the air. So anyway, I looked out through that little peephole thing, and there she was, jumping up and down, laughing her head off." Pincott's face softened. "She looked terrific. What a beautiful woman. I thought . . . to hell with the sheep, this dream's way better'n the last one!"

Pincott emptied his glass into his mouth. He set the glass down carefully on a plate-glass coffee table, collapsed onto the couch next to his wife, shut his eyes, and began to snore.

Rose said, "He's like this, sometimes. I worry about him. He shouldn't try so hard to keep up. What's the rush? He was thirty years older than me the day I married him. That's why I fell in love with him, and that's why I married him, because he was different. Because he was *mature*. Why can't he just relax and enjoy it?"

She was staring at Willows as if actually expecting a sensible answer. He said, "Well, I don't know if he's enjoying it or not, but he sure looks relaxed to me."

Rose giggled. She put a hand to her mouth. A few drops of her martini spilled from her glass onto her husband's thinning hair. She kissed the drops away.

"Do you happen to know a man called Sidney Rothstein?" said Willows.

"Rothstein? No, I don't think so . . ." Frowning, she glanced down at her husband as if for confirmation. But Howard was taking a nap. She said, "Why do you ask?"

"Your husband mixes a good martini. Sidney *orders* a good martini. I couldn't help wondering if it was part of a grander plan, or mere coincidence."

"Mere coincidence, I'd say."

Parker said, "Tell me more about what you heard in the

stairwell. Did either of the men say anything that could possibly help us identify them?"

Rose shrugged. "I really don't know."

"From what you've told us, they were yelling at each other all night long. You must be able to remember *something* they said."

Rose sat up a little straighter. Her husband's head lolled against her breast. She gently pushed him away. "I forgot to mention an important point," she said with a tentative smile.

"What's that?" said Parker.

"Except for the foul language, when they were going down the stairs, neither of them was speaking English."

Parker willed herself not to bare her teeth. She said, "Can you tell me what language they *were* speaking, Mrs. Pincott?"

"Asian," said Rose Pincott firmly. She wet the tip of her finger and lovingly groomed her husband's bushy eyebrows.

Asian.

Parker said, "Don't get up, we'll find our own way out." She dropped her card on the glass coffee table. "Give me a call if you think of anything."

"We will," said Rose. She smiled fondly down at her dozing husband. "Won't we, Howard?"

17

Bo watched TV for a while, half an hour or so, and then stripped down to naked and flounced – there was no other word for it – back out on the deck. Why was it that her favourite part of the house was *outside* the house?

When he'd first reconnoitred the joint, Shelley had noted a lightweight dolly in the garage. Clots of dried earth clung to the wheels and bottom plate; no doubt the dolly was used to move the several avoirdupois tons of concrete frogs, psychotic gnomes and grimly menacing bunnies that were artistically situated all over the garden. He used the dolly to shift the potted plants on the deck so Bo could get a little more sun. And also, by happy co-incidence, to create a bushy green fence to protect her from the neighbours' prying eyes. Bo gave not the slightest indication she appreciated his vigilance or the effort he'd expended on her behalf. What'd she expect him to do, move old Mr. Sun himself? Shelley pleaded guilty to *looking* like a god, but that was as far as it went. His powers over the heavens were nil.

Hot and sweaty and feeling kind of taken-for-granted and low, he went into the kitchen and got some cube ice out of the fridge, two lowball glasses decorated with stylized gold sailboats from the cupboard, the Glenfiddich single-malt whisky. He went back out on the deck, poured a couple of shots into both glasses and set a glass on the deck in easy reach of Bo's trailing right hand. Her eyes were closed, but he knew she wasn't sleeping because her breathing was too fast, a little on the ragged side. He eased down into the same chair in which Mr. Sticks had so recently and so majestically reclined. The man was long gone but his cologne lingered on, smelling like the aftermath of a fire at a used-tire depot. Shelley stirred his Scotch with a finger. He sipped. Bo's throat moved, as if some living thing resided just below the surface of her skin. But it was merely her thundering, adrenaline-powered pulse. She wasn't quite naked – not if you counted her Serengeti sunglasses.

He said, "Mr. Sticks isn't in the phone book. Is that his real name, or did he make it up in one of those lit-by-lightning moments of pure inspiration I'm always reading about?"

"Made up," said Bo after a long pause. She was lying on her stomach with her head turned off to the side, away from him. Seeing no harm in it, he stared boldly. Bo remained oblivious, as the seconds ticked past. Shelley was nonplussed, even scandalized. He'd expected her to somehow instinctively realize she was being ogled.

But then, maybe she did. She rolled over on her back.

He stretched out his legs, drank some more Scotch. He'd vandalized a Jaguar, cold-cocked an offensive little twerp with a baseball bat *and* a brick, and rescued an apparent kidnap victim. Not a bad day's work, even if he did say so himself. And here he was, the payoff, relaxing with a drink on the sundeck of his expensive-but-rent-free house, ogling a beautiful naked woman in the stillness of a perfect Sunday afternoon. Life was more than a bowl of cherries, it was a full-bore fruit cocktail.

Bo said, "Stop staring at my breasts."

"Wasn't," said Shelley.

"No?" Bo's smile was fleeting and cynical. She said, "Andrew told me not long after I met him that Mr. Sticks killed a guy by shoving a bunch of sharpened pick-up sticks into him. Like a demented acupuncturist. This was a long time ago. During the Korean War? Anyhow, that's how he got his name. From then on, everybody called him Mr. Sticks."

Shelley wondered how long it would take people to start calling him *Mr. Bricks*. He smiled at the thought.

"What's so funny?"

"You said it was Andrew who gave you the mouse?"

She said, "Yeah, but it wasn't. He'd never do anything like that. Mr. Sticks punched me, not Andrew. I should've told you the truth, but I didn't want you going after him, because he's so old and fragile, and lethal. Anyway, it probably hurt him more to have his grandson beaten to a pulp."

"*Bricked* to a pulp," said Shelley. "Were you really engaged to the guy?"

"Sort of."

Shelley mulled over the implications of her remark through the bottom of his glass. He poured himself a refill and considered that, like a bad tooth, the truth must out. He said, "How'd you meet him?"

"In the Jag," replied Bo a tad too casually.

Shelley drained his Scotch. He thought maybe he'd let that one slide, rather than dwell on it. But though he kept his mouth shut, his brain was wide open to the possibilities. Which were limited. Riddle. What three professions tend to meet new friends in the comfort and privacy of an automobile? Drug addicts. Hookers. Uh ... He pursed his lips and blew softly across the open neck of the Glenfiddich bottle. An almost subsonic hum ensued. He sounded like a grouse in heat.

Bo hadn't touched her drink. She said, "Mr. Sticks introduced us."

"Right," said Shelley.

"I already told you, it was strictly business." She slid the sunglasses partway down her nose and eyed him over the top of the frame, for more direct contact. "Are you the jealous type, Shelley?"

"How should I know? I've never had a chance to find out."

"You've never been in love?" Bo pushed the glasses slowly back up the bridge of her nose. Before he could answer, she said,

"Neither have I." She stared at him a moment, then turned her face to the slowly wheeling sun.

Shelley's toes nuzzled the boards of the deck. He flexed his stomach muscles. The silences between their words were like the gaps between the thick planks that formed the deck; measured and inevitable. He wondered what he'd have been doing at that exact moment, if he hadn't gotten mixed up with Bo. Probably at this time of the day he'd be down at the beach hustling wallets, or maybe taking a siesta so he could hit the clubs and stay up all night and still look good, as dawn broke and the city rose up out of the blackness, lost its string-of-pearls elegance, it's deceptive simplicity. Night was one-dimensional. What you were meant to see was lit up by neon bright as fireworks. All the rest of it, that great big dirty ball of a world, was blacked out, erased. It had been too long since he'd done any bouncing. Bouncers usually got plenty of work in the summer. The heat made people grumpy. Guys sweltered in a lineup for an hour or two and then went crazy, did some damage.

Bo said, "You know that carwash on Fourth Avenue, that concrete-block place a couple of blocks west of Burrard?"

"The one by the bridge, there's always a bunch of skinny guys standing around outside with towels hanging out of their pants pockets?"

"Mr. Sticks gets his Jaguar washed there every Friday morning," said Bo. "He always leaves a rolled-up five-dollar bill sticking in the ashtray, for the guy with the vacuum, who does the inside work."

"He expects the carwash guy to steal the five bucks?"

"No, Shelley, he expects him to *take* the money. But he also expects him to work extra hard on the inside of the car, to earn it."

Here came another one of those silences, stretching along the neatly laid boards all the way to the far end of the deck.

After a while, when Shelley couldn't take it any longer, he said, "So what's the point?"

"That's where I met him," said Bo. Not quite exasperated, but getting there. "At the carwash. See, the way it works, the customer's supposed to wait outside while his vehicle's being washed. Enjoy a complimentary cup of coffee or maybe stretch his legs, take a stroll around the neighbourhood."

"A *complimentary* stroll around the neighbourhood," said Shelley, smiling.

Bo said, "I got into the car and there he was, in the backseat. Wearing a black hat and a black three-piece suit, with a miniature red rose in the lapel. Like Pierre Trudeau with jaundice. I almost had a heart attack. He was just sitting there, but it was such a shock."

"What'd you do?"

"Maced him at point-blank range with a spray bottle of this stuff we use, it's like quadruple industrial-strength Windex, but a lot worse, very caustic."

Shelley imagined Mr. Sticks sitting cross-legged on the softer-than-butter leather backseat of his Jag; Bo hitting him with a burst of liquid cleanser. He said, "What colour is it?"

"What colour is what?"

"The stuff you sprayed in Mr. Sticks' face."

"Bright yellow," said Bo. She smiled, remembering. "I blinded him. He couldn't see as far as the end of his nose. You should have heard him yell. I dragged him out of there, got one of the guys to turn a high-pressure hose on him. The water blew his glasses right off his face, and we never did find them. The foreman canned me on the spot, the whole crew laughing their heads off. Big joke." She shrugged. "Anyway . . ."

"That's when Mr. Sticks hired you?"

"No, it was about a week later. He got my address from the carwash. I was living in an apartment down on East Sixth, and I came home one night and he was parked out front." Lamely, Bo added, "Listening to the radio."

"Offered you a job?"

Bo nodded. "Five hundred a week, cash. All I had to do was stand around looking beautiful."

"Piece of cake."

Bo ignored him. "Pour the odd glass of wine, smile if somebody spoke to me."

"No matter what they said?"

Bo said, "Nobody was ever rude to me, not even once. Or if they were, it was because they were drunk, nothing personal. Anyway, the next morning, Mr. Sticks took me downtown and bought me almost a thousand dollars' worth of clothes. A new coat, cocktail dress, two pairs of shoes and a whole bunch of other stuff."

"Like what?"

"Some jewellery, perfume. A bra."

Shelley blinked so hard he almost gave himself whiplash. "You hadn't previously owned a bra?"

Bo smiled sweetly across the lawn.

Shelley made another trip to the kitchen, for more ice. When he came back outside, Bo asked him to shift the potted plants again. She was like a mobile sundial, always following the light.

Shelley said, "So when they took you shopping, that was the first time you met the kid?"

"Who?"

"Handy dandy Andrew."

"Are you grilling me, Shell?"

Shelley held up both his hands, palm out. "You don't want to talk about it, fine by me. I thought we were trying to get to know each other a little better, that's all. But you do whatever makes you comfortable. Because I want you to be comfortable, believe me."

"The next day," Bo said, "Andrew drove me to a downtown apartment that Mr. Sticks had leased under an assumed name. I hung around for a solid four hours, in my new high heels and cocktail dress, smiling my little face off, while Mr. Sticks rented the apartment over and over again. We took an hour for lunch and went back to work. We didn't quit until eleven that night."

Shelley frowned. "I don't get it."

"The way it went, Mr. Sticks owned the apartment. I was the

tenant who was breaking my lease because I was getting married. The apartment had two bedrooms and a view of the park, and the rent was eight hundred and fifty dollars a month, well under market value. Everybody who wanted the apartment – and everybody who looked at it wanted it – had to put down a deposit of one-half month's rent, in advance. Cheques accepted but cash preferred."

"Much preferred," said Shelley. He got it now, all right. In more ways than one. Raw emotion skewed his face. In high school he'd taken a couple of art courses. Right now he felt like that painting by Edvard Munch called "The Cry," of a guy whose mouth was open wide in a shout or scream of some kind, and whose hands gripped his head so tight he'd pushed it completely out of shape.

Bo sat up. She said, "It isn't what you think, Shell."

"No? You sure about that?" The house would rent for two grand, maybe twenty-five hundred a month. It'd be a cash-flow monster, while it lasted. And he'd thought all Bo was after was his body.

As if reading his mind, she said, "I'm out of the game, Shell. It's over. How d'you think I got the raccoon eye? Did it ever occur to you to wonder why Mr. Sticks and Andrew came over here and tried to kidnap me?"

Shelley needed to believe her more desperately than he needed to fill his lungs with air. He decided to put aside his doubts. He was no church-goer, but that didn't mean he was incapable of an act of faith.

Bo told him about the apartments they'd rented, all over the city and across the border in Seattle and in Portland, Oregon, across the Canadian prairies and all the way to Toronto, the piles of money, dozens of bank accounts, close encounters they'd had with irate would-be tenants, and sometimes the law. She told him about Mr. Sticks' passion for classical music and about Andrew's burgeoning collection of lethal martial-arts weapons.

She told him that her salary had quickly escalated to one thousand dollars a week, free and clear. If they did especially well, there were cash bonuses. Mr. Sticks liked ritual. He had paid her every Friday night at six; small bills in a large envelope.

"How long have you been working for him?"

"Less than three years," said Bo defensively.

Jeez . . .

Bo told him about the shopping sprees. How easy it was to adjust from minimum wage to celebrity status, at all those trendy little boutiques with hardly any floor space and too much staff.

Three years. Thirty-six months. Approximately one hundred and forty-four weeks. Times, if she could believed, one thousand tax-free dollars per week. It was a hell of a lot better than bouncing, or prowling beaches. Shelley said, "You're staying in my house, driving my car, drinking my single-malt whisky. Acting as if you were broke, when you've been netting at least fifty grand a year for the past three years. What happened to all that dough?"

"My father's terminally ill and requires twenty-four-hour-a-day care. That kind of love costs a small fortune, Shell."

Shelley struggled against a sudden urge to smash himself over the head with the Glenfiddich bottle. A down payment on the punishment he had coming for his terminally stupid behaviour. He didn't know whether to laugh or cry. Both responses seemed equally appropriate.

Bo said, "You don't believe me, do you?"

"I thought the health-care system was supposed to take care of people like your mother."

"Father," said Bo. But she'd hesitated just long enough for Shelley's ear to take measure of it.

"Where did Andrew fit in?"

"If anybody bothered to ask, Mr. Sticks said he was his son and that he was learning the business. But really, he was our insurance policy."

"The Bone-Cracker, or Head-Thumper or Tooth-Smasher or Skull-Buster, the heavy boy. Mr. Brawn. Muscle, if a sucker wanted his money back."

Bo nodded. She didn't look too happy.

Now he got it. Finally. His stomach churned. She'd quit the easy life because Andrew the Bone-Cracker had killed somebody.

He put the question to her.

"*Killed* somebody? Heavens, no. Of course not." Bo tilted her body towards the slip-sliding sun. Down at the far end of the deck, dark shadows inched stealthily towards them, boxing them in. She said, "What makes you think something like that?"

Shelley hunched forward in his chair. He'd adjusted to her nudity, had actually forgotten all about it awhile. But now, he was sure, she was moving around more than the situation called for, using her body to distract him. But from what?

"Shelley?"

"Uh . . . yeah?"

"I'm going inside, to take a shower."

"Yeah, okay."

Bo stood up. She brushed back her hair as she bent at the knee to pick up a stray towel. She slung it over her shoulder in a way that did nothing to obstruct his view. "Is there something you'd like to say to me?"

Shelley frowned.

Bo said, "I'm here because I want to be here, not because I'm hiding out from something. Is that clear?"

Shelley nodded. A drop of sweat trickled down the bridge of his nose and went plop on the deck, vanished into the hot, dry board.

Bo said, "I've got sunscreen all over me."

Shelley looked up.

She smiled. Freckles scrambled to rearrange themselves, get back into some semblance of order. "Will you wash my back, Shelley?" Before he could respond she added, "Please?"

He had to push himself out of the chair, inertia or gravity or indecision or fear holding him down. Bo took his hand, fingers intertwined. As they entered the house, his arm pressed against her free-swinging breast. He felt as if he'd been struck by a low-voltage lightning bolt. The tide rose in his veins, the world jigged briefly out of focus. His poor heart creaked with the strain of it all.

Bo shut the door and locked it, laid Shelley's sawed-off broom handle in the track. In the entrance hall, she checked to make sure the security system was engaged.

Then she led him up the stairs, the delicate muscles in the small of her back and the long muscles in her legs tightening and releasing with every step, her sweet butt hunching up and relaxing; grace and beauty in motion, and Shelley missed not a bit of it.

In the bathroom, Bo turned on the shower, adjusted the water to her satisfaction, stepped beneath the spray. Shelley stripped off his Levi's and boxer shorts. Bo handed him a bar of soap and turned her back on him. Her freckles were the colour of autumn leaves. He washed her diligently but gently. Her flesh was warm and smooth, firm here, silky-soft just there. She slapped his hands away.

"Just the back, Shell."

He felt the bones beneath her flesh. How lovely she was. He knew almost nothing about her but felt somehow that he had known her forever, even beyond the span of his life.

Bo took the soap out of his hand. "Your turn, handsome."

He did his best to be serious and hold still, as she showed him a few special tricks she'd learned when she was a pro.

Back at the carwash.

18

Eddy Orwell sat at his desk, hunched over his paperwork, eyes closed, every nuance of his posture suggesting abject defeat. Orwell's clothes were curiously at odds with his morose demeanour. He wore yellow slacks, a gaudy red leather belt, a pink-and-purple-striped Ralph Lauren short-sleeved shirt with a button-down collar. The pants were too tight, and the shirt fit like a tent. The close-cropped blond hair that covered his bullet head stood at rigid attention over a scalp the same shade of pink as a not-quite-ripe watermelon. His skin had an unhealthy, glossy sheen. He was sweating heavily. A casting director might have given him a role as a sunstroked golfer, but would never have seen him as a functioning homicide detective. He glanced up as Willows and Parker entered the squadroom. His bloodshot eyes focused on Parker.

"Got any Aspirin?"

Parker unzipped her purse. "Headache, Eddy?"

Orwell nodded.

"He caught a glimpse of himself in the mirror, just before it broke," said Ralph Kearns.

Orwell gave Kearns a hard look. "What's that supposed to mean?"

"Catch, Eddy." Parker tossed Orwell a slim plastic box containing a dozen Aspirin. Orwell fumbled with the box, squinted at the directions printed on the label. The container seemed to have been designed to create a greater need for the product rather than to provide quick relief from pain. Orwell's blunt fingers pushed and prodded. The damn box was a bunker. He brought his fist crashing down. Splinters of plastic skittered across his desktop. He plucked five Aspirins from the wreckage, popped them in his mouth and chewed industriously. "What is it you don't like, Ralph. The shirt or the pants?"

"Both," said Kearns promptly.

Orwell swung his castored chair around. His feet were bare – no socks or shoes. A muscle twitched high up on his bony cheek. A vein pulsed just beneath his teddy-bear ear. He ate another Aspirin.

Farley Spears entered the squadroom. Spears' eyes were bright and full of good cheer. He was smiling broadly as he sat down at his desk. Orwell ate another Aspirin. He glared at Spears, and then pushed back his chair and stormed out of the squadroom.

Kearns said, "How was court, Farley?"

"A barrel of laughs. As always. How'd you and Eddy get along?"

"No problems."

Spears frowned. The look Orwell had given him had not been friendly. He said, "Where's Eddy going?"

"My guess, down to the basement, take another shower."

"Coffee?" said Parker.

Spears declined.

"Please," said Willows. He gave Parker a nice smile. On the way to 312 Main, they'd argued sporadically about Willows' approach to Rose and Howard Pincott. Parker thought Willows had been far too easy on them. He felt there was no point in badgering them because neither of them knew anything, except what time every liquor store in the city locked its doors. Parker thought he'd unnecessarily muddied the waters by asking the Pincotts if they knew Sidney Rothstein. Willows had defended himself. He'd had a hunch, taken a shot. No harm done.

The argument had petered out, as arguments do. But it hadn't been resolved.

Spears said, "What d'you mean, *another* shower. What happened?"

"Notice the clothes?"

"I've seen him wearing worse."

"We were down at the Sunrise Hotel," said Kearns. "We got a call from the desk clerk that one of the rooms smelled pretty bad. Stank. The guy who lived in there – it was a monthly rental – wouldn't come to the door. The clerk couldn't get in because the guy'd changed the lock and his key didn't fit."

"The clerk's key didn't fit?"

"Yeah, right."

Parker handed Willows a paper cup. He nodded his thanks. She leaned against his desk and sipped from her own cup.

"We figured somebody'd died," said Kearns. "There was no way in but to kick down the door, which is something Eddy likes to do anyway. So he did, and in we went."

Parker's chair creaked as she sat down.

"We found the guy in the bathroom," Kearns continued. "In one of those big old-fashioned enamel tubs with the slope back and big claw feet. The kind you can lean back with the paper and be nice and comfortable? Anyway, sniff sniff, we follow our noses and there he is, naked as a jaybird, the tub full to the brim of watery brown sludge. There's bits of toilet paper floating on the surface, the smell's incredibly awful."

Willows sipped some coffee. On his desk stood a colour photograph of his children, and another, more-recent photograph of one of the most productive pools in a favourite trout stream. On the near side of the stream there was a grassy meadow. The water was the colour of emeralds. High up in the top right corner of the photograph, the sun in a patch of clear blue sky beamed cheerfully down on him no matter what his mood.

Kearns glanced at Parker. He said, "I've been a cop close to thirty years. My first day on the job, I was working traffic, I got a call from the dispatcher about an old milk truck parked behind an Italian restaurant over on Commercial Drive. The truck's blocking the driveway, the guy owns the restaurant wants it moved. But there's a bad smell coming off it, so he calls the cops. I check it out. The truck's a wreck. Rusty, a flat tire. No plates. It's locked. The windows are painted black so you can't see inside. I break a window, and the stink just about knocks me flat on my ass. The guy that owned the restaurant was standing there, alongside his cook and a couple of waiters, a busboy. I was the only one that didn't throw up. You know what we found in there, Claire?"

"A dead horse," said Parker, who'd heard Kearns tell the same sad tale many, many times before.

"A dead *stallion*," said Kearns. "And the point is that it had been dead a long, long time. But, well, anyway. I figured I'd never run into anything worse, no matter how long I lived." He pinched his thumb and index finger together. "But today, *this* close to my last day on the job, I was proved wrong."

Willows drank some more coffee. "What happened to the guy in the tub, Ralph?"

"Only his nose and eyes were above the surface. He was like a crocodile or an alligator. Eddy and I, we both assumed he was dead. Otherwise, what in hell was he doing there? Eddy went into the other room and broke a leg off a chair. He used the chair leg to try to pry loose the plug on the bath." Kearns shook his head, remembering. "You couldn't see below the surface. Too dark, all that brown scum. Maybe Eddy hit him in the leg with the stick. Anyway, it was like the guy had been in a trance. His eyes pop open . . ."

Parker's phone rang. She reached out and pulled the phone a little closer, picked up, reached for a pen.

Kearns said, "Eddy's leaning over the tub, holding the chair leg with one hand, his nose with the other. The guy sits up straight, grabs his arm, gives him a yank. You should've seen the look on Eddy's face. Total horror."

Parker hung up. She said, "Jack, the preliminary autopsy report came in. No surprises, except the bullet that killed Zagros Galee wasn't fired from the revolver we found in the pond."

"No?"

"It was a copper-jacketed twenty-five-calibre round," said Parker. "The ejection marks are consistent with a semiauto."

Willows wasn't overly surprised. The small calibre of the murder weapon went a long way towards explaining why none of the neighbours had heard a shot.

When Parker had moved her telephone she'd uncovered a pink message slip. She said, "Also, I've got a message here, the Real Estate Board has offered to put up a ten-thousand-dollar reward for information leading to the arrest and conviction of Zagros Galee's murderer."

Kearns said, "The real-estate agent? My opinion, they're gonna have to go a lot higher than that."

Willows leaned back in his chair. Bradley would probably go for it. A cash incentive might kick-start what had become a stalled investigation. He yawned hugely.

Parker said, "Maybe we should take a couple of hours off, catch up on our sleep."

Kearns winked lasciviously at Spears, who suggestively waggled his eyebrows. Parker ignored them both.

Willows picked up his telephone and dialled the number on the solitary message slip that had been left on his desk.

Sidney Rothstein answered on the first ring. Willows identified himself. He told Rothstein he'd got his message and asked him if there was something he could do for him.

"You've got it entirely backwards, my friend. The question is, what can Sidney do for you?"

Willows heard a burst of laughter in the background, the clink of glasses. He wondered if Rothstein was still at the golf course, drinking his way through his crab sandwich. He said, "Well, Mr. Rothstein, what *can* you do for me?"

"Not ten minutes ago," said Rothstein, "I got a call from Julia Delfino. Julia accused me of telling you she'd had an affair with Zagros. I don't mind saying she was a little hot under the collar. In fact she was extremely rude. But that isn't why I called. You see, towards the end of her screech, Julia demanded to know if I'd mentioned her involvement with Zagros' new friends."

"What friends?" said Willows.

Rothstein's voice was muffled as he said, "Jennifer, darling. Would you be so kind . . ."

"What friends?" said Willows again, more forcefully.

"Well that's just it," Rothstein replied. "I have absolutely no idea what she was talking about. But from what she said, I gather they'd involved Zagros in a business venture of some kind, something that might've been a shade unethical."

Willows pressed for more information, but it was no use; Rothstein had given him everything he had.

Julia Delfino's open house had been scheduled from one to three. By the time Willows got off the phone it was three-fifteen. He called the agent on her cellular but there was no answer. He dialled her home and then her office number, and left messages on her machines. He tried her pager number. The answering service told him her whereabouts were unknown.

The dregs of his coffee were cold and grim. He pushed away from his desk, asked Parker if she wanted another cup. She nodded. Spears had left. Kearns told him thanks but no thanks, he was on his way home. Willows walked down to the machine at the far end of the room and poured two fresh cups. Parker took her coffee with real milk, no substitutes accepted. He added powdered creamer to his own cup and returned to his desk.

Kearns waved goodbye.

Parker drank some coffee. She yawned. The beach seemed a lifetime ago.

Willows picked up the phone and dialled his own number. No answer. He tried the vet. The receptionist told him Barney had lost a leg but the rest of him had been saved. She asked Willows if he wanted to speak to his daughter.

Willows said, "Hey, Annie. How's it going?"

"Dad, Barney lost his left front leg."

"But he's going to be okay, isn't he?"

"Dr. Larkins said he'd be just fine. She won't let me see him, though." Annie was subdued, but had her emotions under control. Willows was a little dismayed to realize how much he had come to depend on her unstinting good nature, her constant cheer.

He said, "Is Sean around?"

"No, I don't know where he is."

Willows pondered. "I wish I could be there, Annie. We've got a witness we're trying to track down . . ." He massaged his temple. "How long is Barney going to be at the vet's?"

"Dr. Larkins said probably four or five days, at least. It sort of depends on Barney. She said some cats come out of surgery acting as if they never knew they had four legs, but that others take a long time to recover."

"Barney's an extra-smart cat. He'll be fine."

"He better be," said Annie with uncharacteristic force. She added, "Is Claire around?"

"Yes she is, and she wants to talk to you. Annie, take care of yourself, okay? I'll be home just as soon as I can get there."

"I know." Annie sounded resigned. He didn't blame her.

"Love you, sweetie."

"I love you too, daddy."

Willows handed his phone across to Parker. Claire was always very good with the children, patient and kind, firm when firmness was required. Parker did a lot of listening and not much talking. She advised Annie to go home, rather than hang around the vet's feeling sorry for Barney. She told her she loved her, and hung up.

Outside, a gull perched on a telephone post and the brick walls of the remand centre were a dull, glowering red.

He wasn't sure why, but Willows always felt slightly claustrophobic when the squadroom was empty. Where was everyone? Off-duty or solving crimes. He reached for his coat.

Parker stifled a yawn.

Julia Delfino lived in a top-floor corner unit in a sprawling three-storey complex a block to the east of Richmond's oddly misnamed main drag – Number Three Road.

There was guest parking at the rear of the building, but Willows parked on the street, where the unmarked Ford was out in the open and less likely to be broken into. The lobby door was unlocked. Parker waited by the elevator, as Willows took the fire stairs down to the underground parking lot. He prowled the rows of parked cars until he found the agent's black Mercedes, and then went back upstairs.

"She's home."

Parker thumbed a button. The elevator doors slid open. Screwed to the side walls of the elevator were metal-framed advertisements for local fitness clubs, restaurants, an oil-and-lube franchise. Overhead, a dying fluorescent tube hissed venomously.

Delfino's apartment was to the right, at the end of a long hallway that was not one inch wider than the fire code required.

Parker knocked. She stood directly in front of the peephole. On the other side of the door a dog growled unhappily.

"Doberman?" said Willows.

"More like a Rottweiler. With horns, a spike collar, glowing red eyes and a bad case of rabies."

"And a ravenous appetite," said Willows with a smile.

The door swung open. Julia Delfino stood there, looking resigned. The dog struggling frantically in her arms was a dwarf or miniature chihuahua. It's teeth were tiny but sharp, like a piranha's. The creature's eyes, gormless and bulging, threatened to fall out of their sockets. The agent stepped aside. She said, "Sidney couldn't keep a secret if you stuck his stupid head in a bucket of quick-drying cement and dropped him in a lake."

Willows smiled. Apparently Julia Delfino's cocktail party had been cancelled. He and Parker entered the apartment. Delfino said, "Let me just take care of this stupid dog." She strode rapidly down a hallway to an open door. Willows glimpsed a line of black lingerie hanging above a pink bathtub. The chihuahua's nails skittered on enamel. Delfino stepped out of the bathroom and slammed the door shut.

She led her two guests into the living room. The chihuahua yapped ineffectually. Willows was fairly sure he wouldn't have even heard it, if he hadn't known it was there.

Through the living-room windows there was a nice view of the three-storey condominium across the street. Beyond the condo's tar-and-gravel roof lay the endless strip of multi-coloured neon that was Number Three Road.

Julia Delfino had shucked her power-salesman outfit in favour of a pair of baggy green shorts and an oversized dark blue Nike T-shirt. She offered that the dog's name was Gorgeous and that it had been bequeathed to her by her mother, who obviously hadn't loved her after all. Collapsing but not blending into the tiger-lily sofa, she lit a cigarette and energetically exhaled.

Parker said, "You're aware that we're investigating a murder, Miss Delfino."

"Yes, of course."

"When we talked to you this afternoon, why didn't you mention that, at the time of Mr. Galee's death, he'd become involved in a new project."

"With a couple of shady characters," said Willows, deadpan.

"Is that how Sidney characterized them?"

Parker took a step towards her, stared down at her. "Let's get this straight. Our job is to ask the questions, and your job is to provide concise, but detailed, answers." Parker sat down on the sofa's overpadded arm. Intimidation by proximity. She said, "Tell me, how would *you* characterize Mr. Galee's new friends?"

Delfino flicked cigarette ash on the pine Ikea coffee table. Was there a high-tech ashtray there, that only she could see? Or was she a tad nervous?

From the bathroom, Gorgeous loudly registered the fact that he was one discontented chihuahua.

"That damn dog." Delfino blew a stream of smoke at the ceiling. She said, "I never actually met Zagros' new business associates." She flicked a little more ash into the invisible ashtray. "He tried several times to get us together for lunch, but I kept putting him off."

"Why?" said Parker.

The agent shrugged. "I don't know why I got involved with him in the first place. I'm not usually attracted to the slope-shouldered, swarthy type. But I'd just ended a relationship, and I was bored, I suppose. Don't misunderstand me. Zagros could be a very charming fellow, when he was in the mood. But he was too intense for my taste. Too desperate, really. Desperate in the sense that he was being pursued by inner demons."

"It wasn't an inner demon who shot him," said Willows. He smiled. "We ruled out inner demons right off the bat."

Parker gave Willows an over-the-shoulder look. In the bathroom, nails scrabbled too loudly on the sides of the tub. Visions of Barney danced in her head. Lack of sleep had begun to take its toll. "We're not particularly interested in your personal relationship with Mr. Galee," said Parker. "We do want you to tell us whatever you can about Mr. Galee's new business associates."

"As I said, I never met them. Zagros didn't say much about them either. He was quite careful not to mention their names, for example. All I know is that they were involved in some kind of borderline-illegal scam. At least, that's the impression Zagros gave me. 'Maximum profit maximization,' he called it."

"Why did he approach you? What made him think you might be interested in something 'borderline illegal'?" said Parker.

Julia Delfino's hazel eyes skittered around the room. A length of ash was deposited on the pine table. "I have no idea," she said at last.

Parker said, "None at all?"

"My best guess is that he may have hoped I'd dissuade him, that he was looking for a way out."

"You say you never met these men?"

"Yes, that's right."

"But you're fairly sure there were two of them?"

The agent nodded tersely. The tip of her cigarette glowed bright. She exhaled with a rush.

"He must've said *something* about them," said Parker. She smiled down at Delfino. "I wonder what we can do to help jog your memory. Would a drive downtown help?"

"Not really. Let me think . . . Zagros did mention that they were Chinese, recent immigrants, and that he was fairly sure they were father and son. There was a woman, too. Zagros said they were very serious and dependable. That they'd been involved in the same sort of project many times before, had a great deal of experience, and knew exactly what they were doing." Delfino stared out the window. "I think Zagros was afraid of them," she said. "It wasn't anything specific that he said, but I think he'd gotten himself mixed up in a situation that was beyond his experience and completely out of control."

"Did he say how he'd met them?"

"They came to him, I think."

"And he never mentioned any names?"

"I'm afraid not." The agent leaned forward to extinguish her cigarette in the non-existent ashtray. She blinked comically at the untidy pile of ash that lay on the table.

A heavy green glass ashtray was perched on top of the television. Willows carried it over to her. She glanced up at him, nodded her thanks. He dropped his card on the table. "If you should think of anything, anything at all . . ."

"I'll be in touch."

Willows' eyes were solemn. He said, "If Mr. Galee's new friends should happen to call, we'd like to know about it right away. Immediately."

"I don't know why they'd want to see me."

"There's a chance they may be looking for a new partner," said Parker, "now that the old one isn't any use to them."

Julia Delfino nodded. Not because she followed Parker's logic, but simply because she was in no mood for an argument. She got up to show them to the door. In the bathroom, Gorgeous whined frantically. Delfino said, "Do you know what he does when he gets mad at me – if I leave him alone too long, or forget to fill his water dish or feed him at the appointed hour?"

"Probably," said Willows.

"That's why I put him in the tub, because it's easier to clean up after him."

"Remember," Parker said, "call us if you think of anything."

"Promise," said Delfino as she slowly shut the door.

Willows started laughing before the elevator doors had slid shut. Parker asked him what was so funny. He explained that the threads of the case were beginning to come together. Sidney Rothstein and the Pincotts shared a taste for martinis. As for Gorgeous and Eddy Orwell . . .

19

Bo changed into black silk shorts and a red-and-white diagonal-striped miracle fabric tanktop that didn't make her look at all like a barber pole. She wore a different pair of gold sandals. Her hair had that self-inflicted windblown look of a raging three-alarm fire. Around her narrow waist she wore a genuine Boy Scout belt in dark brown leather, with a brass buckle. Shelley lacked the nerve to ask her how she'd happened to acquire it.

All he knew, because Bo had emphatically told him it was all he needed to know, was that they were going out, to eat dinner at her favourite Vietnamese restaurant.

At the curb, Bo offered her hand in such a way as to encourage Shelley to fall to his knees and kiss her ring. She snapped her pretty fingers. "The keys, Shelley."

"You left something in the house?" Shelley smiled. "It's okay, I'll get it."

Bo moved in on him. "Get this – I'm driving."

Shelley grinned a foolish grin. "Driving what?" The grin faded, tooth by tooth. "My car?" As soon as the words had left his mouth, he knew that they were true. The last faint traces of his good humour had vanished, wiped away as abruptly as if drawn in chalk. Though he could still feel where the grin had stretched his jaw muscles, it was gone.

172

Bo effortlessly read the paint-by-numbers look on his face. "I know where we're going," she said. "You don't."

"Maybe so. But nobody drives my car but me. Especially when I'm in it."

Bo moved up against him. She put her arms around him and clung tight, her nipples hard as marbles against his chest. She shifted her hips in a complex pattern that was not at all plausible, given what he knew about human anatomy. He tried to retreat but she clung fiercely to him. Her hands slid deep into the back pockets of his dark blue Dockers. His shirt was partly unbuttoned. She licked his chest. He stopped hyperventilating long enough to say, "You want to go back inside for a while?"

Bo put her arms around his neck. She jumped lightly up, and wrapped her smooth brown legs around his waist. "No, I don't want to go back inside 'for a while,' or for anything else. What I *want* is to drive your car to the restaurant." Her eyes were bright as a sparrow's. Her voice was hard as an anvil. She said, "I *always* get what I want, Shell. That's the kind of woman I am, and if you didn't already know it, you sure as hell know it now."

Bo gave him another loving squeeze. Her deceptively muscular thighs compressed his ribcage. Without a word, he handed over the keys, slid into the passenger seat and buckled up. It felt stranger than strange. The perspective was all wrong. He fidgeted, trying against all odds to make himself comfortable. Bo turned the key. The tachometer needle swept like the red hand of a manic clock across the face of the dial, fell just short of the red line, and dropped back. Bo depressed the clutch pedal and shifted into first gear. The sx jumped away from the curb.

Bo was nobody's grandmother. You could tell by the way she drove. All that bobbing and weaving, spine-tingling acceleration and borderline-suicidal cornering had made him fear for his life. Like a modern-day Gretel, determined to find her way back out of the urban forest, she left treadmark spoor all across the city.

The restaurant was high up on Commercial, a mile south of the cluster of fashionable and sometimes-overpriced Italian joints that crowded the street for block after block below Broadway. The owner smiled his way out of the kitchen as they arrived, arms spread wide, all happy-happy. The relaxed, effortlessly and endlessly cheerful type. He tilted up his cheek and Bo gave him a kiss, and he turned the other cheek and got that one smooched too, while his wife looked on, smiling bashfully from behind her hands. The guy's name was Bill. Bo introduced him to Shelley. The wife was Arlene. First names aside, Bill and the missus might or might not have been Vietnamese. Virtually everything Shelley knew about the country and its inhabitants had been learned at the foot of the big screen. He tried to picture Bill in *Platoon*. It worked, kind of. They shook. Bill's hand was soft, cool as a milkshake.

Bo must have phoned ahead, for she had somehow managed to reserve a prime window table at a restaurant that – as a political statement – had a policy of refusing reservations. The menu was in English, but Shelley couldn't make much sense of it, so Bo ordered for both of them. He toyed with his chopsticks in a mostly useless attempt to distract himself from the after-effects of their wild ride across the city. The chopsticks were made of a light, pale-coloured wood, and to his untutored eye were pretty much identical to chopsticks that you'd find in Chinatown or at a Japanese restaurant. He made scissor motions until Bo reached across the table and batted down his hands.

She said, "Do you fool around like that with your knife and fork, when you're eating North American cuisine?"

Shelley placed the chopsticks neatly down on his paper napkin. Arlene brought them tall water glasses full of pale orange tea, which you were supposed to drink straight up, without milk or sugar. Shelley was strictly a black-coffee man, but under Bo's watchful eyes what choice did he have but to pick up his glass, sip, and swallow.

She smiled. Her lipstick was a delicious shade of pink that just drove Shelley wild. Mary Kay Cadillac, but purer.

Arlene brought spoons to the table, and two odd-shaped bowls of a thin broth containing a few small pieces of unidentifiable meat, pale green sprigs and a handful of exotic, medium-green spheres that Shelley eventually realized were common garden-variety peas. He waited until Bo picked up her spoon and then followed suit. The soup was delicious, hot and beefy, substantial to the palate even though when you looked down into the bowl you could plainly see that there was almost nothing there.

He chased the last pea around the bowl until he trapped it with his spoon. He'd heard on the radio that women tended to eat less when they were nervous or upset, or angry. Men took a different route; they gobbled, and gained weight. Not him, though. He had discipline, and he'd always taken too much pride in his body to try to chew his way out of his problems.

Until now, anyway.

Bo said, "There's nothing I like more than a man with an appetite."

"For what, exactly?"

"Life," said Bo. Shelley was busy wondering what that ruled out when she asked him how he got into the house-sitting business. It was a story he liked to tell.

"It was an accident," he said, with not the trace of a smile. "I was working at a club downtown that got fire-bombed a couple years ago, burned out in some kind of insurance scam."

"You were bouncing?" said Bo.

Shelley nodded. He said, "There was a woman that worked there, worked behind the bar, and she had a brother in Los Angeles, who was in the movies." He frowned. The name was coming to him. Brent. He said, "Her brother's name was Brent."

"He was a movie star?"

Shelley laughed. "No, nothing like that. The guy, Brent, drew pictures, black-and-white drawings, sketches of the actors. Where they'd stand or sit or whatever, and how the scene should look. Storyboards, they were called. They helped the director work out where he was going to put the cameras, what angle he'd film from."

Bo drank some tea. She seemed interested, even though he'd got himself sidetracked, somehow, so he continued.

"She showed me some of his work, that he'd sent up to her for a birthday present," said Shelley. "It was for a movie called *Maverick*."

"I saw it."

"Yeah, you did?"

"I'm a James Garner fan."

Shelley couldn't tell whether she was serious or yanking his chain. He said, "So anyway, this guy Brent draws the movie scenes on big pieces of white cardboard, in panels, like a cartoon. But different."

"He draws in colour?"

"No, I don't think so. Like I said, mostly black and white."

"He's an artist."

Shelley nodded. He said, "I thought I was going to be an artist, for a while."

Now it was Bo who thought her chain was getting yanked.

Shelley smiled, caught himself toying with his soupspoon. He let it drop into the empty bowl before she gave him a rap on the knuckles. He'd taken both of them by surprise, confessing to his frustrated ambitions. He said, "A painter, I wanted to paint."

"Watercolours?"

She was teasing him, but in a nice way. He said, "No, oils. Oil paints. I painted in high school, in art class. And then for a year at Emily Carr, down on Granville Island."

"You went to art school?" Bo's eyes were wide. She was amazed. He might as well have told her he'd trained to be a rocket scientist.

"Yeah, but just for a year, before I dropped out. Gravitated, or maybe I should say fell, into the bouncing game."

"I'm a dropout too," said Bo. "UBC. I was an economics major, for a couple of years, until somehow I drifted into being a party-girl with a C-minus average." She smiled, wryly. "So your friend at the nightclub went down to Los Angeles to visit her brother, and she asked you to take care of her house, is that what happened?"

"Studio apartment," said Shelley. "Her brother had broken his arm in one of those zillion-car freeway pile-ups. So naturally she wanted to go down there and cheer him up. But she'd just split up with her boyfriend, who was the bitter and threatening type, and still had a key to her apartment."

"Why didn't she change the lock?"

"Well, she meant to, but never got around to it, probably because she was worried that he'd kick down the door, if that was the only way he could get in. It was one of those unresolvable conflicts. I was her insurance policy against him trashing the place."

The main course arrived. Unidentifiable vegetables. Chunks of dark meat skewered on thin bamboo sticks.

Shelley trusted the place now, because of the soup. He dug in. The food was hot, mildly spicy, very good. Arlene brought two fresh glasses of tea. He chewed and swallowed, said, "Ever think about going back, taking classes again, finishing your education?"

Bo laughed. "Can you see me in a cap and gown?"

"Bet your ass," said Shelley without hesitation. A blind man a mile or more distant could have easily seen he meant every word.

Now it was Bo's turn to scrutinize her plate. She was blushing. Her skin was almost as pink as her lipstick. Her ears burned. And then, in the face of all that heat, a glistening teardrop welled up out of the corner of her big green eye, steamed slowly down the postcard sunset of her cheek and plunked into her tea. Bo reached across the table and held Shelley's hand, chopsticks and all, tighter than it had ever been held before.

"That's the nicest thing anyone's ever said to me," she told him, her eyes emerald-green now, damp as a rainforest.

Shelley realized, was shocked to realize, that his love for his new babe kept on getting deeper and deeper. He had not believed it was in his nature to exchange secrets, but he'd been dead wrong.

Following a lifetime of silence, he had indulged in a spilling of the guts, and been converted in an instant to the credo that silence ain't manly. What an enormously easy pleasure, how simple and seductive and sweet, the transaction had been. He could see no end to his appetite for true confessions. How he yearned to disclose the fat catalogue of failures and disappointments of his life had been trapped deep inside him, all his years. He wanted nothing more than to delineate, in vast and sordid detail, the traumas that made him tick tick tick. In a slow and elaborate striptease, he would peel off tight-wrapped layers of pain until he'd bared his very soul.

For dessert they had hot deep-fried bananas and vanilla ice cream.

By way of compromise, Shelley drove home. En route, he talked more or less nonstop, as if he'd been stockpiling conversation for years and years. He told Bo about his only sister, Vicki, who worked downtown, buying and selling children's books.

"She married?"

Shelley nodded. "Yeah, she's married."

"Any kids?"

Did Bo sound wistful? Shelley had run into that kind of girl before. His sister had three children. The youngest was only a couple of years old, packed to the rafters with high-voltage energy. It wore him out, watching the kid race around. Was this Bo's fatal flaw, the bloated raincloud that faithfully trailed her wherever she went: that she was willing to sacrifice her perfect figure for the dubious pleasure of dumping a few more pounds of inedible meat on this already overburdened planet? To be scrupulously fair, Shelley had to admit he might be less judgemental if *he* was cast in the role of Mr. Happy Dad. But still, it was a risky topic. Changing the subject, he observed that the night was young. Would Bo care to go somewhere and have a drink?

She smiled. "Somewhere? What kind of destination is that?"

Shelley named a few places, bars he knew of that weren't too bad. Bo briskly eliminated them one by one. Too loud. Too small.

Too quiet. Too big. Too meat-marketish. Wrong music. Wrong crowd. Too stylish. Too smoky. Too this. Too, too that.

Shelley tried another half-dozen bars, watering holes, hangouts. Same response. Discouraged, he said, "Okay, look, let's just forget it."

"I know a place that'd be absolutely *perfect*," said Bo.

Shelley downshifted into third. He goosed it, ran a yellow. "Yeah? Where's that?"

Bo's hand perched light as a peregrine falcon's feather on his thigh. Her nails might have been talons, as she tested the firmness of his flesh. She gripped him a little tighter as she said, "Why don't we just go home. Stop on the way, pick up a bottle of gin and some fresh-*squeezed* orange juice. Sit out on the deck, and get bombed."

"Count the moons and stars," said Shelley mock-whimsically.

"Relax, be ourselves," said Bo.

It was a pretty extreme idea; a novelty to both of them. Shelley detoured slightly to a government liquor store on Dunbar, at Eighteenth. There was a convenience store next door to the liquor store, and a Block Brothers real-estate franchise. Something for everybody. As he parked, Shelley tried to think of the last time he'd seen that overweight actor, Raymond Burr, ex-*Ironside*, pitching the Block Brothers' product on television. A long time ago. He killed the engine. Bo said she'd get the orange juice if he got the gin. They got out of the sx and, like an old married couple, went their separate ways.

Outside the door a guy with less than minimal talent brutalized a cheap guitar. Shelley brushed past him. Inside, he bought a bottle of Beefeater, paid the clerk. Outside, the musician was beating an old Dylan tune to death, slaughtering chords, bruising the air. Bo wasn't in the car or the convenience store. He suddenly felt, as lovers of insufficient faith so often do, that dreadful sensation of drowning; that he was taking on too much water. His stomach churned. But there she was, standing in the fluorescent glow cast by the Block Brothers window, looking at a display of for-sale photographs of expensive houses.

Shelley went over and stood beside her. She said, "I couldn't get fresh, all they had was reconstituted. Whatever that is."

"It'll be fine."

"What brand of gin did you get?"

"Beefeater."

Bo snuggled up against him. She said, "That house you're living in, I bet it's worth close to eight hundred thousand dollars."

"Somewhere in there," said Shelley disinterestedly, as they turned away from the window crammed with snapshots of a much better life – or at the very least a better box to contain the life you had. He was aware, and took a certain distorted pride in it, that he was living in a very expensive neighbourhood. But then, the entire city, east side and west, was exorbitantly pricey. If you found a rathole under three hundred grand, you were laughing.

It was only a few minutes' drive from the liquor store to Shelley's home sweet home. Shelley parked where the Miata used to park. He wondered if the cops had the axe in their property room, or if they'd let the girl keep it. Hadn't she earned it? He took Bo's hand. They strolled past the wisteria, which Shelley had come to think of as an octopus with roots. An erratic summer breeze tickled the bamboo; the sword-like fronds rustled together with a faint sound that was almost metallic.

Shelley unlocked the front door. In they went. He shut and locked the door behind him. The house was silent. A gauzy curtain slow-danced across an open window. He was slightly alarmed. Was it possible he'd forgotten to lock the windows before they'd left the house? The muscles in the small of his back clutched tight to his spinal cord. He imagined the kid, Andrew, waiting for him with a handful of death stars.

The living room and den and dining room were empty. Standing in the kitchen doorway, he saw that the door leading down to the basement was shut tight, chained and deadbolted. He handed Bo the gin, told her he had to make a quick trip to the bathroom and asked her if she'd mind mixing the drinks.

"I'm a mixologist from way back," said Bo, smiling.

Shelley said, "I believe it. You had me all mixed up in the first ten minutes."

Upstairs, he checked the bathroom, then toured the master bedroom and walk-in closet, the other bedrooms and closets. He felt not the slightest sense of embarrassment as he got down on his knees and peered under the beds. In the hall, he yanked open and slid shut the drawers in the built-in linen closet. As he prowled, he wondered what he would do if he actually encountered an intruder. Andrew would not be a problem. He'd smack the kid between the eyes with the equivalent of a brick and then stomp on him until he was reduced to the consistency of, say, pudding. But Andrew's dear old dad was another kettle of fish. Shelley had a natural disinclination for thumping the elderly. Yet Mr. Sticks clearly wasn't your average harmless old coot. It wouldn't be easy, but he had an obligation to Bo and to himself to put Mr. Sticks out of action lickety-split. When he'd investigated every nook and cranny that a small and immorally flexible human being could squeeze into, he trotted back downstairs to the kitchen.

Bo had poured a generous slug of gin into two glasses half-full of orange juice and ice, picked up the glasses and bottle. Hips swinging, she led Shelley out onto the backyard deck.

By now the sun had bellied up to the horizon, and the light was rapidly dwindling. Shelley had blocked out much of his largely expropriated childhood, but he remembered that, when he was a kid, this was the time of night when he had to turn his back on high adventure, tuck his tail between his skinny legs and voluntarily return to the low-level disaster that was his home. He turned a deck chair so he'd be able to spot anyone skulking in the backyard shrubbery. Bo handed him a glass. She said, "I checked the paper. There's a fingernail moon, but it won't come up until a few minutes past eleven." She clinked glasses in a toast. "What time is it?"

Shelley lifted his arm. He peered myopically at his watch.

"Let's do it as soon as it gets dark," said Bo.

"Do what?" said Shelley. He gulped half his gin.

"In the meantime," said Bo, "there are a few things I think I'd better tell you about."

Shelley nodded. He'd known since dessert that the evening's agenda included some seriously ugly stuff. It was inevitable. Bo was smart, gorgeous, determined. She was sitting so close to him that he could have reached out and touched any part of her, and it didn't make any kind of sense at all. What was she doing, wasting her time with a guy like him? Deep in the secret confessional of his heart, he knew full well that he wasn't worthy of her. Yet her presence was no mystery.

She was going to use him. She was going to test him. She was going to give him a chance he didn't deserve, to prove that he deserved her. What if he couldn't cut the mustard? What if he failed her? What if he brought both of them crashing down? He tilted back his head to drink some more gin. High above him in the vast and immeasurable distance, a few stars glimmered palely. His glass was empty. He put it down.

Bo made a small sound of pleasure. She'd finally discovered that she was close enough to reach out and touch any part of him.

Even his heart.

20

Willows phoned home. The machine picked up. He left a brief message for Annie and Sean, and then he and Parker drove to the emergency animal clinic. The glass front door to the blue-painted cinderblock building was securely locked. Willows peered inside. The decor was mini-hospital; overbright and easy to clean. Posters of various purebred dogs and cats hung upon the walls. Willows knuckled the door and a moment later Annie came into view, rubbing her eyes and clutching a battered copy of *Equestrian*. She unlocked the door, gave Willows a big hug and then hugged Parker, and told them both how glad she was to see them.

Willows said, "I'm sorry we couldn't get here sooner, Annie."

"It's okay." Annie's cheeks were flushed, her eyes red and swollen with grief. Barney was a middle-aged cat, but they'd only had him about eighteen months; he'd escaped a winter cold snap by hopping uninvited into Willows' car, curling up on the back-seat, and staring him down.

Parker said, "How's Barney doing?"

"He's okay. Dr. Larkins is working a double shift because she had a few things she needed to do, so she let me stay. Barney's sedated. He's sleeping and she said he won't wake up until some-time tomorrow morning." Annie smiled bravely. Tears welled up in her eyes. "But the operation was a complete success. Barney's going to be just fine."

"That's wonderful news!" said Parker.

When they'd first got him, Barney had been emaciated, host to a galaxy of fleas. It had cost almost two hundred dollars to have him inoculated and bathed. It had seemed a lot of money at the time, but it was small potatoes compared to the bill the cat had just racked up.

A walk-on scale stood against the near wall. Willows lowered a brogue. Seven kilos.

Beyond the receptionist's desk, a glossy white-painted door swung open.

Annie said, "There she is!" with such unrestrained enthusiasm that Parker felt a sharp twinge of jealousy.

Dr. Pamela Larkins was in her mid-thirties, slim and athletic-looking. Her blond hair was cut very short. She wore no makeup, oversized glasses, a white labcoat. She offered her hand. "You must be Claire. And you're Jack. Annie's been telling me all about both of you." Her handshake was businesslike but friendly. She said, "Barney's going to be just fine, but he'll have to stay in the hospital for at least a week, and possibly longer."

Annie groaned. "A week . . ."

"When you do take him home," said Dr. Larkins, "he'll need a lot of care and personal attention for quite some time, until he regains his strength."

Willows nodded. He considered asking if he could view the patient, but decided against it. A cat with a recently amputated leg probably wasn't a whole lot of fun, especially for a child. If visiting Barney was a good idea, Dr. Larkins no doubt would have suggested it. He put his arm around his daughter. "There's nothing more we can do here, Annie. Let's go home and get something to eat."

"Pamela bought me a cheese sandwich, and a Dr. Pepper."

"That was very nice of her," said Willows, smiling. "All the same, though, I don't think we should skip dinner."

On the way home, they stopped at the worn-out IGA on Forty-First, and bought Boboli pizza shells, tomato sauce, green pepper, pepperoni, mushrooms, and a half-dozen other ingredients vital to any self-respecting pizza. Parker showered, while Annie and Willows prepared the meal. Willows had just taken the first of the pizzas out of the oven when Sean ambled into the house. He sat down at the table as if he'd known to the minute when dinner would be served.

Without preliminaries, Annie told him about Barney's accident.

Despite the heat, Sean was wearing his black leather motorcycle jacket, stylishly ragged jeans, heavy black boots. His buzzcut was dyed bright yellow on top, red on the sides. He wore a gold hoop in his left ear and had shaved his eyebrows. He looked tough, capable of easy violence, the kind of kid who'd much rather rip your watch off your wrist than give you the time of day. But his face crumpled when Annie told him what had happened to the family pet. His slice of pizza lay on his plate, untouched, as he listened to her detailed explanation of Barney's injuries, Dr. Larkins' prognosis.

"Can I see him?"

"He's been sedated," said Willows.

"So what?"

"He wouldn't know you were there."

"How d'you know?"

Parker said, "Barney's been through a lot, Sean. Dr. Larkins thought it would be better for him if we let him rest, just for a day or two, until he regains some of his strength."

"It doesn't seem right not to visit him."

"You're right," said Parker, "it doesn't. But we have to consider Barney's needs, more than our own."

Much to Willows' surprise, his son nodded thoughtfully. He'd not only listened to Parker, he'd actually agreed with what she'd said. Willows bit deeply into a wedge of pizza. He popped the tab on his beer. Barney's medical costs were going to set him back about a thousand dollars, but the minor tragedy had somehow brought the family together. He was the only one who had an appetite, but, for the first time that summer, all four of them were sitting at the table. Willows swallowed. He glanced around. Everyone had begun to eat, even Sean. The pizza was vanishing rapidly, slice by slice. But what was really amazing was his sudden realization that, without giving it a moment's thought, he'd included Parker in his definition of "family." How would she feel about that? Maybe it was time he saw a lawyer. Sheila had abandoned the children for her new lover, but how long would the relationship last? More and more, Parker was becoming emotionally involved in his life and the lives of Annie and Sean. What would happen to the kids if Sheila decided she wanted them back? He decided he'd better find out, and quickly.

Later that night, the perfect fingernail moon that floated outside the window so brightened the bedroom that Willows was able to read Parker's expression in her chocolate-brown eyes. As delicately as he knew how, he broached the messy subject of divorce.

Parker was quick to cut him off. "I don't know why you'd want any advice from me, Jack. It's none of my business. I've never been married. What would I know about separation or divorce? Hell, I've never even been *engaged*."

She snuggled a little closer. The moon had drifted out of frame by the time they finally fell asleep.

At five minutes past eight, they parked next to Sidney Rothstein's reserved double-wide slot. The office was already up and running. People could be seen inside the building, moving around behind the plate glass.

Inside, Willows asked for Rothstein, and was told by the receptionist that Rothstein wasn't in the office but was expected at any moment. It was obvious that the woman had assumed Willows and Parker were potential clients, cash in the bank. He flashed his tin and explained the purpose of their visit. She said, "I wish I could help you, but I hardly knew Mr. Galee."

"Did you ever socialize?" said Parker.

"Certainly not!"

Parker smiled. "He never celebrated a sale by taking you out to lunch, or anything along those lines?"

"No, never." The receptionist turned a photograph sandwiched in clear plastic towards them. A handsome, curly-headed, deeply tanned young man in a Speedo bathing suit flexed his considerable bulk. "Cute, isn't he?"

"A hunk," said Parker. The receptionist wasn't wearing a ring. "Your boyfriend?"

"I've never met him. I bought the picture at Cannon Beach, for a dollar fifty. It's a postcard. But Mr. Galee and all the other agents *assumed* the guy was my boyfriend, and I never told any of them otherwise."

Willows, getting to the point, said, "We'd like to see Mr. Galee's office."

"Fine with me." The woman hesitated. "No, wait. Shouldn't you have a warrant, if you want to do a search?"

"Only if you insist on it," Willows pointed out. He smiled. "Mr. Rothstein has been extremely cooperative, so far. I can't believe he told you to give us a hard time."

The receptionist pushed away from her desk, straightened her skirt. "This way, please."

The late Zagros Galee's office was borderline claustrophobic, robustly functional, so clean it might have been a brand-new display model. The desk was bare except for a computer monitor and keyboard, a well-thumbed calendar, the requisite family photograph and a stack of the dead agent's business cards. The walls were bare.

Willows sat down in the fake-leather swivel chair. He slid open a drawer. Empty. He tried another, with the same result. He deliberately opened the next drawer out of sequence.

Empty.

"Nice try," said Parker. Zagros' window faced the parking lot. She watched a pale green Rolls-Royce ease, ponderous as an ocean liner, into the parking slot next to their unmarked car. The driver's-side door swung wide, and Sidney Rothstein got out. He slammed the door shut. Parker heard the *thunk* through the double-glazed window. Rothstein looked up. He waved, and Parker waved back.

In the desk's bottom drawer, there was a box of Zagros Galee's business cards, a neatly folded paper bag from *The Bread Garden*. Willows flipped the bag over, rotated it so he could read the few words that had been scrawled on the rumpled paper.

Andrew. Two o'clock.

Willows slipped the bag into his jacket pocket. He shoved a waterfall of loose business cards into the drawer and slid it shut.

Parker heard Sidney Rothstein's booming, overly cheerful voice as he greeted the receptionist. A few moments later Rothstein appeared, smiling broadly, in the doorway.

"Hunting for *clues*, are we?" He waved away Parker's response. "Please excuse my undue frivolity. A man's dead. The fact that nobody liked him very much or misses him at all is entirely beside the point, I'm sure."

Willows said, "Who cleaned out the office? Was it you?"

"Zagros' rent is paid through the end of the month. I talked to his wife on the telephone yesterday evening. When I told her I'd return the balance of the month's rent if we were able to find another agent to take the office, she told me to go ahead and give it a shot. But no, I haven't touched a thing."

Willows drummed his fingers on the desktop. "There's nothing in here, not even a paper clip. His telephone's gone. The monitor's bolted down or it'd be gone too. Somebody's strip-mined his desk, Sidney. So tell me, who did it?"

"Beats me. I fired him a week ago, told him to get the hell out. Like I said, the office was rented through the end of the month. But he hadn't been working for us for a week." Rothstein ran his fingers through his thick white hair. He looked out the window. He rubbed his jaw.

"Why'd you fire him?" said Willows.

"I found out, a little after the fact, that he'd tried to sell a house at far below market value, to another agent. His intent was to make a quick sale, pocket a few dollars on the side. The home's owner was an elderly widow. She suffered from Alzheimer's disease. I don't know what he told her, but the deal probably would've gone through if the old lady's daughter hadn't given us a call." Rothstein added, "But it wasn't Zagros who cleaned out his desk. He never came back, after I canned him. You've got to remember that this is a very tough business. Only the strong survive."

Parker said. "What's that supposed to mean?" She smiled. "Sidney, try not to be so enigmatic."

"Paper clips cost money," said Rothstein. "Hard, cold cash."

"You're suggesting another agent, to save himself a few dollars in office supplies, cleaned out Mr. Galee's desk?"

"It's possible."

"Even likely?"

Rothstein shrugged. "It's a hypothetical question. You'd never get anyone to plead guilty. I'll tell you this much, though. I guarantee there was nothing of real value in there, or it'd have been pinched before he left."

Willows said, "Let's back up a bit. When Mr. Galee tried to unload the widow's house for less than it was worth, shouldn't the lawyer he'd hired to do the conveyancing have spoken up?"

Rothstein thought it over, shrugged. "Yeah, I suppose so. I never gave it much thought, since the deal had fallen through anyway."

"What's the lawyer's name?"

"Zagros always used Patrick Gordon, of Turnbull, Connaty and Gordon. It's a downtown firm. We've been doing business with them for years."

Willows said, "What about Mr. Galee's files? Where are they?"

"In the computer. It's all in there, all the property he ever listed, everything he sold."

"Can you bring up his files?" said Parker.

"Whatever your heart desires, detective." Rothstein came around behind the desk, leaned over the keyboard, and tapped busily with his index fingers and the thumb of his right hand. The screen came to life. He tapped a few more keys. Three columns of text filled the screen, white on blue. "There you go. Use the arrow keys to scroll up and down. I'm going for coffee. Maybe this'll be the cup that wakes me. Anything for you?"

"A cup of coffee would be great," said Parker. "Black, please. No sugar."

"Detective Willows?"

"I'm fine, thanks." Willows used the down arrow to scroll slowly through the first file and into the next. In April of 1993 Zagros Galee had sold a detached home on West Twenty-Third for $452,000. He had split the commission down the middle with another agent. The following June he'd scored again, selling an east-side single detached home for $303,000. Again, he'd split the commission down the middle. The next sale hadn't come until November. During all of 1994 he'd listed five homes but made only three sales; a condominium that had sold for $135,000, another condo at $178,000, and an east-side house on a small lot for $280,500. The commissions from the house and the second condo had been split with other agents. Willows got out his pen and notebook and did some rough math. It didn't take him long to figure out that Zagros Galee should have died of starvation at least six months before he was shot to death.

Rothstein came back with the coffee, in paper cups.

"I see what you meant about Mr. Galee not exactly being a ball of fire," said Willows. "Did he have another source of income – that you're aware of?"

Rothstein sighed. He rolled his eyes. "He had a reputation for hitting on the ladies. In this business, you tend to meet a certain number of single women, divorcees and the recently widowed. A woman's husband leaves her or dies, the cash flow dries up, and suddenly the house is too large. She thinks about selling, calls a couple of agents. Or they've been watching the obituaries, and call her. I heard that Zagros sometimes spent too much of his energy trying to get laid, instead of lining up a sale."

Parker said, "He preferred sex to money? Wasn't that kind of unusual for someone in his line of work?"

"Highly unusual. Unheard of, actually."

"Were there any formal complaints regarding his conduct?"

"Not that I knew of. And if there'd been any, I'd have heard about it."

Willows indicated the computer. "Can I get a printout?"

"Yeah, sure. Just take a minute."

"The agents he worked with on the sales he made, the agents he split the commissions with, their names aren't in the files."

"No?" Rothstein leaned in for a better look. Willows could smell his cologne. Ralph Lauren, one of those. Rothstein said, "I could probably get that information for you, but it'd take a while."

"How long?"

"Depends how busy the computer is. An hour or two should do it."

"Make it a priority, would you?"

"No problem," said Rothstein. He smiled at Parker, as a mark of his sincerity.

"The apartment in which Mr. Galee was killed," said Parker, "isn't on the list of properties he'd worked on or sold. Why is that?"

Rothstein was clearly startled. He peered at the screen, as if hoping to conjure up the needed information by sheer force of will. "You're referring to the penthouse apartment at BeachView Towers?"

Parker nodded.

Rothstein's laugh was clipped, nervous. "To my knowledge that apartment isn't for sale. We're talking about a valuable property, one-five, somewhere in there. The penthouse is the building's flagship unit." Rothstein's dark eyes flicked from Parker to Willows and back again. "Trust me, I'd know in a minute if it was listed." Rothstein was gaining momentum. "There's no chance that an agent with Zagros' track record would be involved, even peripherally, in a sale of that magnitude. He'd be completely out of his depth." He frowned. "What led you to believe the apartment was on the market?"

"Did Mr. Galee ever mention the name 'Andy' or 'Andrew'?"

"No, I don't think so. Not that I recall. Is it important?"

"Could be," said Willows. He slipped one of Zagros Galee's business cards into his pocket. "We'll call in an hour or so, for that list of names."

As Parker got into their unmarked car, she glanced up. Rothstein leaned into Zagros Galee's window, fingers splayed, palms flat against the tinted plate glass. Willows started the engine, backed slowly out of the parking slot.

Parker said, "Look at him. So serious. But I doubt if he's a murderer. Could he be worried that you might dent his Rolls?"

"Sid isn't going to worry about anything," said Willows, "until the world runs short of martinis." He turned left on Dunbar. There was a Chevron station at Alma and Broadway, one of the self-serve joints that was more restaurant than gas station. But the kid behind the counter would have a copy of the Yellow Pages. He might even let Parker use the phone, save the taxpayers a quarter.

Willows wondered what Patrick Gordon looked like. Not much different from any other honest and hard-working lawyer, he supposed.

21

In bed, Bo was loud and boisterous, completely uninhibited, absolutely amazing.

Shelley could hardly believe it. Never in his life had he heard anyone snore so raucously, or with such vigour. He tried everything he could think of to drown out the noise – stuck his fingers and wads of toilet tissue in his ears, buried his head in the pillow, hummed loudly, imagined his favourite MuchMusic videos. Nothing worked. He was in the sack with a high-balling asthmatic freight train. He tried pinching Bo's nose, tickling her, poking her gently and then not quite so gently in the ribs, rolling her over on her side.

Nothing worked. The train rolled on.

He lifted his head so he could see the red numerals of the alarm clock. Time: dead of night. He lay there, trying not to listen to the hurricane that whistled and churned through Bo's nasal passages. To divert himself, he tried picking out and identifying the sounds of the night. It was the audio equivalent of dropping an anvil on your foot to relieve the stress of a headache. On Forty-First, a large truck passed by, fat tires ripping the pavement, fading into the distance. Somewhere very far away, a siren wailed. The dull roar of a departing jet was engulfed by Bo's discordant harmony. There was a moment of unnatural quiet, and then a mosquito charged into

Shelley's ear. He slapped himself so hard the retort made Bo falter. Soon enough, she started up again.

Shelley rolled out of bed. He went into the bathroom, shut the door, and vented perhaps two or three ounces of urine. He flushed, ran some lukewarm water over his hands, towelled off, and went back into the bedroom.

When they'd gone to bed Shelley had been in the mood for love, but Bo had a book she'd found in the den, a telephone-book-sized novel by Norman Mailer that she'd always meant to read. She'd fallen asleep somewhere in the middle of paragraph one, page one. No wonder Norman was such a popular guy.

Bo snored on, regular and just about as musical as a metronome. He ran his hand across the curving swell of her hip, down and down. A sharp elbow caught him in the ribs. Bo kept snoring.

To be fair, her trumpeting probably wouldn't have bothered him at all, under normal circumstances. But he was kind of tense at the moment, and who could blame him? It wasn't a whole lot of fun, twisting and turning in the sheets while you waited for the downstairs door to get kicked in, a bomb with a burning fuse to crash through the window, dark shapes to materialize in the doorway, the evil hiss of death stars, small-calibre gunshots, self-generated cries of pain in the night. The more he thought about it, the more real and immediate the danger seemed.

Shortly after taking possession of the house, during the course of his discreet basement-to-attic search of the premises, he'd found an ordinary-looking small brass key and a stubby cylindrical steel key – similar to a bicycle-lock key – taped to the back of the clothes dryer. The cylindrical key had the words DO NOT COPY stamped on it. Shelley was confident it would fit the dual locks in the door of the huge brown-enamelled metal gun safe that was flush-mounted to the rear wall in the master bedroom's walk-in closet, and he was right. The safe was about five feet wide by five feet high by approximately thirty inches deep.

Inside, he'd found thirteen rifles of various calibres, a few shotguns, half a dozen revolvers and semiautomatic pistols, thousands of rounds of ammunition, and a quantity of jewellery – loose gem-stones and two pounds of gold in shiny one-ounce coins. There were also eight litres of Evian water, a cardboard box of mixed tinned goods, two can openers, a dozen candy bars. There were small fluted air vents at the top and bottom of the safe. Welded brackets and a sturdy steel bar made it possible to secure the safe from the inside, in the event the vault's owner – who was obvi-ously a closet survivalist – wanted to be alone so he could commune with his firepower. Or if the North Koreans or Iraqis or even a revitalized Russian mob threw caution and their ICBMs to the winds.

Shelley had laid the guns down on the carpet, artistically fanned them out the way the cops did, whenever – and this seemed to happen fairly regularly in the city – they displayed for the televi-sion cameras a batch of illegally imported weapons seized from a black Honda stuffed with imported thugs. If you looked closely, with an objective eye, guns were kind of neat. The fine woods were beautifully shaped and finished, ditto the precision-fitted pieces of polished metal. Pick a gun up, and the impression that it was a cleverly disguised piece of functional art was doubly strengthened. The weight was pleasant, the balance superb, the design astonish-ingly complex, the purpose devastatingly obvious.

When he was a kid, Shelley'd had a friend whose father was a hunter. He'd dropped by after school one fall day and found the guy hunched over the kitchen table, smoking his pipe and drink-ing coffee as he cleaned and oiled his rifle. Shelley had never before seen a real gun up close. Fascinated, he sat down. The rifle was in pieces. He watched in silence as it was reassembled, elegant chunks of metal sliding into each other, tight but easy.

"What's it shoot?" he'd asked his pal's dad.

"Bullets."

"No, I mean what can you shoot with it?"

"Anything you point it at, kid, as long as the damn thing's loaded, and you don't choke up and forget to squeeze the trigger."

For the second time that night, he eased out of bed. The

carpeted stairs made whispery-soft stepping-on-mice sounds as he descended. Bile-yellow light filtered in from the street, staining the walls and furniture a truly repulsive colour. He went into the kitchen, unlocked the basement door, and switched on the light. A spider with more legs than brains was trapped in the laundry tub. It scuttled hither and yon as Shelley tore the DO NOT COPY key free of the tape. Taking pity, he trapped the spider in a cone of paper and let it free, then killed the light and went back upstairs. The tenor of Bo's snoring had not changed, but the rhythm had slowed to the point at which it was almost danceable. He slid open the wide, mirrored closet door. The interior light automatically clicked on. He stepped inside the closet and slid the door back along the rails until it was only open an inch or two, just wide enough to keep the light on. He pushed aside dozens of pastel-coloured plastic hangers and a ton of expensive clothes.

The gun safe/bomb shelter squatted at the end of the closet, brawny and malevolent. Or was he projecting? He unlocked the door, quarter-inch-thick sheet steel, and swung it open. The interior of the safe had been lined in foam that was a dark, silvery grey. The rifles stood upright on their wooden butts. The handguns were laid out on narrow shelves, nestled into more foam. Each firearm was equipped with a trigger lock but Shelley had learned his first time into the safe that the same small brass key fit them all.

There were many guns to choose from. Particularly appealing were a stainless-steel Smith & Wesson .44-calibre revolver and a Russian-made AK-47, equipped with a fully loaded banana magazine. The two guns hadn't a lot in common, other than their lethal nature. Neither was particularly suited to urban warfare or point-blank mayhem. It was just that he liked the way they looked; their appearance.

In the end he chose a 12-gauge Remington "Home Defender" shotgun with a matt-black eighteen-inch barrel and black nylon stock. The Remington had a pump action and a five-shot magazine. The brass and red-plastic shells were about as long as his index finger and slightly thicker than his thumb. Each shell was stuffed with BB-sized environmentally unsound lead shot. It took only one or two of these balls to drop a goose at fifty yards. At close range, the full load would blow a Chunnel-size hole in the average human being. Shelley harboured no doubts about the Remington's ability to chop a couple of featherweights like Andrew and Mr. Sticks pretty much in twain. He unscrewed the cap from a bottle of Evian, drank thirstily, screwed the cap back on, and shut and locked the steel door.

The Remington's bead front sight was neon-green and glowed brightly in the dark, for easy sighting on and accurate visceral dismantling of would-be rapists and burglars and other late-night chaff. He eased out of the closet and tiptoed over to the bed, hoisted up the kingsize mattress and slid the shotgun underneath, slipped into bed.

Bo had stopped snoring but now, as if on cue, she started up again. He rolled over on his side, so he was facing her back. Enough horrible jaundiced light seeped into the room for him to dimly make out the luscious, mouth-watering shape of her body. She was wearing pink satin babydoll pyjamas. He slipped his arm around her, stealthily cupped a perfect breast. She continued to snore. Her nipple beneath the satin felt soft and sweet as a fresh raspberry. He tweaked her with his thumb. Her warm breath stirred the golden hair on his forearm. A fluttering hand batted him away. He yawned loudly. Rolled over. Tossed and turned. Bo slept on. In desperation, he rolled out of bed for the third time that long night, yanked on his jeans and a T-shirt, and went outside and washed his car. When he finally climbed back into bed, the train was still rolling. He snuggled into her, fell asleep furtively copping a feel.

The alarm woke him at seven. He reached for Bo but couldn't find her. He rubbed sleep from his eyes. She was gone. Downstairs, he could hear Mr. Coffee chuckling happily, as if the machine had just been told a mildly funny Juan Valdez joke. He ambled naked into the bathroom.

The water pressure fluctuated oddly as he showered. Had Bo learned how to operate the dishwasher? Back in the bedroom, he dressed in jeans and a faded black T-shirt, then pulled the curtains so he could check the weather and assure himself Bo hadn't taken the sx again.

Mr. Sticks' black Jag was parked so close to his car that he was sure the bumpers must be touching. The Jag's top was down. Mr. Sticks slouched low behind the wheel, eyes closed. He had the stereo cranked up and was a Dire Straits fan, apparently.

Shelley retrieved the Remington from beneath the mattress. In the harsh, uncompromising light of day, the gun had turned mean-spirited and ugly. He revisited the phrase "blow a Chunnel-sized hole" and found it wanting. He was no gunslinger. Falling in love had mellowed him. If he couldn't charm Andrew out the door, he'd bless the little bastard with a swift kick in the nuts. He put the gun back under the mattress and went downstairs.

The pot was full – and overflowing. A river of coffee ran the length of the granite counter and tumbled in a steaming black waterfall down the vertical face of the genuine-oak cupboard all the way to the gleaming linoleum, then turned a corner and followed the line of the baseboard until it abruptly disappeared down a hot-air vent. The toaster popped. Shelley twitched nervously. Two slices of burnt-to-hell toast shot high into the smoky air, tumbled back, and fell upon an untidy heap of previously-scorched slices. Half a loaf or more had already been laid to waste.

He became aware of a larger gurgling. Downstairs, in the laundry room, the washing machine was hard at work. The basement door was open. A dull metallic clunking floated up the stairs. Something was in the dryer that didn't belong in the dryer. Shelley mopped up the spilled coffee, emptied the pot into the sink and made some fresh. He adjusted the toaster to light brown, the way Bo liked it. Got an Indian River grapefruit out of the fridge, sliced it in half and then used a special knife with a curved and serrated blade to separate the half-grapefruit into bite-sized triangles. He placed the half-grapefruit in a bowl, and sprinkled a teaspoonful of sugar over the glistening pink pulp.

Maybe he should have brought the shotgun downstairs with him after all. It was all very well for him not to be too concerned about his own ass, but what about Bo's, vulnerable as could be in that shiny pink satin? He tore a paper towel from the dispenser and wiped pink flesh from the grapefruit knife. Was slashing Andrew's throat in any way superior to Chunneling him? Shelley was in no mood for philosophy. He slipped the knife into the back pocket of his jeans and trotted lightly down the stairs to the basement.

Andrew stood by the manhole-sized open door of the Maytag dryer, a large white towel in his small jaundiced hands. He wore a vested double-breasted Hugo Boss suit that was at least two sizes too large. He'd been interrupted as he'd emptied the dryer. To ensure that he hadn't overlooked anything, Shelley took a peek inside. Bo had not been stuffed in the Maytag. The stack of folded white towels Andrew had piled on top of the dryer tilted slightly to one side, but was in no danger of toppling.

The washer churned sluggishly. Andrew made a small-but-intense sound of disapproval as Shelley lifted the lid. Soapy, reddish-brown water. Lots more towels. The unmistakable perfume of bleach. He let the lid drop.

"What're you doing in my house?" said Shelley.

"Penance." Andrew chuckled grimly. "It's grandfather's idea of a joke, I think."

He added a towel to the pile, snatched another from a pale blue plastic laundry basket, and expertly shook it out. A rust-red smear curved diagonally across the fluffy material like a rainbow from hell. He snorted in disgust, flipped open the lid of the washing machine and tossed in the towel. Almost as an afterthought, he upended the bleach bottle and emptied the last of it into the machine. A heap of red-smeared towels lay on the floor, partially hidden by the dryer. These towels had not been washed. The red

was crusty and sometimes lumpish. Whatever the stuff was, quarts
and quarts of it had been spilled.

"Where's Bo?"

Andrew shrugged as best he could, given the scant width of his
shoulders. "Why ask me? You're her boyfriend."

"Fiancé," lied Shelley. "But not for long. We're flying to Vegas
first thing tomorrow morning. Bo wants to get married at one of
those chapels on the strip."

Andrew's smile lacked sincerity. He plucked a towel from the
washing machine, snapped it at Shelley's face.

The washing machine segued into the spin cycle. A gush of
frothy red water splashed into the laundry tub.

A bright red welt bloomed on Shelley's cheekbone, just below
his eye. He moved in, swung from the floor and hit Andrew flush
on the mouth, so hard that the blow lifted him off his feet. A tooth
glanced off the white enamelled side of the dryer and made it ring
like a bell. Andrew's eyes rolled up in his head. His upper lip had
been split. He bled without much enthusiasm, as unconscious men
will do.

Shelley rolled him over and yanked off his suit jacket. He held
the jacket upside down and shook loose a storm of weapons.
Death stars. A dozen steel balls that clattered and rolled. A folding
slingshot. A three-pack of scalpels. A jelly donut wrapped in clear
plastic. A plastic bag of small bullets. A bundle of pick-up sticks
fastened by an elastic band. Numerous sharp metal objects that
were beyond Shelley's sphere of knowledge and that he could not
identify or even begin to categorize. He dumped the suit jacket
and all the towels, clean, dirty and wet, on top of Andrew. He bent
and picked the kid up in his arms, staggered as he carried him upstairs, through the house, out the front door and down the sidewalk towards the black Jaguar.

Mr. Sticks stared at him. The towels were piled so high he had
no way of knowing his grandson was hidden beneath them or who
might be carrying that bloody bundle towards him. His close-set
eyes were wide with alarm. He tried to turn off the radio, but in

his panic spun the knob in the wrong direction. The car vibrated. The speakers shuddered. Shelley dumped Andrew and the mountain of towels in the backseat. The Jag listed. He leaned across the front seat and killed the radio, pushed a button that popped open the trunk. If Bo was hiding, he hadn't found her. Mr. Sticks gave him a tentative smile. Shelley took his hand. Mr. Sticks' fingers were long and slim, hairless. His skin was very smooth and almost inhumanly soft. Shelley pressed Andrew's tooth into Mr. Sticks' soft and wrinkled palm. He curled Mr. Sticks' fingers into a fist. Mr. Sticks kept smiling, with teeth designed to rip and shred and tear asunder.

Andrew had regained consciousness. He wept softly.

Shelley found Bo upstairs, in one of the kids' bedrooms, sound asleep beneath a *101 Dalmatians* coverlet. He went back downstairs to the kitchen, made toast and poured coffee. The grapefruit still looked pretty good. He picked the morning newspaper up off the front porch and carried the paper and her breakfast upstairs.

He kissed her lightly on the mouth. Her eyes fluttered. She smiled up at him. While she ate, Shelley read to her, bits and pieces of the news he thought she might find interesting. He told her about Andrew and the pile of dirty towels and she told him it was Mr. Sticks' style to clown around, soften you up with a dumb joke and then hit hard, while you were still wiping tears of laughter from your eyes. So that was something they could look forward to, and soon. Without waiting to be asked, he fetched her another cup of coffee. When he came back, the pink satin babydolls lay in a shimmering pile at the end of the bed. Bo apologized for her nasal thunderstorm. She told him, between kisses, that she'd moved into the kids' bedroom so he could get some sleep.

Shelley asked her to *please* never do that again.

22

The city's downtown core was a griddle, but the wind that came steadily in from the west had been cleansed by its flight across the Pacific Ocean. The wind swept across the city, blowing tons of suspended particles and noxious fumes into the soft green flatlands of the Fraser Valley, where it drifted silently down upon the region's scenic fields of green, herds of dimwit dairy cows, dense pockets of suburbanites who, perhaps unaware of the prevailing winds, had taken full advantage of toothless land-use codes and settled their dream houses upon the lush black soil.

But that was there and this is here.

Willows braked hard to avoid colliding with a white Toyota that had run the red at Seymour and Georgia. Driving in the city was a high-risk business, but at last he knew why. The latest statistics indicated that as many as ten thousand Lower Mainland drivers had received their licences illegally in the past few years, by bribing Motor Vehicle Branch and various driving-school employees. To date, only one MVB employee had been charged with bribery. Every last one of the illegally licensed drivers was still wandering around out there, accelerating hard on a steep learning curve.

The offices of the law firm of Turnbull, Connaty and Gordon were located at suites 605–607, 347 Pender. Willows made a left. He let Parker out of the car and then parked on the shady side of the alley, tight against a scabrous brick wall and close behind a battered dumpster. It had been in a similar alley that Barney had made his first appearance, mewling piteously but showing his yellow fangs in the event plan A didn't cut any ice. Willows got out of the car and shut the door. A quintet of pigeons flapped nervously on the overhead wires. Though it hadn't rained in weeks, green water dripped sluggishly from a twisted drainpipe on the far side of the alley. The alley had a reverse camber; a sort of built-in gutter. The asphalt was darker where it was wet.

As they walked down the alley towards the sunlit street, Willows thought about lawyers. Most of the lawyers he knew were prosecutors, but he'd met more than his share of defence lawyers, over the years. None had specialized in family law or had spent much time – other than on their own behalf – in divorce court. He wondered if Turnbull, Connaty and Gordon restricted their practice to the simple art of conveyancing. It seemed unlikely. As they said at the police-union meetings, dollars bought donuts.

Number 347 Pender was typical of that part of the city – a medium-sized brick building that hadn't had a lot of money spent on it, other than to modernize the façade at street level, slap some veneer on the lobby walls, install an elevator that didn't require an operator.

Willows punched the sixth-floor button. The doors slid shut with the sound of grinding metal teeth. Parker said, "I can't remember how long it's been since I was kissed in an elevator." Willows checked the indicator light. The elevator meant well, but it was slow. Two hadn't yet lit up. He put his arms around Parker and kissed her, giving her 99 percent of his attention, but at the same time closely monitoring their upward progress through the soles of his shoes.

The law office's heavy oak door had been recently refurbished; the carpet was so new you could still smell the chemicals. The receptionist's desk was ten feet long, slightly curved. A long hallway ran off to her left. On the wall behind her, stern men in black suits scrutinized all visitors from behind panes of nonglare glass. The receptionist wore a bright red suit, a slim gold chain, red lipstick and nail polish. A dual-purpose employee, she was decorative as well as functional. "May I help you?"

Parker identified herself, and Willows. Flashed her tin.

The woman laughed. She might have been at a cocktail party. She said, "I thought you were in sales – office supplies or computers. Colour me wrong!"

Willows matched her smile tooth for tooth. He said, "We'd like to speak to Patrick Gordon."

That sobered her up. She said, "In reference to . . ."

"Confidential police business."

The receptionist reached for a phone. Her bright nails flashed in the light. Links of gold slithered across smooth white skin.

Patrick Gordon looked puzzled and slightly worried as he waited for the two detectives in the doorway of his cramped, over-burdened office. The lawyer was in his late twenties, still a decade or more away from a corner unit. He was of medium height, fashionably thin. He shook hands, invited them into his office, shifted a stack of battered legal-size files from a chair to his desk. A silver flute lay across his blotter. He moved the flute aside. Busy work, to give him time to arrange his thoughts. He said, "Sit down, please. Make yourself comfortable."

Parker sat. Willows leaned gingerly against a glass-fronted oak bookcase. Gordon eased into the swivel chair behind his desk. Slats of light and shadow fell across his long, narrow face. The lawyer's ears stuck out prominently. His nose was a little too thick across the bridge, heavy and aggressive. His black hair was cut to within an inch of his scalp. His off-the-rack suit was midnight blue with white pinstripes. His shirt was white, his tie the colour of a ripe plum. If you squinted, he looked distantly related to a genetically manipulated zebra.

The simple act of sitting behind the bulwark of his desk gave Patrick Gordon added confidence. Willows had seen a similar transformation occur in lesser men as they slouched onto a familiar stool at the friendly neighbourhood bar. Gordon screwed the cap onto a fat gold fountain pen. His gold watchband gleamed against his tanned wrist as he closed a file and pushed it aside. He wore a gold band on the third finger of his left hand. A tiny gold hoop hung from his left ear. Parallel strands of light and shadow rippled across his face as he leaned forward, adopting a pose of professionally detached interest. Willows was a little nonplussed. An unexpected appearance by the cops usually meant bad news. Patrick Gordon didn't seem the least bit concerned that a tragedy might have befallen a member of his family, or that he himself might be in deep and dangerous waters. But then, maybe he didn't have a family, and maybe his conscience was clear.

He said, "I assume you're here to question me about the murder of Zagros Galee?"

"What makes you assume that?" said Willows.

Gordon held out his hands, palms up, slowly turned them over. His nails had been professionally manicured. He said, "I read about the shooting in the newspaper, heard about it on the radio, watched a report on television. It was obvious that you'd get around to me sooner or later. Am I a suspect?"

"Absolutely not."

Gordon used one of his sparkling clean fingers to press the intercom button on his speakerphone. "Carla, would you ask Bill Turnbull if he'd mind dropping in for a moment? Thankyou, my dear."

"Did Mr. Galee's death surprise you?" said Willows.

The lawyer picked up the flute. He said, "And now for a brief musical interlude," and began to play. Mozart? Willows didn't recognize the tune. Gordon had talent. If there'd been a hat on his desk, he'd have made a dollar or two.

There was a light tap on the door. Gordon put aside the flute. He stood up, extended a hand. "Bill, I'd like you to meet detectives Parker and Willows." He smiled at Parker. "Bill's our senior partner."

Turnbull shook hands. He was a big man, in his mid-fifties, with heavy features, longish blond hair streaked with grey at the temples. He wore a pinstripe vest but no jacket. His shirtsleeves had been rolled halfway to his elbow. He'd loosened his tie. Bifocals dangled from a thin, shiny blue cord. He was the very picture of a harried, overworked lawyer, but when he spoke his voice was calm and unhurried. "What can I do for you, Patrick?"

"Detectives Parker and Willows are here to question me about that real-estate agent we had a problem with last spring. Zagros Galee."

Turnbull smiled. He said, "You're investigating his murder?"

Willows nodded. He offered his card. Turnbull slipped the card in his vest pocket without bothering to look at it.

"Is Patrick a suspect?"

"No, not at all," said Willows.

Turnbull shot Gordon a quick look that might have meant almost anything. He said, "I'm not a criminal lawyer, but in the event we should feel the need to establish an alibi, it would be convenient to know exactly when Mr. Galee was murdered. I understand the body was discovered sometime Saturday night?"

Willows nodded.

"Mr. Galee was killed that same night?"

"Yes, he was."

"May we take it that, if Patrick is able to provide you with an alibi, the nature of his alibi will remain strictly confidential?"

"Unless he was involved in criminal activity of a serious nature."

Turnbull glanced at Patrick Gordon. He nodded almost imperceptibly.

Gordon said, "I was at St. Paul's. In emergency."

Willows couldn't help wondering why the lawyer had needed to visit the emergency ward, so close to the time of Zagros Galee's murder. He decided to let it slide, for now. He moved slightly to his left, away from the hard spine of a protruding book. "How did you come to know Mr. Galee?"

"We'd been doing business with his firm for many years. As

favoured clients, they receive a very favourable rate. It was only natural that he should come to us."

"As I understand it," said Willows, "Mr. Galee had arranged the sale of a home, at considerably under market value, to a fellow agent. You nixed the deal."

Gordon nodded. The sun had shifted in the heavens; the bars of shadow and light slanted more acutely across his face. His eyes were dark.

"Was this the first time he'd come to you?"

"No, I'd performed work for him on several previous occasions."

"Conveyancing?"

"Yes."

"Nothing else?"

"Not to my recollection."

Bill Turnbull stood by Gordon's desk, silent but attentive, at his ease, solid and implacable.

Parker said, "From our point of view, Mr. Gordon, you did exactly the right thing. There's no need to worry about client-solicitor privilege. You know as well as I do that there's no law against libelling the dead. Believe me, Zagros Galee is about as dead as a man can get."

Patrick Gordon blanched. He reacted as if Zagros Galee's ghost had just sauntered into the office. Parker glanced at Turnbull. The older lawyer's face was expressionless. She pressed on. "All we're interested in is the identity of Zagros Galee's killer. I'll be candid with you. We don't have a lot of leads. Anything you can tell us, no matter how insignificant it might seem to you, could be very helpful."

Gordon nodded. He picked up his flute and turned it end to end and put it down again. "I didn't know Mr. Galee personally, not at all. When I queried him on the price of the house he'd sold – a price I felt was considerably below market value – he offered me a thousand-dollar cash bonus to complete the deal. As you might well imagine, alarm bells rang." Gordon's chair creaked as he leaned back. He glanced at Turnbull, but Turnbull was looking out the window, at something very far away.

Parker said, "Was that the end of it?"

"No, it wasn't. He told me the thousand dollars was small potatoes, that he was very close to completing a seven-figure deal, and that I'd walk away with fifty grand minimum if I did the conveyancing work. But first, of course, I had to roll over on the deal we had on the table."

"The elderly woman's house."

"Yes, that's right."

Parker waited. Willows appeared to be studying the contents of Gordon's bookcases.

Gordon said, "I told him I wasn't going to touch the original deal, not for a thousand or even five times that much. But fifty was another kettle of fish. I told him if he needed me for fifty, I'd be there."

After a moment, when Parker was absolutely sure that Gordon wasn't about to correct himself or add any postscripts, she said, "Did he get back to you?"

"A week ago today. We had lunch at the Four Seasons with the owner of a million-plus condo for which Mr. Galee had an exclusive listing."

"The penthouse unit at BeachView Towers?"

"He didn't mention an address, and I didn't ask."

Willows turned away from the bookcase. "Tell us what you remember about the condo's owner."

"The owner and his son. Charles and Andy Zhang." Gordon smiled. "By sheer coincidence, Bill has a client named Zhang."

"Develops golf courses," said Turnbull. "Known him for years. No connection."

Gordon said, "Zhang's the most common surname in China. There are about a hundred and twelve million of them, and counting. It's like Smith, but a whole lot worse."

Willows asked for a physical description of the Zhangs.

Gordon's description was infuriatingly vague – not much better than Rose Pincott's. Willows wondered what the lawyer'd had for lunch. One too many martinis, maybe.

Parker said, "Did you get an address?"

"A Hong Kong box number. Mr. Zhang said they spend most of their time overseas."

Parker said, "Did Mr. Galee ever mention the penthouse apartment at BeachView Towers?"

"No, never."

"Any other address?"

"No."

"Anybody he was working with, other than the Zhangs?"

Gordon shook his head.

Willows popped the big question. "St Paul's. Would you mind telling us what you were doing there?"

"Seeking medical assistance for a health problem that, I assure you, is entirely unrelated to the Galee case."

"Is there someone at the hospital can verify you were there?"

"Yes, certainly."

"Can you give us a name, Mr. Gordon?"

The lawyer shot Willows a look of frustration and despair.

Turnbull moved aside so he could quietly shut the office door. With great affection and concern, he said, "Patrick . . ."

"My physician, Michael Dewdney." Gordon took a deep breath. He let it out in jagged bits and pieces. He stood up and cracked the mini-blinds, peering out the window, down at the hectic streets. With his back to them all, he said, "I'm HIV positive. Complications arise, from time to time."

As they waited for the elevator, the music of the flute came to them with extraordinary clarity, liquid and silver as a jiggerful of mercury.

Descending, Willows volunteered a six-storey hug.

23

Bo fell back, sighed contentedly, rolled away from Shelley's *bon voyage* kisses. He watched, utterly fascinated, as she drank some lukewarm coffee, wet her thumb, and cleaned the last of the toast crumbs from her plate. He almost told her he loved her. As if she sensed what was on his mind, Bo scrambled out of bed and made a beeline for the shower. While she was sluicing herself off, he went down into the basement with a dustpan, broom, and a plastic Safeway bag. He whistled tunelessly as he swept Andrew's weapons into the dustpan, deposited them in the Safeway bag, and tied the plastic handles in a knot. The razor-sharp points of the death stars and pick-up sticks poked through the plastic here and there, but the bag held.

He crouched so he could see inside the dryer and learn what horrors had been bumping around in there.

An empty, plastic one-litre Heinz ketchup bottle.

He thought about the red stains on the heap of unwashed towels. He'd assumed bloodstains, but maybe he'd been wrong. Once he started looking, it took him only a few moments to find the cardboard box marked top and bottom with the Heinz logo. Inside, sheets of waffle-design cardboard interlocked to form a dozen identical compartments. Eleven were filled with empty one-litre Heinz bottles. Shelley dropped in the twelfth bottle. What had Andrew and Mr. Sticks been up to? The old white-towels-and-ketchup trick. He smiled. Mr. Sticks had hoped to intimidate him with a little sleight of hand, and he'd nearly succeeded. The washing machine full of frothy red liquid had been a genuine stomach-turner, top-notch trickery . . .

Shelley carried the box full of plastic ketchup bottles upstairs and out the back door. The upstairs bathroom window was partly open, curtains swinging in the breeze. Bo was singing a tune from *Oklahoma!* A few houses down a trio of kids in raggedy shorts and T's and hundred-dollar sneakers were playing lane hockey with a flimsy net and a bright orange ball. Shelley dumped the plastic bottles into the city's blue recycling bin. Every once in a while the city left a notice reminding him to stomp things flat, but he never bothered. Dancing on a four-litre milkjug was, to his way of thinking, a pathetic and even a somewhat demented thing to do. A picture of the mayor and several city councillors had appeared in the newspaper a few months ago, above an article promoting the benefits of recycling. None of *them* looked like jug dancers.

The bright orange ball skittered across the asphalt. Shelley stopped it with his shoe. He picked it up. The kids eyed him warily. Axeman, they called him, from a distance.

Shelley pointed at the goalie. The kid was nine or ten years old. In his featherweight foam pads, he was slightly wider than he was tall. Shelley brought back his arm. The distance was about eighty feet, and he gave it everything he had, his best shot. The ball was an orange streak as it curved in and down, hit the pavement in front of the net and took a crazy, unpredictable bounce towards the far top corner. The kid reached out. The ball vanished into his trapper. Shelley stood there, feeling deflated, a has-been. The kid's save had been effortless.

He went back into the house, shut the door but could still faintly hear the shrill jeering that would probably never stop.

He was stuffing dirty plates into the dishwasher when Bo strolled into the kitchen wearing – if that was the correct word – a sunflower-yellow bikini in a thin, clingy cotton material. She posed, and turned and posed again. "What d'you think?"

Shelley said, "What do I what?" He smiled. "My eyes are full but my brain is empty."

Bo posed her way over to him. She wrapped her arms around him and let him take her weight. She slipped her hands into his pants pockets, groped him ineffectually.

He said, "Can I help you, ma'am?"

"Gimme your keys."

"Going somewhere?"

"To the beach," said Bo. "Want to come along?" She hadn't stopped looking for his keyring. Triumphantly, she said, "Got 'em!"

Shelley grunted.

"Oops!" said Bo. "My mistake."

A couple of hours later, she wheeled the sx into the parking lot by the Kits beach tennis courts, cutting it close as she backed into a tight slot. Shelley had forgotten all about it until now, but until the early eighties an old steam-powered train engine had stood on a strip of grass between the parking lots, on a short length of track. If the train had still been there, they'd have parked under its shadow. Generations of children had scrambled over the engine, fantasizing God knows what triumphs and disasters. Then, overnight, a few well-meaning but mentally disenfranchised adults had spirited the engine away. Fifty tons of iron. The city's biggest toy, vanished. Shelley had no idea what had happened to the damn thing. All that mattered was that it was gone. He stuffed money into the greedy maw of the Parks Board's ticket dispenser. In Vancouver, the parks were for everyone. Who could afford them. He tossed the ticket on the dashboard, secured the steering wheel with his Club, locked up. Bo shimmered in the distance. In hot pursuit, he jogged lightly towards her across alternate strips of asphalt and scrubby, heat-blasted grass.

The beach was crowded, and why not? It was mid-summer and it wasn't raining. The proper application of sunscreen had all but eliminated carcinoma. Tanning was a relatively cheap, low-maintenance activity. There were acres of flesh to be ogled. The restless sea was conveniently located, for those who felt in need of a dip.

Bo was enthusiastically greeted by quite a few darkly tanned men, as she made her way across the dimpled sand. Room was made for her near the end of a choice log not far from the concession stand. Shelley finally caught up. He turned his back to the offshore breeze. The tartan blanket billowed like a spinnaker. Bo dumped her wicker beach bag. Heads turned as the Mailer novel landed with a mighty thump.

Bo lay down on her belly, positioning herself so the sun fell, hill and dale, all along her length. She adjusted her sunglasses and cracked open her novel. The top right corner of page one had been sharply folded. She turned to Shelley, cocked her head. The glasses slid partway down her pert nose. A glade-green eye dissected him. She blew him a kiss. "Slather some of that gunk on me, handsome."

Shelley dropped to his knees. He popped the cap on the sunscreen and squirted a little too much viscous white fluid into the palm of his left hand.

Bo pushed the glasses back up her nose. Her lipstick seemed to have reached meltdown. In the dizzying heat, her mouth glowed like neon. "Try not to be a shadow, okay?"

Shelley shifted a little to the side. He dipped his fingers into the pool of sunscreen. Bo began to read. He started at her neck, and slowly worked his way down her shoulders, the stubby angels' wings of her shoulder blades, along her spine, over her ribcage. As if reading his mind she said, "Don't worry about the bikini, it'll wash out." Her freckles were a soft dun colour, not much darker than the deerskin chamois he used to wash his car. He bent and sniffed the perfume of her body, her bottled scent and the stronger smell of sunscreen, a wonderfully exhilarating bouquet that made him weak with desire.

Bo said, "You still there? Don't stop now."

She spread her legs, the better that Shelley might apply the lotion to the inside of her thighs. He bent to his task. It was hard work but somebody had to do it.

Bo roasted for half an hour or so, and then strolled down to the ocean for a refreshing dip. When she was hip-deep in the water she slipped smoothly beneath the surface. It may have been bird cries or the keening wind, but it seemed to Shelley that, in the moment of her disappearance, a sigh of frustration travelled all along the beach.

Back from her swim, Bo towelled herself dry, lay down on her flip side, and resumed reading. By now she was deep into chapter one. Shelley poured on the sunscreen. Men of all description dropped by to say hello, make laboured small talk, and eventually drift away. Now and then a page was turned. Old Mr. Sun reached the apex of his journey and began his long, slow descent towards the distant horizon. At regular intervals, Shelley followed Bo's instruction to slap on some fresh sunscreen. What a slender thread it is, that separates sweet ministration and gross indecency.

It was about three o'clock when Bo sat up, negligently brushed a few grains of sand from her forearms, kissed Shelley tenderly and asked him if she could get him something to eat or drink. Not that she was going anyway, and could she get something for him. But simply, did he want anything.

Shelley was a little surprised, somewhat suspicious. Had he heard her correctly? Up until now he had been doing most of the stepping and fetching. But he held his tongue, except to say he'd like a diet something.

"Coke?"

"Whatever," said Shelley. "Pepsi's fine."

He watched her move as she strode away from him. Those long legs, the sassy flow of her hips, the way she moved her arms and held her head, paying no attention to the breeze that messed her hair.

She was a stunner, and Shelley had always considered that skin-deep was plenty deep enough. The city had as many beautiful women as its beaches had grains of sand, almost. But Bo was extra-special. He marvelled at how effortlessly she'd wriggled her way into his life. What was there about his new sweetie that was so utterly irresistible? Shelley furrowed his handsome brow. He narrowed his eyes and watched a sailboarder scoot across the water, hit the crest of a wave and rise up, catch good air and touch down at too sharp an angle, vanish in a welter of spray. In moments she was back on her board again, hoisting the sail. What a wonderful sport. You could crash, but you could not burn.

What had attracted him to Bo, and what he'd most loved about her, in the beginning, was her apparent need to be rescued. When they'd met, he'd still been pumped up by his exchange with the Mustang full of dorks. All that high-octane adrenaline racing around his veins with nowhere to go until *presto*, there she was, in need of a white knight. The timing had been perfect. But for whom? Imperceptibly but with blazing speed, a casual pickup had evolved into a lifelong commitment. He remembered that the beach trash she'd claimed were irritating her never did materialize. The sudden appearance of Andrew and Mr. Sticks had been ample compensation. He'd pictured himself a hero. There were still plenty of opportunities on the horizon. Bo had his number all right. When they'd gone out to dinner, she'd driven him exactly where she wanted to go. He had a feeling their future held more of the same.

What it came down to was personalities. She had one. He didn't. It was a question of willpower, strength of character. All the things he lacked. He didn't have the guts to stand up to her, and that was, for now, exactly what she wanted in a man. It was as simple as that. Or maybe it wasn't. Maybe it had nothing to do with Bo. Maybe it was a karma thing. Life had taught him not to be overly optimistic.

Bo rose up out of the distance. A shapely mirage that dissolved and reformed, broke up, undulated weirdly in the rippling waves of heat with every slow step she took. There she was. High-stepping across the burning sands. Plenty substantial, now. Chili-pepper hair, tanned skin, yellow bikini, those long, slim legs. Out of all the thousands of guys on the beach, she'd homed in on *him*. It was a miracle, sort of. He felt a sharp pang, as if someone – God, maybe – had driven a white-hot rivet through his heart.

He'd almost told her he loved her. Come *that* close and never felt so vulnerable. He'd felt since the moment he'd first seen her that he'd fallen in love with her. Now he knew it was true.

Bo squatted down on the blanket in front of him. Her skin was firm. She radiated heat. Her hand touched his knee. She said, "I really liked the way you looked at me, just then."

"It was the Coke," said Shelley. "I was looking at the Coke."

"He put too much ice in it, but I made him dump it out."

Shelley strawed some Coke. Or Pepsi or whatever. "I just bet you did," he said with a smile.

Bo offered up her mouth. He kissed her and she kissed him back. Her lips were unseasonably cool but unmistakably friendly. When they'd temporarily smooched themselves out, she said, "The way I see it, we have three choices."

Shelley nodded. His agile brain shifted gears. In a flash he came up with: *let's get married right this minute* or *we better live together until we're sure it's going to work out* or *sorry pal, my mistake*.

Bo was thinking along strikingly dissimilar lines. She said, "They kill us, or we kill them. Or we give the money back and hope they let us go."

"What money?" said Shelley. "Go where?" His agile brain flopped around like a tadpole in a little boy's bucket.

"Go on living," said Bo. She toyed with her straw and then inhaled some more soft drink.

"Why would they . . ." Shelley started over. "You're talking about Andrew and Mr. Sticks?"

Bo nodded.

"Why would they want to kill us?"

"Two reasons." Bo held up one finger. "First but least important, they think you stole me away from them." Smiling, she reached out and rumpled his hair. "It's bullshit, Shell. But the only truth that matters is the truth they believe to be true."

He nodded. It made no difference if you were Christ reincarnate or the number-one loony in the bin. No matter who you were or hoped to be, all that mattered, at times, was what you happened to believe in that crucial moment.

"Reason number two," said Bo, holding up two fingers, "is they think we've got some money that rightfully belongs to them."

"Ah," said Shelley. "I see." There were three windsurfers out there now, a quarter-mile from shore, running with the wind, skimming gaudy as a flight of one-winged parrots across the waves. He said, "What money is that?"

"The money they were supposed to split with Zagros Galee."

Now there was a name that rang no bells. Shelley said, "Who's he?"

"A dead, twice-crooked real-estate agent. Mr. Sticks shot him, or it might've been Andrew."

Shelley rubbed his forehead so hard you might have thought he was intent on rubbing himself right out of existence. "They were involved in some kind of scam?" He corrected himself. "You were involved in something you haven't told me about, right?"

"Mr. Sticks and Mr. Galee sold a deluxe waterfront penthouse that didn't belong to them, to a wealthy Hong Kong businessman. It was a fire-sale, all-cash deal." She kissed him again, fleetingly. "It took months to set up. Mr. Galee was a big help, but then he got kind of greedy."

"He wanted a larger commission?"

"And me," said Bo. "Anyway, he got shot, and I kind of panicked, and took the money. Mr. Sticks would've done something awful by now, if Andrew wasn't so crazy about me." She hastily added, "Remember, Shell, all I did was serve tea and cookies, show a little leg."

Shelley nodded. Something else he remembered was that he'd told her within an hour of meeting her that he was babysitting a big house in Kerrisdale, right through Christmas. Bo stared into his eyes. He saw that she was crazy about him. But then, maybe there wasn't a whole lot she wasn't crazy about. She rested her hand on his shoulder, for balance, and tongued a sticky drop of Coke from his lower lip. In an instant, he absolutely despised himself for his base and cowardly thoughts.

"Legally and morally," said Bo, "there's no way one thin dime of that money belongs to them." She adjusted the strap of her bikini. "But on the other hand, I've got a garbage can full of cash they *believe* belongs to them."

A garbage can. Shelley tried to imagine it. He resisted the urge to ask her where she'd hidden the money. What garbage can out of all the city's tens of thousands of cans had gotten lucky? "How much is that in round figures, exactly?"

"Quite a lot," Bo replied.

She was being evasive, but what did it matter, after all. Mr. Sticks and Andrew had already vividly demonstrated that the sum in question was large enough to kill for. Ten thousand monkeys working ten thousand calculators for all of eternity couldn't come up with a more substantial number.

Shelley said, "So, in a nutshell, it's us or them?"

"You got it, handsome."

"Give up the money."

She nodded thoughtfully. Light moving in her eyes as she looked out at the harbour. "You really think that's a good idea?"

"Call it the best of a bad bunch." He took her hand, but she pulled away. He said, "It isn't just you and me and them, Bo. If somebody's been murdered, there's cops out there, doing their job and doing it well."

"Beavering away even as we speak," said Bo. Her smile was thin.

"If he got nabbed, would Andrew turn you in?"

"Not if we still had the money and he thought he eventually might end up with it. But otherwise, yes."

"What about Mr. Sticks – what'd he do?"

"Make bail and then do what he's going to do anyway, as soon as he runs out of patience. Hunt us down. Come after us with a double handful of needle-sharp pick-up sticks. Shove them into me or you or both of us until we told him how to get his hands on the cash. Then kill us, quickly or slowly, depending on his mood and how crowded his calendar happened to be."

Shelley said, "Have you got any way of getting in touch?"

Andrew never went anywhere without his Nokia. Mr. Sticks had a cellphone in his Jaguar.

Shelley's mind whirred like a beanie's propeller in a force-ten gale. He plotted and schemed. Was it possible that Bo had a key to the penthouse apartment? Of course she had a key. She was the babe in charge of tea and cookies. How could she not have a key? He said, "Have you got a key to the penthouse?"

"I sure do."

The *I do* words. Shelley would not be distracted. He said, "Where's the garbage can, Bo?"

Her smile was wonderfully enigmatic. She bent to her straw. Her soft drink made a horrible gurgling noise as she finished it off.

"Don't you trust me?"

Laughing, Bo said, "More than anybody."

As so often happens in the summer, the wind picked up as if for one last gasp just at the time that dusk began to fall. The sea moved with more spirit. The sky paled and then darkened to violet, tincture of iodine, cobalt blue. The sun, a molten blob of gold, touched down upon the horizon and was distorted by the burden of its weight. Streaks of orange and red light fell across the restless water. The mountains turned to lumps of black, speckled low on the flanks and down along the shoreline with tiny pin-pricks of light. Insects sizzled and died on the lights along the promenade. Men – reduced by the darkness to eyes and teeth – prowled in search of the things they needed. The city pulsed like a living thing. It glowed incandescent beneath mischievously twin-kling stars.

By then, of course, Bo and Shelley were long gone.

24

Willows' beeper sounded as he and Parker walked down the alley towards their car. Willows unlocked Parker's door, slid across the seat, started the engine, and used the Motorola to call the dispatcher. Parker eased into the car, rolled down her window. The Ford had been parked in the shade but the interior was hot and stuffy. The radio crackled. Willows was put through to Farley Spears.

Spears said, "Hey, Jack. The name Alex Findley mean anything to you?"

Willows' head was still full of Patrick Gordon's music.

Spears said, "The old guy at the beach, the retired milkman."

"What about him?" said Willows.

"He's got a hot tip. A *hot* tip. I asked him for details, but he'll only talk to you. And your lovely partner. That last bit's a direct quote. Want his number?"

"Let's have it, Farley."

Spears gave Willows Alex Findley's address and phone number. Willows wrote it down on the dashboard pad. Spears added, "He said he'll be out in the garden, so let it ring. Hey, Jack? You gonna make it to Ralph's retirement party?"

"I'll do my best."

"The way Eddy sees it, he wouldn't have been yanked into that bathtub if Ralph'd been paying attention. Could be fireworks."

"See you later, Farley."

Willows fastened his seatbelt. He shifted into reverse, backed away from the dumpster. He drove until he came across a pay-phone, dropped a quarter. Findley's phone rang and rang. Willows got back in the car.

Parker checked the address. Findley lived in an apartment block in the 2300 block West Third. If he lived in an apartment, where was the garden? She said, "Think it's worth driving over there?"

Willows was in a grim mood. The first twenty-four hours of a murder investigation is crucial, and time was flying. So far, it had been a resounding dud. The interview with the dying lawyer hadn't improved his mood. He said, "Got any other ideas?"

Parker glanced at her watch. Quarter past three. "A late lunch?"

Willows smiled. He was always the hungry one. Breakfast for Parker was rarely more than a quick cup of coffee. She often skipped lunch as well, or, if she did eat, nibbled on a salad. He turned off Georgia, made a left on Burrard. Lunch could wait. Alex Findley had a *hot* tip.

Findley's complex was in the middle of the block, a tan-coloured stucco box with wood trim, balconies that many of the tenants had converted to open-air storage closets. Willows parked as far away from the fire hydrant as he could get. The apartment's lawn had been recently mowed. The narrow strip of dwarf shrubs was well-tended. The glass doors to the vestibule were locked. He tried the intercom. No answer. He buzzed the manager, identified himself. A slow, disembodied voice told him that Findley was expecting him and that he was in the garden at the rear of the building.

Willows followed Parker around to the side. A tall cinderblock wall had been built between the apartment and the neighbouring building, but there was a wrought-iron gate, and it was wide open.

Parker heard the sound of a shovel in gravelly soil.

Alex Findley stood in the middle of a small patch of earth to the left of the driveway that descended steeply to the apartment's underground parking lot. His "garden" was about six feet wide by ten feet long; not much larger than a grave. There were tomatoes, herbs in clay plots, a few scraggly plants Willows couldn't identify. Findley was digging a hole and had his back to them. He wore a floppy, wide-brimmed hat, long-sleeved white shirt, jeans that had been hacked off at the knee, heavy scuffed boots. His small white dog – Betsy – lay off to one side beneath a flowering rose bush. The dog's close-set eyes were wide open. Her pink tongue lolled. Findley bent his knees. The tendons of his wrists stood out. He grunted. A shovelful of moist black earth dotted with small stones joined the heap a little behind him. Willows noticed that a brown paper bag had been partly buried by the growing mound of earth.

Willows had a strict rule about men with shovels: tact was preferable to a dented forehead. He delicately cleared his throat.

Betsy was up in an instant, snapping and snarling. She raced towards him, teeth bared. The rose bush swayed violently, and a shower of petals drifted down, as she reached the end of her leash.

Alex Findley said, "Don't even smile, or she'll never forgive you."

Betsy danced erratically on her stubby hind legs. Her choke chain was tight. Parker couldn't decide whether the dog was growling or asphyxiating. As they'd approached Findley, Parker had thought the dog was dead, that Findley was about to bury her. Given the dog's disposition, Parker thought she might've had a good idea.

Findley said, "You got here pretty quick. Hope I ain't wasting your time."

"What did you want to see us about, Mr. Findley?"

"The fella that busted into your car on the weekend. I seen him again. In that pay parkin' lot at Kits beach. By the tennis courts, where that old train used to be? Settle *down*, Betsy! Laughin' his fool head off, havin' the time of his life with his girlfriend."

The dog circled, and lay down. It stared malevolently at Parker.

"They was gettin' into that snazzy black car of his just when I arrived. I wrote down the licence number, and then I figured, what the hell, might as well follow 'em and see where they went."

Findley dropped his shovel into the hole. He worked it around a little, hauled up a cupful of earth and deposited it on the pile.

"Followed 'em to a liquor store. The woman was driving, fella went in and bought a case of beer. She stopped again at a grocery store on Dunbar. This time he bought a bunch of flowers. Kiss kiss. Then off they went again, didn't stop this time until they got home. Big house in Kerrisdale, on West Thirty-Ninth. Young but rich, drivin' a car like that, livin' in a place like that. Great big garden. Wisteria and rhodos all over the place." Grudgingly he added, "Well taken care of, I got to admit."

Parker said, "What's the address, Mr. Findley?"

"The house's set way back on the lot. I didn't want to stop. Couldn't make out the numbers from the road." Findley grinned. "But I got the address of the house next door, and the woman parked that little black car right out in front, so if she's still there, you got 'er made."

Findley handed Parker a scrap of paper on which he had carefully printed the sx's licence-plate number. Parker asked him to describe the house. Findley made a show of rubbing his unshaven chin. He was able to describe the garden with a great deal more clarity than he recalled the house, which he vaguely recalled as being sharp-roofed, painted dark grey, with white trim. There was a stone retaining wall at the front that was in danger of collapsing. A hedge of evergreens on the righthand side. Willows wrote it all down in his notebook. When he'd finished, he and Parker thanked Findley for his help. Willows offered his hand. Findley held on tight.

"*Crimestoppers* got any money out on this?"

Willows said, "I'll look into it, and give you a call."

"Yeah?"

"We won't forget, Mr. Findley," promised Parker.

"You got my number?"

"We've got it."

Findley wasn't finished yet. Maintaining his grip on Willows' hand, he said, "Know why I'm digging this hole?"

Willows shook his head.

"Take a guess!"

"To get to the bottom of things?"

Findley stepped closer, so close that Willows could feel the old man's breath on his cheek. "Sometimes you find things," he said, "that it just wouldn't be right to put in the garbage. Get what I mean?"

"No," said Willows, "I don't think I do."

Findley released Willows' hand. He stepped back, used the shovel to neatly scoop up the brown paper bag. He turned slightly away from Parker and opened up the bag and tilted it towards Willows.

"Okay?"

"Okay," said Willows.

"Don't you forget about that *Crimestoppers* reward, understand? You might not believe it to look at me, but I sure could use the dough!"

As soon as they were safely out of earshot, Parker said, "What'd he have in the bag, Jack?"

"Something he didn't want you to know about, obviously."

Parker slipped her arm through his. She smiled sweetly at him. Her elbow nudged him sharply in the ribs.

Back in the car, Willows passed Parker his notebook. He drove to the end of the block, turned right. Parker radioed dispatch and gave the operator the licence-plate number – VAV 457 – that Findley had given them.

Parker removed her jacket and laid it neatly on the backseat. She said, "Where d'you think you're going?"

"West Thirty-Ninth."

"To bust some kid for letting the air out of your tire?" Parker smiled. "Get serious, Jack. We're in the middle of a murder investigation."

"Are we?"

Parker put her arm out the window to deflect a bit of wind into the car.

Willows said, "What've we got? Nothing. No leads. No suspects." He braked for a stop sign, made a right on Fourth Avenue, drove to the end of the block and turned left. "Tell you what – you're not hungry and neither am I. Instead of taking a break for lunch, let's drive over there and get the address. Take it one step at a time, okay?"

Parker hesitated.

Willows accelerated past a rusty pickup truck and changed to the inside lane, pulled into a 7-Eleven and parked. He walked into the store, returned a few minutes later with two cans of Diet Coke. He popped the tabs and handed a can to Parker. He said, "Yeah, I want to bust the silly bastard who broke into my car. Know why? I'm tired, frustrated, totally pissed off. My son seems to have vanished off the face of the earth, my daughter's at home all by herself, crying her eyes out, and it's going to cost me a thousand dollars to bail out a three-legged cat." Willows' face was grim. "If Findley can be believed, the idiot had a chrome-plated crowbar. A chrome-plated crowbar! Can you believe it? What a nitwit!" His smile was mirthless. "Right this minute, I can't think of *anything* I'd rather do than slap a pair of cuffs on him."

"If I understand the situation correctly," said Parker, "you're telling me you need an outlet for your aggression." She patted his knee. "Why didn't you say so in the first place?"

Willows had drained half his Coke when their call number came over the radio. Parker picked up. The dispatcher told them the licence plate belonged to a 1995 Datsun 300sx. The car was a lease. The insurance had been purchased by Shelley Byron Cooper. Cooper's address was a downtown mail drop.

Parker said, "We need a warrant."

"Okay, fine. But we can't apply for a warrant until we've got the address, can we?"

Parker leaned back. A few minutes earlier she'd caught a glimpse of the temperature readout on the Molson tower at the south end of the Burrard Street Bridge. Twenty-seven degrees Celsius. Somewhere in the mid-eighties. She was melting into the Ford's naugahyde seat. She said, "I'm dying in here. Let's get rolling."

Willows turned the key.

The house was pretty much as Alex Findley had described it: dark grey, in the Tudor style, with a sharply sloped roof and plenty of white trim. The house had been built at the back of the lot, about fifty feet from the sidewalk. Findley had been right about the stone wall, wisteria, and rhododendrons. There was no sign of the black car.

Willows had parked on the far side of the block, a few houses down. Now he cruised slowly up the street. Cooper's neighbour was in the front yard, working her garden. Willows drove to the end of the block and made a left. There was a firehall at the mouth of the lane that ran behind the houses. He drove down the lane, past the house. No sx. He parked again, out of sight of the house, in the shade of a maple tree well past its prime. He and Parker strolled up the sidewalk. The gardener was in her early forties, blonde, good-looking. She wore a plain white T-shirt, faded blue shorts, battered sneakers. She was on her hands and knees, loosening the soil of a flowerbed with a stainless-steel gardening fork.

She stood up as Willows and Parker entered the yard.

Parker smiled. "Good afternoon," she said cheerfully.

The woman nodded, a little uncertain. She held the fork loosely in her right hand.

Parker glanced towards the Tudor. Thick shrubbery blocked the view. For added insurance, she turned her back to the house before she showed the woman her badge.

"You're police officers?"

Willows nodded.

Parker introduced herself, and Willows. The woman's name was Mimi Rushton. Smiling disarmingly, Parker said, "Mimi, what can you tell us about the boy next door?"

"His name's Shelley. He smashed my daughter's windshield with an axe."

It was a good opening line. Suddenly, everybody was paying attention. Willows wouldn't have been all that surprised if the pansies and marigolds had turned their pretty little heads.

"Tell us about it," said Parker.

Mimi launched into her tale of woe. She told them about the argument over the parking space, the axe in the Miata's windshield, that the cops had come, done nothing. How infuriated and helpless she'd felt when Shelley had grinned and held up a couple of empty beer cans, as the constables drove away.

Parker said, "He told you they drank his beer?"

"No, he didn't say a word. But his *meaning* was certainly clear."

"Is your daughter home?"

"She's at work."

"Have you had any other problems with Shelley?"

Mimi told them about the redhead who liked to wander around on the sundeck stark naked, for all the world – including her husband – to see. Bo. She told them about the weird Chinese father-and-son team, the loud fights over the redhead, at least one failed kidnapping attempt, the ominous black Jaguar, how Shelley had dumped the kid and a big stack of red-streaked towels into the Jaguar's backseat. Each revelation triggered a flood of questions that were never asked, because Mimi answered them before they could be put to her.

They were still talking when the sx roared up to the curb. Bo was driving. She and Shelley got out of the car. Shelley applied The Club. He rolled down his window a fraction of an inch, just enough to let the hot air out and protect the leather upholstery. They'd apparently been shopping. Shelley carried several plastic Safeway bags and a six-pack of beer. Hand in hand, they ran up the sidewalk and into the house. The door slammed shut on a burst of laughter that was, somehow, downright lewd.

Willows caught Parker's eye. He smiled a tiny smile.

Parker said, "Well, thanks, Mimi."

"Would you mind telling me what this is all about?"

"You'll be the first to know," said Parker. She pointed at a stand of tall, bright-orange flowers. "In the meantime, mum's the word."

Willows made a short side trip home. Annie was in the kitchen, cooking spaghetti and listening to her Walkman. No sign of Sean. Pamela Larkins had called. Barney was recovering nicely. Willows told his daughter he'd be home late. He gave her a hug, and a peck on her upturned cheek, and told her he loved her. Annie turned to Parker for more of the same.

On the way back to 312 Main and the Q & A with Inspector Bradley that Willows hoped would result in permission to apply for a search warrant, his enthusiasm for the bust began to flag. Parker was right. They were working a murder case. He had no business taking out his built-up frustration on a petty criminal. But at the same time – probably it was just his cop's brain hunting around for justification – he couldn't stop thinking about Mimi Rushton's hot-blooded Chinese duo. Was it at all possible that they and Rose Pincott's Asian shadow dancers were one and the same? And what about the woman Rothstein had told them about, who'd rolled around in her black Jaguar to visit Zagros Galee at his office? Rothstein's description of her had been vague at best. But he'd stated emphatically that she was young, gorgeous, and a redhead. Shelley Byron Cooper's girlfriend was a perfect three out of three.

Willows rubbed his sweaty palms against the upholstery. He believed in coincidence, but mistrusted luck. He made a mental note to run the name "Bo" through the CPIC computer. The other name, "Andrew," was too common; he'd end up with a dot-matrix printout a half mile long.

Parker said, "Jack?"

He glanced at her. They were halfway downtown. He'd been driving by rote. "Yeah, I'm back."

"Let's stop somewhere, grab a bite to eat."

"What, now?"

Parker nodded. "Yes, now." Something caught her eye. She

turned and looked behind her and then turned her attention back to him. "We need to sit down and talk this over."

"Talk what over?" said Willows, frowning. Was she backtracking, having second thoughts about the warrant?

"The two Chinese guys, the beautiful redhead." The breeze from the car's open window played with Parker's hair. Smiling, she leaned towards him. "I know exactly what you're thinking."

"You do, huh?"

"And I think you could be right."

Willows kept quiet. When in doubt, mute.

Parker said, "But now the situation's a lot more complicated. We've tied a murder investigation to a simple petty theft. You know Homer. He's going to have some serious doubts about giving us the green light, and I can't blame him. That's why we need a restaurant," she added. "For the paper napkins. So we've got something to write on, as we work out a strategy."

"El Patio," suggested Willows. It was on their way, and the food was good.

Parker nodded. They could order a selection of *tapas*, and she could pick away at her own pace, while Willows ate as much as he pleased. A cool, refreshing bowl of *gazpacho* to start, followed by a slice or two of fresh bread, a single glass of wine. Maybe some chicken or prawns, a few of those delicious, chunky, deep-fried potatoes. If things went well, it was going to be a long night.

Her stomach growled in anticipation.

Willows hit the gas.

25

It might've been the perfect weather or the dreadful certainty that sooner or later Mr. Sticks and his tame grandson would be back for an unexpected visit. Whatever, the house made him feel claustrophobic. Shelley had never indulged in the habit of analysing himself or the events that set him in motion. What he thought was that it would be a good idea to go downtown and catch a movie.

"Why?" said Bo from behind the wheel. She ran her fingernails down the length of his arm, and then leaned over and kissed his fingers.

Shelley slumped low in his seat. Why, indeed? The sx's air-conditioner blasted him. He shut his eyes. Minutes rolled by on the dashboard clock. He was so quiet he might've been dead.

Bo waited.

"Because," he said at last, "it's such a wonderful day."

"Too nice a day to squander inside a theatre?" said Bo, catching on fast.

"Yeah," said Shelley.

"There won't be anybody there," said Bo. "No line-ups for popcorn. Nobody sitting behind us crackling candy wrappers or making stupid remarks."

"Or, if there is, we can move."

"We'd probably have the balcony all to ourselves," said Bo. "It'd be our third date. We could get as passionate as we wanted."

Shelley's eyes popped open. He couldn't think of a single theatre in the whole city that still had a balcony.

They batted that one around awhile, as Bo drove them downtown. She parked in the DPC lot at Seymour and Georgia. More than a dozen of the city's screens were located within a few blocks of each other, in multiplexes on Granville Street. Shelley and Bo walked down Georgia to Granville. The corner had been locally famous for its Birks clock. The clock had served as a meeting place for generations of Vancouverites, but had been ruthlessly uprooted a year or so ago, when the jewellery store had moved to a different location. You could still see exactly where the clock had stood, because the city had done a shoddy job of patching the sidewalk. Hand in hand, Bo and Shelley strolled south on Granville. Across the street, the white tile wall of the Eaton's building ran the length of the block. The wall reminded Shelley of a urinal. It was a mark of the city's artistic despair that the tiles were so rarely targeted by the spray-can mob.

They ended up at the Paradise, because Bo had heard from a friend that the seats slid back and forth, so you could sit bolt upright or scrunch down low as a weasel, according to your mood. She liked the theatre's sparkly neon, too, when she saw it. Thumbing a fifty off a wad fat as a jelly roll, she told Shelley it was her treat, and paid for their tickets. A bald guy in a pink tuxedo that made him look a little like a sunburned penguin stood just inside the door. He pushed open the thick slab of glass and gave Bo a dazzling smile. Inside, she sprung for a couple of bags of popcorn and a large-size Pepsi, helped herself to extra straws. They entered the darkened theatre. Shelley counted eleven heads. He and Bo sat in the back row directly beneath the projection booth, nothing behind them but dark-painted wall. A beam of light played upon the screen, illuminating a beautiful young woman who lay in an antique bed, close beside a handsome young man. A second handsome young man entered the room. He wore a striped nightshirt and carried a breakfast tray loaded with steaming cups and dishes. A folded newspaper was tucked beneath his arm. When he had placed the tray carefully down on the bed, he crawled in next to the woman. After some heated but good-natured discussion, the newspaper was split into three sections. The three began to eat. Knives, forks, salt and pepper, cream and sugar; all were passed back and forth with great good humour. Time was sped up, so the actors' movements were swift and jerky, oddly fragmented. Eventually the breakfast tray was put aside. The woman lifted the comforter from her body to shake away the crumbs; the men shared a quick peek. In unison, they leaned towards her for a kiss.

The woman shut her eyes and pursed her lips. The scene faded to black.

Credits rolled, and the lights came up. A bloodred velvet curtain fell silently down, until the blank screen was hidden from view. The lights came up.

Bo said, "What d'you think, Shell?"

"Short movie."

Bo smiled. "They'll roll it again. I meant, what do you think about threesomes?"

"Wouldn't work for me."

"Ever tried it?"

Shelley shook his head. He felt miserable. A man in an aisle seat stood up. He wore a pale blue short-sleeved shirt, plaid shorts, and a pair of cheap rubber thongs. He coughed loudly, without lifting his hand to his mouth. The thongs made a clapping sound as he went out the door.

Bo had plunged one straw into another until she had a monster straw that was almost a yard long. Her cheeks collapsed. She took a deep breath. The straw darkened all along its length.

She swallowed.

"Me neither," she said at last. The sunburned penguin walked down the aisle to the front-row seats, lingered for a moment, kicked at something stuck to the floor, and started back up the aisle again. Bo ate some popcorn. She rested her head on Shelley's shoulder. Her fireball of hair tickled his ear. The penguin broke waddle to inform them that the movie would be starting soon, and that he hoped they enjoyed every minute of it. Bo saluted him with a fistful of popcorn. His eyes blew her a sultry kiss.

Chalk up another broken heart, thought Shelley. He said, "A garbage can full of money *sounds* like a lot."

Bo slurped up some Pepsi.

"But how much is it, exactly? I don't need a specific dollar figure – what I want to know is if it'd be worth it to Mr. Sticks to come after us."

"From his point of view," said Bo, "a dime'd do it." She smiled. "Mr. Sticks got the short end of the stick. I know what he's like. He got screwed, and now he wants to get even."

The lights faded. Behind and high above them, the projectionist stirred. The velvet curtain was slowly raised.

"What about the kid?"

"He thinks he's in love."

Bad news, and worse. Shelley flicked a piece of popcorn up into the bright beam of light from the projection booth. It came swirling down like a grotesquely misshapen snowflake. He snatched at it but missed. "So, in your opinion, there isn't much chance they'll lose interest in us?"

"None at all," said Bo. She snuggled up against him. A nipple grazed his rib. His heart felt as if it was being dragged at high speed down a cobblestone road. He said, "Maybe we should leave town for a while."

"It wouldn't do any good. Wherever we went, they'd never be more than a step or two behind."

The film was rated PG13. Someone hidden in the gloom whistled shrilly. Credits rolled.

Shelley thought about telling Bo he had to use the washroom, sprinting to the sx, racing home, grabbing his clothes and everything edible that was in the fridge, taking a bead on the Trans-Canada Highway. He'd had a lifelong ambition to drive solo across the country, spit into Niagara Falls. Maybe now was the time. But – he was crazy in love.

Besides, Bo had driven them downtown, and his keys were safely tucked away in the bottom of her bottomless purse.

Plus, make no mistake about it, he loved her.

Bo experimentally slid her seat back and forth, up and down. She stayed low as she moved over to Shelley's lap, straddling him. They pressed against each other. She put her arms around him, and sighed, and whispered explicit directions into his ear. When they were both as comfortable as circumstances allowed, Shelley braced himself and pushed down with his legs. The seat slid back. He let it slide forward again, and pushed away. They picked up speed, as he got the hang of it. The seat bucked and chattered. Bo hung on for dear life. Shelley's lap was full of loose popcorn. Buttons rolled away into the distance. Bo's sweet breasts gleamed palely in the light. Her breath came harsh and ragged. Shelley kept moving. Bo bit his neck and mussed his hair. An image of Zagros Galee lying naked on his deathbed flashed through her mind. She thought about the message she'd left on his home answering machine. Had the cops found it? Did they have her voice on file? There were always loose ends, weren't there?

Shelley kissed her everywhere his mouth could reach.

It was close to seven by the time they left. Despite the popcorn, Shelley's stomach was in disarray. He suggested dinner. Greek? Chinese? Mexican? Bo suggested Zefferelli's, an Italian restaurant on Robson Street that was within easy walking distance. Shelley was happy to let her lead the way up the steep flight of stairs that led to the restaurant. She effortlessly charmed the maitre d' into giving them a window table overlooking the street.

A waitress recited the day's specials. Shelley ordered pasta for both of them, a bottle of white wine. Service was prompt despite the crowd, but by the time the food arrived, he'd lost his appetite. He leaned back in his chair and watched Bo eat. Bo was a polished dawdler. She could dawdle with the best of them, when she was in the mood. He sipped his wine. Expensively coiffed heads bobbed comically on the sidewalk almost directly below him.

He searched his mind for a topic of mutual interest, something that would take her mind off their problems, set fire to some idle, harmless conversation. Their furtive sexual antics seemed to him to be a subject that was not quite appropriate to the cheerful atmosphere. Plus, en route to the restaurant some of the starch had been taken out of him when he'd realized that his left pant leg was soaked through, stained dark and sticky just below the crotch. In the theatre he'd spilled Bo's Pepsi all over himself and never felt a thing. Such were the wages of lust.

What were Mr. Sticks and Andrew up to? He needed a plan, didn't he? He picked disinterestedly at his congealing pasta. More than anything, he was acutely aware of the watch upon his wrist. Time was on the limp, but marched on nevertheless. Bo paid the bill at nine-fifteen sharp. As he trotted happily down the stairs to street level, Shelley tried to remember where he'd parked his Datsun.

Home again. Bo led him upstairs and into the shower. She tossed her scant clothing over the pebbled glass door. He kicked off his Birkenstocks. The steamy water beat down on them. She gave him a thriller of a kiss, broke away giggling as she hit him in the crotch with a spurt of lime-scented shaving cream.

Downstairs, wood splintered and glass shattered. A blood-curdling howl rent the air.

Shelley took a moment to rinse himself off. He slid back the shower door and stepped cautiously out of the tub. Bo reached for the tap to turn off the water, but Shelley caught her arm and stopped her. He threw her a fluffy orange towel that clashed loudly with her hair. She tossed the towel right back at him. He passed her the neutral beige. The sound of two hands clapping floated up to them, as their unwelcome guests high-fived triumphantly.

Downstairs, things that were breakable were being efficiently broken. There was no need for quiet. First thing that morning, Andrew had toured the block in the guise of a servile B.C. Hydro employee. Every household within earshot of a tortured scream had received a voucher in the sum of one hundred dollars, good

that evening only at a popular downtown restaurant. Andrew
had claimed that the voucher was Hydro's way of apologizing for
grief caused by the unscheduled and no-doubt-untimely disrup-
tion of service. The apology was bogus, but the vouchers were
good as gold.

Andrew leapt high into the air. His heel drove viciously into the
plump, pablum-smeared face of a six-month-old child. The anodized aluminum frame buckled. Splinters of glass were driven
into the wall. The face was torn to papery shreds. Andrew landed
light as a feather.

Mr. Sticks, meanwhile, used a broom to wreak unimaginative
havoc in the kitchen, then unholstered his new pistol, attached the
noise-suppressor he'd made of a ten-inch length of plastic pipe
lightly stuffed with steel wool, and ruthlessly shot to death the
major appliances and microwave, the coffee pot and even the
toaster. When he'd finished with the kitchen he went into the living
room and emptied a clip into the antique Steinway baby grand,
shielding his eyes against the sharp splinters of ivory that clattered
against the walls and windows. He reloaded, killed the television
and stereo, then wandered about, firing randomly into the ceiling.
Drifts of plaster dust gentled the rose-coloured light. In the
kitchen, Andrew helped himself to a beer from the bullet-riddled
fridge. Entirely by accident he found Mr. Sticks' precious Titan
Tigress hidden in an empty milk carton. He gave Mr. Sticks the
gun and had his hair affectionately tousled. Back in the living room,
he chucked a five-pointed death star at the antique bevelled-glass
mirror over the fireplace. Shards of silver rained down upon the
carpet and gleaming oak floor. His eyes were dark and full of
thunder. He kicked a triangular splinter of glass so hard it embed-
ded itself in the baseboard.

Mr. Sticks thumbed bullets into the Tigress' magazine until it
was full. He slid the loaded magazine into the butt of his beloved
pistol. It had been years since he had killed a man. During all that
time he had lived by his wits and he had lived very well indeed.
Then Mr. Zagros Galee had stumbled into his life. Mr. Galee with

his greedy mouth full of stupidities, and his arms spread wide to take whatever might fall into them. Poor Mr. Galee. He had thought he was God's gift to women, but lovely Bo had disagreed.

Andrew was close behind him as he trudged up the stairs. He could feel the boy's breath, hot and fetid and quite pleasant really, on the back of his neck. At the landing, he stepped aside so Andrew could take point. The beige carpet was soaked; he could feel the wetness seeping through his shoes. The steady roar of the shower came to him from the wide-open bathroom door. The hallway was thick with steam and each stair was a miniature waterfall. Andrew shrieked and rushed full-tilt into the bathroom. Mr. Sticks leaned against a peach-coloured wall. Predictably, Andrew's experience with Zagros Galee had given him an appetite for blood. Mr. Sticks permitted himself a fleeting smile. Andrew was a lazy fellow, always ready to practise the black arts of distillation, simplification. It was likely that his penchant for violence had been an integral part of him, repressed but thriving, since he'd broke free of his mother's womb.

He lit a cigarette with his gold Ronson. Andrew appeared, wraithlike, in the roiling mist. The left side of his body was wet from the shower. His hair lay flat across his dripping skull like a beaten dog, and though it must have been a trick of the light, his eyes seemed a little smaller and more close-set than usual. He sneered at Mr. Sticks, lurched down the hallway. Mr. Sticks crossed to the master bedroom. He paused in the open doorway. Two pairs of wet footprints led to the walk-in closet, where a damp towel lay in a crumpled heap. As he stared at them, the footprints seemed to shrink, faded to a lighter colour as they evaporated into the summer air. Soon they would entirely disappear.

Too late, however.

Andrew padded down the hall towards him. He pointed.

Andrew danced into the bedroom. It had broken his heart to pieces when Bo traded him in for the bronzed beach bunny. Love, or something that must pass for love, had sent a tsunami of blood thundering down his veins, washing over his heart. Mr. Sticks had counselled him that he must hold his patience and bide his time, and now his time had finally come. Vengeance! He kick-boxed the bedroom walls to smithereens. His dervish hands shattered the furniture. A flurry of death stars shredded the bed. A leaping kick shattered the ceiling light fixture. He hurled himself at the mirrored closet doors and smashed them and every vile thing they'd witnessed into a thousand pieces. Coat hangers rattled like poisonous snakes as he worked his way to the walk-in gun safe at the far end of the closet. Bo's endearingly small handprint, highlighted by a few beads of water, lay upon the dusty, enamelled surface. Andrew snarled. His knuckles rattled on the steel. The lip of the door was curved inward and offered no purchase. He slipped the blade of his knife in an inch or two, wriggled and pried. The door held solid. He saw that the metal box was bolted to the building's frame; the very bones that held the house together. It did not budge. Vexed, he stepped back and drove his heel into the metal, but failed even to chip the paint.

Mr. Sticks gave him the Jaguar's keys and told him to fetch the propane torch from the trunk – and whatever else caught his manic eye.

On his way to the car, Andrew slashed with his new knife at the rhodos and wisteria. He bent and uprooted a small palm tree, spun on his heel and decapitated a cluster of daisies. He was blinded by a vision of his treacherous beloved and her beach-bunny bimbo, pressed naked together in the close confines of the gun safe. How could she!

The street was quiet, the houses all along the boulevard dark and silent. Not even a dog barked. Andrew unlocked the Jag's capacious trunk, grabbed the propane torch and a spare canister of fuel, two pairs of handcuffs he had bought at a sleazy downtown sex shop. Returning to the house, he hacked and chopped and kicked and bit and spat at every living thing within his reach, laid waste to a hundred vases' worth of flowers.

Mr. Sticks wielded the Ronson. He lit a fresh cigarette and then the propane burner, rotated a knurled knob to adjust the flame.

When the flame was three inches long and burned pale blue, he scrolled it across the brown enamel. The paint bubbled, turned black. He used the torch to cut a silk blouse into several pieces, set the pieces ablaze, and shoved them through the air vents. A slim tendril of smoke rose to the ceiling. He hunkered down, set the burner upright on the floor so the point of the flame splashed against the metal. The close air inside the closet stank of burnt paint and scorched clothing. A smoke alarm began to screech.

Mr. Sticks lost patience. He whipped the safe with a wire coat hanger, screamed at Bo to come out. He described in graphic detail the terrible sadistic things he and Andrew would do to Shelley when they finally got their hands on him. The torch hissed steadily. Andrew finally noticed the air vents on the exposed flank of the safe. The vents were about six inches above the floor. He grabbed the burner and pointed the flame directly at one of the holes. His scalp was alive with sweat. Five minutes crept past, then ten. The smoke alarm had begun to falter. Mr. Sticks would surely kill Bo even if she returned every penny she had stolen. It was a shame, but inevitable. He sniffed the air. A sour odour – burning flesh? – made his nostrils flare.

How much longer could Bo and her bimbo take the heat?

26

Zagros Galee's girlfriend had been a redhead. Shelley Byron Cooper's girlfriend was a redhead. Rose Pincott and Mimi Rushton had both had close encounters with a hot-blooded Asian duo. What more evidence did Bradley need that Shelley Byron Cooper might be a murder suspect?

Plenty. Warrant in hand, Willows asked Homer Bradley for an ERT – Emergency Response Team – presence. Bradley wasn't convinced by Willows' arguments. Two coincidences were worse than none. He told Willows to forget the ERT team, but that he'd involve a couple of patrol cars. As an added bonus, he volunteered to go along for the ride.

Willows parked his unmarked Ford across the street from the firehall at the far end of Shelley's block. Two blue and whites pulled in behind. The Ford's engine muttered quietly.

Willows said, "If you and the two uniforms go in the back door, Parker and I'll take the front. That suit you, Inspector?"

Bradley lit his cigar, tossed the match out the window. "Sounds good to me, Jack."

Ten minutes later, Willows and Parker were crouched behind the granite retaining wall that ran across the front of the property, and Bradley and the two cops he'd borrowed from traffic division had taken up positions at the back of the house. A black Jaguar convertible was parked on the street directly in front of the house. Willows had palmed the Jag's long, sloping hood. The metal was warm; he estimated the car had been driven within the past half-hour or so. He assumed Shelley's 300sx had been put away for the night in the locked garage at the rear of the property.

Parker's radio crackled. She adjusted the squelch, signed on. Bradley told her about the open French doors, the gleam of broken glass on the sundeck and inside the house.

In a top-floor room of the house, shadows jolted across the walls and ceiling. Downstairs, nothing moved.

Parker consulted briefly with Willows. Dense shrubbery growing between the houses would allow them to approach the front porch undetected by anyone inside the house, but it would take them a few minutes to get there. Parker thumbed her walkie-talkie and spoke briefly to Bradley. "You ready to go, Inspector?"

Willows held his breath, as he listened to Bradley chew on his cigar. Finally Bradley said, "'Kay, go ahead. But watch your ass, understand?"

Parker grinned at Willows. "You heard him, Jack."

Andrew was fast losing patience. He got down on his hands and knees and thrust the burner's hot nozzle deep inside the gun safe. Peeking through the adjacent vent, he was able to see by the blue light of the flame row upon row of gold-coloured disks. Coins? Bullion? His imagination ran wild. The tip of the flame touched burnished metal, but the smoke and heat made his eyes water, and so he was unable to see that the "gold coins" were actually several hundred rounds of large-calibre ammunition.

Willows duck-waddled along the stone wall. When he reached the cover of a tall hedge, he stood up, and happened to be looking directly at the house when a fine white mist – thousands of pebbles of safety glass – accelerated into the purple void. A skylight had exploded. In that same fraction of a second a massive explosion tore through the upper floor of the house.

The hedge bent flat. Branches snapped, and the air was filled

with debris. The concussion punched Willows in the chest and
knocked him down. To Parker, who was crouched down low
behind the stone wall, it felt as if a 747 had passed a few inches
overhead. The Jaguar rocked on its springs. The car's alarm
shrieked. All the way to the far end of the block, the street was lit
up by a roiling ball of fire. Everything turned orange. Jetblack
shadows lurched across the lawn. Parker was on her knees, her
hands clasped to her head. The streetlight vibrated. Skinny green
leaves from the rhododendron spiralled crazily through the air.
Tiny pieces of glass rained down thick as hail. Every leaf had been
stripped from the wisteria. Dust clouded the lights. Parker staggered to her feet. Willows was up, moving slowly towards her.

Beneath the peaked roof, a raggedy section of the house's outer
wall had been blown entirely away. The dust of a thousand
different things mingled in the light of several small fires. There
was more fire on the lawn and in the bushes and on the neighbour's roof. Parker's dark eyes were crammed with flame. A
burning shingle skittered erratically down.

Willows peered into her eyes. She couldn't hear a word he said.
Then, it was as if someone had flicked a switch. He was shouting.
Predictably, he wanted to know if she was all right.

Parker nodded. Inside the house, many small fires had already
begun to merge into one. Wood crackled. Flames and black smoke
shot through the hole in the roof where the skylight had been.
Each piece of glass that lay upon the lawn glowed a luminous
orange.

Her back was warm. She glanced behind her and saw that the
Jaguar was on fire. Sirens wailed. Willows was running hard
towards the house. She hurried after him, gun in hand. Secondary
explosions rattled the air. As she entered the house, she caught a
glimpse of Willows on the landing. She called his name but he
didn't respond. She followed him upstairs.

In the bedroom, Mr. Sticks lay where the blast had flung him,
square in the middle of the kingsize bed. The explosion had
stripped him down to his shirt and skivvies, and his thin body

from mid-thigh down had more holes in it than ten yards of chicken-wire. His button eyes were wide open. He opened them a little wider as Willows burst into the room, and he blinked like a half-bright owl when he saw Parker. The room's ceiling was buried in pink smoke. The air stank of burnt clothing and over-done Andrew. There was not a shard of glass in any of the win-dows. Paint bubbled. Wallpaper smouldered. A fractured electrical circuit tossed sparks across the floor. Willows could feel the heat sucking the moisture from his skin. Mr. Sticks' arm came up.

"Jack, he's got a gun!"

Willows saw it – a small-bore semiauto. The muzzle looked him in the eye, drifted away, and then jerked back and held steady.

"Drop it!" shouted Parker.

Mr. Sticks flinched at the brute force of her anger. He smiled to hide his embarrassment, teeth flashing in the weirdly flickering light. Parker's shadow twitched. Once again, she shrieked at Mr. Sticks to drop his gun.

It was a no-brainer, if you went by the book. Willows' life was in jeopardy. It was Parker's responsibility, her *duty*, to use deadly force.

But Willows complicated matters by holstering his revolver. Slowly and tentatively, he moved towards the bed. He said, "You've been hurt. You need help."

Mr. Sticks licked his lips. "Where is Andrew?"

Willows strained to hear him. "Who?"

"My little boy, my dear sweet child . . ."

Parker said, "In the ambulance. He's in the ambulance."

Mr. Sticks smiled. His teeth gleamed orange, streaked with red. "Andrew knows nothing of this. I did all the bad things."

Willows took a single slow and cautious step towards the bed. Outside, he heard the hiss of air brakes, clank of heavy machinery, shouts. Flashes of red light strobed the cloudy room.

"Very bad things." The old man made a clucking sound. "The money was in there with them, I bet." He looked down at his shat-tered legs. "Hidden in the big metal box." His bloody fingers clawed at the sheets as he wriggled into a sitting position. His skull thumped against the headboard. His eyes rolled up in their sockets and his head lolled. Willows took another step towards him. The pistol came up. After a moment Mr. Sticks said, "Andrew had nothing to do with it. It was me, only me. He was angry because Galee had intended to seduce Bo, but all that mattered to me was that he had intended to steal my hard-earned money. I shot him. I shot him dead with a single bullet from my nice little gun."

"What gun?" said Willows, for the record.

"My Titan Tigress. Like Andrew, it is small but efficient."

The old man stared suspiciously at Parker, but Parker had temporarily lost interest in him. The floor had given her a hotfoot. She glanced down. The carpet was scorched and smoking.

Willows coughed. "We've to get out of here. The fire . . ." He offered his hand to Mr. Sticks. A stream of water leapt out of the darkness and knocked him right off his feet. Startled, Mr. Sticks fired into the space Willows had so recently occupied.

Parker instinctively fired back. Her first shot drilled the oak headboard. She adjusted her aim. But Mr. Sticks had already forgotten her. He whooped shrilly as he shot a fireman off his ladder. Willows tackled Parker, hit her low, and sent her tumbling towards the bedroom doorway. They rolled across the smoking floor and into the hallway. The stairwell was nothing but fire. Coils of dense black smoke gyrated crazily. Behind them, the old man fired and fired again. Willows dragged Parker down the hall, into another bedroom. Red light pulsed on the walls. Dozens of stuffed toy animals perching on a bookcase stared solemnly at them. Willows couldn't stop coughing. He kicked the door shut, crawled across the carpeted floor. A cone of light swung across the ceiling and swerved away. Willows kicked open a window, slung Parker over his shoulder and carried her outside, onto a narrow deck that ran across the width of the house. The air was sweet and cool. Parker wondered why she felt so tired.

An aluminum ladder banged against the rail. Bradley squinted up at them as he held the ladder steady. The inspector's white shirt was riddled with pinprick burn holes and his skin was raw and parched. Across the street, a telephone pole smoked all along its length. Bradley helped take Parker's weight as Willows reached the ground. They trotted side by side across the lawn. Behind them, a section of the roof caved in with a marrow-vibrating roar. A galaxy of bright sparks crackled and popped, and scurried wildly up into the ebony sky.

In the festering light, Parker saw that Willows' shoulder was wet with blood. She reached out to touch him and found to her surprise that she couldn't lift her arm. She tried to make sense of this as he lowered her onto a gurney. A paramedic leaned over her. His breath smelled of mints. High above her, the moon wobbled crazily. The ambulance swallowed her up. She had a moment of rising panic as she thought about what happened to people who let themselves be trapped in metal boxes. A bubble of plastic was pressed firmly down over her mouth and nose. Willows smiled grimly down at her. He kissed her fingers. His words were drowned by the enormous thumping of her heart.

She realized at last that she'd been shot.

27

There is a hat for every rabbit, a welcoming sleeve for every black-hearted ace of spades.

Every pea has its pod, and everybody has to be somewhere.

Sleight of hand is, when the dust finally settles, merely sleight of hand. Even so, Shelley'd always had a special place in his heart for vanishing acts. Lucky for him and Bo that he'd remembered that his obnoxious neighbour, the fisherman across the lane who'd had the balky boat motor, was gone to the high seas for the rest of the summer. Lucky as well that the guy had mentioned he was a bachelor and lived alone, with not even a cat to keep him company. And wasn't it lucky that Shelley had decided it would be a good idea to leave town pretty soon, and to stay at the fisherman's in the meantime. And wasn't it convenient that the fisherman's living-room window overlooked the back of Shelley's ex-residence.

Shelley and Bo snuggled on the couch, nipped at a bottle of Australian Chardonnay, and watched the fire.

Bo said the *F* word when the miniature armoury in the gun cabinet blew sky-high. The fisherman's house shook, the windows rattled, and at least one pane cracked. Shelley swallowed hard. He hadn't exactly killed Mr. Sticks and Andrew, but he hadn't done anything to save them, either.

As if reading his mind, or perhaps to reassure herself that what they had done was unavoidable and absolutely right, Bo said, "They would have killed us."

"I know," said Shelley. Though of course he didn't. Nothing was a certainty until you could speak of it in the past tense. Even that small window of opportunity was soon slammed shut. Life's hard knocks had taught him how little time it took for the fog to roll in. Memory soon faltered and lost step. You became uncertain of everything all over again.

Bo gave him a peck on the cheek. "Killed us dead," she dolefully assured him.

Shelley went over to the window. He rested his palms against the sill as he looked out. The flames were fifteen or twenty feet above the peak of the roof, inclined slightly towards the east. Shrubbery and the neighbour's dogwood tree had caught fire. He tried to remember who lived on that side. A guy who owned a gold Volvo station wagon and a slim black leather briefcase. His wife was a recluse. Shelley had caught a glimpse of her now and then.

There were a bunch of guys running around in the alley. Cops, most of them. Their badges flashed in the firelight. Shelley turned his head and saw a fireman running down the alley. The hook and ladder was right behind. Another firetruck pulled up in front of the house. He unlatched the window and pushed it partway open. The *sound* of the fire came to him; a malicious, ill-tempered hissing and crackling and low-down dirty growling. The owners had told him when they'd interviewed him that the house had been built in 1912. The way things were going, if the firemen didn't get their hoses untangled and their heavily padded asses in gear, the joint wasn't going to get a whole lot older. But since bits and pieces of arsenal kept exploding, he couldn't blame them for hanging back. The cops had bulletproof vests, but all the firemen had to protect them were their gumboots and silly hats.

Burning asphalt shingles fluttered down on the lawn and in the alley and on the steeply pitched roofs of the neighbouring houses. A cop tried to stamp a shingle out. The melted tar stuck to his shoe. He danced a one-legged jig in the glare of the fire truck's headlights.

A fireman gaped at him. The cop kicked off his shoe. The fireman hit it with a blast of carbon monoxide and walked away laughing. Shelley was glad to see someone was having a good time. He hoped like hell that the fire didn't get too far out of control, because Bo's money was in the fisherman's garage and so was his sx, nose pointed at the double doors for a stylishly quick getaway.

A box of twenty rounds of ammunition exploded like a string of extra-strength firecrackers. The firemen in their bulky yellow coats shot through with silver reflecting tape abandoned their equipment and ducked down behind their vehicles. Most of the cops stood fast.

His view of the front of the house was blocked by the house itself and by the rising wall of flames, but he was able to see that the street had been turned into a snakepit. There was plenty of activity down there. Cops. Firefighters. Passersby with a taste for disaster. His eye was attracted to the white glare of a television light. The extra-cool guy from CKVU's 23:30 was front and centre, yakking calmly into his microphone.

The largest of the firetrucks directed a mechanical ladder into the yard. A fireman with a limp hose draped over his shoulder climbed up the ladder and waved his arm. The hose grew fat. A dense stream of water that the light had turned sparkly phosphorescent was directed towards the fire, and vanished in a sudden burst of tangerine steam.

The fireman raised his arms in triumph. His face was a tiny white oval. Suddenly he fell backwards off the ladder and plummeted silently out of Shelley's line of sight. For a moment or two the abandoned hose bucked spasmodically in the glare of the lights. Then it, too, fell away.

Shelley's fingernails scraped across the windowsill. His breath fogged the glass.

In the darkness behind him, Bo made a small sound of utter dismay. Her ghostly reflection swayed in the glass. Shelley pushed away from the window. He took her in his arms and gave her a hug that was meant to stiffen her spine. Down in the alley the cops shouted into their walkie-talkies, ran in aimless circles and pointed their weapons skyward. There was nothing to shoot at, no targets of opportunity upon which they might vent their frustrations. The heat of the fire and expanding gases blew out the top-floor windows one by one. The shot fireman had dampened his colleagues' enthusiasm for battle. Unchecked, the fire had followed the open stairway down to the main floor. Another section of roof collapsed in slow-motion. The fire rumbled and groaned. A lace curtain drifted out from an exploded window, was roughly snatched back and swallowed whole in a flash of red. Discs of yellow light winked among the shrubbery. Snipers. The firemen regrouped.

Shelley and Bo retreated to the couch. There was nothing they could do now but stay sober, keep an especially low profile, and wait for things to cool down.

When the happy diners started to roll in, Bo and Shelley began to argue about the best time to bail out. Shelley wanted to wait until the wee hours of the morning. Bo was in favour of taking advantage of the moment. Soon enough, she had her way. Shelley tucked the fisherman's house key under the flowerpot on the back porch railing, and they nip-and-tucked it down to the fisherman's double garage. The alley was deserted except for a couple of blackened firemen smoking cigarettes and telling grim off-colour jokes.

Shelley pushed open the garage door. He blessed the fisherman's tendency to grease everything. Three dark-green plastic garbage cans stood in a row against the wall of the garage. He picked up the middle can and carried it into the garage. Bo unlocked and opened the sx's trunk. Two tartan suitcases lay there, mouths agape. Shelley tore the lid off the garbage can. He dumped out several small plastic bags of garbage and there it was, money enough to die for. Bo had told him she'd walked off with close to every last cent the gullible Hong Kong millionaire had paid for the BeachView Towers penthouse apartment. The cash had gone to Zagros Galee, who'd unwisely tried to keep the whole wad instead of being satisfied with his commission. Even worse, in Shelley's opinion, and lethal Andrew's too, the unwise real-estate agent had tried to buy Bo's love on the instalment plan. Shelley picked up the can. He tilted it and gave it a shake.

The sx's trunk filled up with money. Bo quietly shut and locked the trunk and they got into the car.

The smell hit Shelley as he was unlocking The Club. It was the smell of something that had been left in the oven far too long. It was the smell of burnt clothing, scorched hair, and heat-seared flesh. It was the smell of someone on a day trip from hell.

It was Andrew.

Shelley started the car. He reminded his passengers of their legal obligation to buckle up. Then he switched on the lights and drove out of the garage and sedately down the lane. A fireman stared hard into the windshield as he eased past. Bo rolled down her window. She blew a kiss to anybody who happened to be in need.

Shelley glanced at the rearview mirror. Andrew bobbed and weaved. His Hugo Boss suit was in ribbons. The whites of his eyes were not very white. Patches of his skin had the colour and texture of roast duck. A tendril of smoke escaped from a tear in his jacket beneath his armpit. Parts of him glistened, but most of him was charred a dull black. The garbled sounds he made could have been interpreted any number of ways. "I'm a goner," seemed the most likely interpretation. Shelley headed east, towards the rising sun.

A few blocks before they hit the turnoff for the Trans-Canada Highway, he pulled into a PetroCan gas station for a fill-up. Canadian flags hung dolefully in the sluggish air. Bo said she thought she'd better use the washroom. Shelley got out of the car, filled the tank with premium. Inside, he paid for the gas, a six-pack of Diet Coke, and an assortment of candy bars. He was in the mood for confession but the attendant paid him no attention at all.

He gave Andrew a hard look as he climbed back inside the car. Andrew stared fixedly back at him, giving no ground. He didn't take Shelley up on his offer of a Coke. Shelley started the car and drove around to the side of the gas station, parked opposite the door to the woman's washroom.

Bo came out of the washroom. She walked straight over to the car and got in. Andrew's mushy skull lolled against the side window. He was fading fast, but not nearly fast enough. Bo apologized to Shelley for keeping him waiting. She guided his hand to her breast. Her heart was racing like a tiny bird's. She kissed his fingers each in turn.

The highway carried them safely past mile upon mile of urban sprawl, and then over the Port Mann Bridge, the Fraser River a stream of highly diluted mud that lay far below them in the moonlight, the sx surging up a steep hill and into altogether different terrain, open farmland that was marred every so often by a small town, a strip mall, or acreage of used cars. They passed out of the valley and into the mountains. For some distance the highway kept alongside the river. Moonlight romanticized the sandbars and trees that lined the riverbanks, and made the water gleam as it if was a strip torn from a roll of aluminum foil. In time the moon and river fell away. Shelley ate a candy bar. Bo drank her Coke. They gained altitude steadily as they penetrated inland, away from the sea. The traffic thinned out. From time to time they passed a dusty pickup or an eighteen-wheeler. The wind that rushed through the car's open windows carried the scent of cooling earth, pine needles. At the top of a rise, Shelley pulled over to the side of the road. Two or three hundred feet directly below them a creek wound tortuously through naked rock. A dozen miles away, the lights of a small town or perhaps a mine glittered shrill and bright.

Shelley left the engine running. He unlocked the trunk and he and Bo shovelled money into the suitcases. Stars glimmered overhead. He wished he'd thought to single one out, and make a wish. When they'd packed the suitcases full, Bo wandered away into the moonlit night, and Shelley turned on the sx's dome light, took a deep breath and gingerly reached into the backseat. Andrew had stopped moaning a little after three in the morning. It was a

wonder he'd lasted so long. He belonged in a grave or on a barbe-
cue, and stared at nothing at all as Shelley diligently searched for
a nonexistent pulse. When Shelley was certain that the kid was a
goner, he poked him gently and then not so gently in both eyes,
for insurance.

Andrew neither flinched nor blinked.

Shelley rolled up the windows. He popped the sx's lid, scorched
his knuckles getting a good grip on the line that ran from the fuel
pump to the carburetor. He yanked on the line, turned and twisted
it until it broke free. High-octane fuel spurted onto the cylinder
block. The gasoline smoked, but refused to burst into flames.
Shelley got a packet of nightclub matches out of the glove com-
partment. He struck a match and tossed it on the jet of fuel. The
gasoline went *poof.* A smoky orange ball of fire rose slowly up into
the crisp mountain air. He put the car in gear, released the emergency brake, slammed shut the door, and gave it a push to get it
rolling. The car followed the fall line for a little while, until a front
wheel hit a rock or soft patch of earth. Traversing the slope diagonally, it continued to pick up speed, jolting and bouncing across
the rock, until finally it rolled over on its roof. It trailed a shower
of sparks and noise as it skidded down the last hundred or so
nearly vertical feet. Finally it came to rest against a boulder at the
water's edge.

The fire seemed to have gone out, but then it started up again.
Shelley checked his watch. It was quarter to four. He drank some
Coke. At six minutes to four the sx's gas tank exploded. Shelley
couldn't bear to watch. He carried the two suitcases full of hard-
earned cash over to the side of the road, plunked them down.
He and Bo cuddled and kissed until the fire had burnt itself out
and his beloved sx had been reduced to a twisted heap of blackened steel. Into the silence that followed leaked brittle smalltalk
made by many unseen creatures of the night. Thousands of stars
twinkled high above them, untouched by the fates that played
out far below.

False dawn had brightened the sky when a glossy black raven dropped silently down to the road. The bird picked at the flattened remains of some tiny creature that had fallen prey to a passing vehicle. The click and scrabble of its talons on the asphalt came to them with preternatural clarity. The raven lifted off a full minute before a truck full of chickens rocketed past, trailing a pillowful of chicken feathers in its wake. Bo offered her thumb, but the driver was myopic or altogether blind, for he did not stop.

At quarter to six a heavy crackling of undergrowth and swaying of small trees was followed by the appearance of a low-slung, densely bearded old man on a morose, sway-backed burro. Rider and beast exited the bush and followed the road awhile, and then crossed the double solid and crackled back into the trees. Bo said she thought that the old man looked a little like Ernest Hemingway's dwarf brother. There seemed little point in wondering what he had been up to or where he had gone.

At a little past eight, the truck they'd been waiting for – any truck that would stop – finally huffed into view. The driver's name was delicately painted on the side of the door. Earl Wainwright wore black cowboy boots, tight black jeans and a black shirt with fake mother-of-pearl buttons. His muscles bulged as he threw the two suitcases in a cubbyhole behind the bench seat. Bo smiled and shook his gnarly tobacco-stained hand and said her name was June and that her husband's name was Tracy. Earl introduced himself and his guitar, and then his dog, a cockapoo named Esmeralda. He was too polite and taciturn a man to ask them what the hell they were doing way out there in the epicentre of nowhere, and neither Bo nor Shelley was inclined to tell the truth or even a convenient lie. It was easier to listen to the radio and watch the white lines drift monotonously by, or count the yellow signs that warned of sharp curves and slow-witted deer. The dog had curled up on Bo's lap. Every hour or so she sat up, looked inquisitively around until she had her bearings, and then licked Bo's face and went back to sleep.

Earl let them off at a down-at-the-heels restaurant on the out-skirts of 100 Mile House, a town that was considerably smaller than its name indicated. He blushingly refused Bo's offer of cold hard cash, and drove away singing of the women he loved, who were waiting for him only a few miles down the road. Bo took one suitcase and Shelley the other. They entered the restaurant and sat down in a window booth. A tired-looking waitress in her late thir-ties shambled over to their table with a menu. Shelley ordered dry whole-wheat toast, coffee, and fresh orange juice. He and Bo held hands and stared into each other's eyes for half an hour or so, until Shelley judged he had enough caffeine in his veins to think rea-sonably straight. He waited until the waitress had her broad back to them, grabbed a handful of cash from a suitcase, kissed Bo goodbye, and went off in search of the local used-car lot. Bo leaned against the sun-warmed window. She pressed her cheek hard against the dusty glass so she could keep him in sight for just one more step. When he had passed irrevocably from view, she idly turned her attention to the mirrored-glass display shelves behind the counter. The shelves were loaded with fresh-baked pies and cakes and a wide choice of donuts that a hand-lettered sign boldly declared were made fresh daily on the premises.

Bo hadn't indulged in a donut or piece of cake or pie, *à la mode* or not, since her twelfth birthday, which was when she'd first decided she wanted to be a model.

Maybe now was the time.

28

Inspector Homer Bradley couldn't stop smiling. The pain was gone. It was late, but he'd come straight to work from Dr. Doug's office, where his offending tooth had been gutted and capped with gold. Better yet, the VPD's dental plan had paid every last cent of Doug's outrageous bill. Cigar in hand, Bradley slapped Ralph Kearns on the back and told him he'd been a great cop and that he wished him nothing but the very best. Kearns shrugged away the compliment. He looked down at his tan Hush Puppies and then across the crowded, party-time restaurant. He'd got a pretty fair turnout, for somebody who was bailing out early and hadn't been all that popular in the first place. But then, he was willing to admit that the helium balloons, two free beer tickets, and Szechuan cuisine might've pulled in a few extra bodies. He stared across the bobbing sea of heads at Bobby Dundas. Now there was a popular guy. Bobby had worked vice and then narcotics. In late May he'd tripped over a multimillion-dollar bust, come up smelling like a dozen long-stemmed roses and immediately applied for a transfer to homicide. The golden boy's paperwork had landed on Bradley's desk just in time to catch the updraft created by Kearns' decision to take early retirement. Kearns thought about his own tortuous climb through the ranks to homicide, the not-particularly-illustrious career that followed.

His thoughts drifted to his alcoholic ex-wife, Barbara. The re-
lentless, never-ending bi-monthly alimony payments took such a
massive bite out of his paycheque it'd make a great white shark
gnash its teeth in jealous rage. It was the alimony that had finally
made him decide to quit, take his pension and head for the hills.

He drank some beer. Life could be terribly unfair, when it was
in the mood. Bobby Dundas was thirty-two years old but had the
complexion of a baby. His chestnut hair was thick and glossy. His
eyes were a piercing blue. He had great teeth, a nice smile. One of
those tall dark and handsome types, and, brother, did he know it.
Bobby dressed well, too. Or you could say he dressed too well.
Kearns drained his beer and snatched another from an inattentive
waiter's tray. He knew to the last dime how much Bobby earned,
and was pretty sure that somewhere in the city a browbeaten tailor
was giving Bobby a below-cost deal on shiny three-piece suits.
Kearns angrily downed half his beer. His younger brother had
found work for him at a fly-in fishcamp in the Queen Charlottes.
The camp was so far north that, when the wind was right, you
could lean off the dock and spit on Alaska. The plan was that
Kearns would help cook, tend a little bar. A season or two down
the road, he could get into guiding. Make some serious bucks off
fish-hungry American tourists. The downside was that no matter
how far he ran, Barb would get a piece of his pension until the
day one of them died. The upside was that neither he nor Barb
was going to live forever. Kearns stared bitterly at Dundas as the
new dick field-tested his charm on Claire Parker. Like they said,
some guys had all the goddamn luck.

On the far side of the squadroom, Parker shook hands with
Bobby. She released, but Bobby wouldn't let go. He locked eyes
and never blinked, as he breathlessly told her he'd heard a lot of
good things about her and had been keeping an eye on her for a
long time and sincerely hoped – squeeze, squeeze – that she'd teach
him everything she knew. About working homicide. Squeeze,
squeeze. He lightly touched her sling and asked her how her arm

was coming along. She told him she was doing fine. A few more weeks and she'd be back at it. Working with Bobby. Wonderful.

Willows emerged from the crowd. Bobby finally let go of Parker. In a kidding-but-serious voice he said that he understood Willows was Bradley's favourite dick, but that he'd better reach out and grab a new number, because wherever Bobby had gone, he'd always been number one.

"Number-one what?" said Eddy Orwell, who'd been loitering. He'd tied the string from a silver helium balloon to his stud earring. Someone – probably Orwell – had printed BADYEAR on the balloon with a black felt marker. The balloon wobbled erratically as Orwell added, "Or would you rather not say?"

Bobby clenched his jaw muscles. Eddy stopped cackling as he spotted Bradley striding purposefully towards the group.

Bradley got straight to the point. The report had finally come in from ballistics on the Titan Tigress found in the ashes of the West Thirty-Ninth Avenue bedroom. He took the stub of cigar out of his mouth and looked at the damage he'd done to it. He smiled at Parker and said, "Mister Sticks did it, in the bedroom, with a single bullet from a Titan Tigress twenty-five-calibre semi-auto. Case closed." He smiled at Bobby Dundas. "Nice suit, Bobby."

"Thanks, Inspector."

Kearns had been hanging on the periphery. He fingered Bobby's lapel. "Silk, huh?"

Bobby shot him a look. Kearns let go of the lapel. Bobby said, "Yeah, well. It's hot out there."

Bradley frowned. Parker noticed that the wrinkles became shallower as they climbed up towards the crown of his balding head. Bradley caught her eye and turned towards her. "I don't know if Jack told you, but so far we've got nothing on the missing redhead."

Kearns said, "The woman next door, what'd she say her name was?"

"Bo."

"Yeah, Bo."

Willows said, "As far as we can determine, she vanished the same night the fire broke out."

"Along with her boyfriend, Shelley." Bradley snapped his fingers. "They both disappeared in a great big puff of smoke." He clamped his jaws together, testing his tooth. Perfect. He said, "I got a fax from Hong Kong a couple of hours ago. Are those guys quick? The guy we believe dropped a million on the apartment flatly denies any money changed hands. The Hong Kong cops figure he'd rather lose the money than lose face. Also, he's connected."

Parker said, "Connected in what way?"

"Narcotics."

"He's got a record?"

"Not yet, and I bet he's in no hurry to get one. The assumption is that he'd rather take the loss than file a complaint and have to explain where all that cash to buy the apartment came from in the first place." Bradley rubbed his nose. He ran his tongue around the inside of his mouth.

Kearns said, "The novocain wearing off?"

Bradley nodded. "I've handed Bo and her boyfriend's files over to fraud, but I'd be surprised if they followed up on it. What can they do, when there's no complainant?"

"Not much," said Kearns, as he turned to intercept a beer-carrying waiter.

Parker gave Willows a nice smile. They'd talked it over and decided to let slide the thirty grand advance commission Zagros Galee had inadvertently deeded to his long-suffering wife.

Soon afterwards, the party broke up. Ralph Kearns, Eddy Orwell, and Farley Spears headed for a nearby bar, where Kearns planned to do some deep thinking while enjoying a couple of complimentary end-of-career beers.

Willows and Parker drove back to Willows' house. Sean was in the den, sprawled out on the couch watching bowling on TSN. He wore tight black jeans, a black T-shirt with the sleeve rolled over his pack of cigarettes. Sean had brightened the picture in preference to removing his sunglasses. Willows was too tired to argue about it. Sean glanced up. He waved languidly.

"Hey, dad. Hi, Claire."

"How's it going?" said Jack.

"Third frame. A real nail-biter, but my money's on the bald guy."

Willows nodded. He said, "They're both bald, Sean."

"Yeah, but one's balder. Would you mind getting me a Pepsi out of the fridge?"

"Quite a lot," said Willows.

Annie was in the living room, stretched out on the couch reading a paperback copy of *Moby Dick*. As Willows and Parker entered the room, she jumped to her feet, startled. Her face cleared. She marked her page, tossed the book on the couch, and came to greet them.

"Guess what, dad? I've got some good news and some bad news."

Annie wouldn't look Willows in the eye. Her face was solemn. He had a feeling it wasn't because she'd reached that point in the narrative where Ahab got it. He said, "Why don't you give me the bad news first, sweetheart."

"Barney's been apprehended. I got a phone call. He's at the SPCA on East Seventh."

It had all come out in a rush, and Willows wasn't sure he'd heard her correctly. He said, "Barney's at the SPCA?"

Annie nodded.

"What's he doing there?"

"Somebody turned him in Saturday afternoon, just before closing time. They said they'd phoned and left a message, but I checked the machine and they didn't. Then I remembered that you got an unlisted number a few months ago, when that weirdo kept calling. But we didn't get Barney a new tag, did we?"

Parker said, "Annie, are you telling us that Barney's been at the SPCA since Saturday?"

"Since late Saturday afternoon. He had grease and oil all over

him. They said he was probably sleeping on the engine of somebody's car when they drove off, and didn't jump out until he was
too far away to find his way home."

Parker said, "How is he, other than in need of a bath?"

Annie smiled. "He's fine, just fine."

"But whose cat is at the vet's?" said Parker.

Willows said, "What difference does *that* make? Larkins has got
my credit card. I'm into her for almost a thousand dollars!"

"But now we've got two cats," said Parker. She winked at Annie.
"Or I should say about seven-eighths of two cats."

Willows sighed. Next time one of the family pets made an unscheduled trip to the vet's, he was going to insist on a positive ID
before he cracked his wallet. He went into the kitchen, poured a
glass of water, and got some ice cubes from the fridge.

Moments later Sean tramped loudly out of the house. He had
apparently decided it was a propitious time to do a little yard work.

Annie's expression was pretty much inscrutable as she told
Parker that she was going tidy up the flowerbeds, that she and
Sean would do the front yard as well as the back, and that they
were going to take their time and do it right. She added meaning-
fully that it would take them at least an hour.

Parker smiled. "You're leaving Jack and me alone for a whole
hour, Annie?"

Annie nodded. "At *least* an hour," she said firmly.

Two weeks into September a tourist with a weak bladder discovered the sx's fire-blackened hulk. The RCMP detachment at Cache
Creek was notified just as dusk fell. At dawn the following
morning a constable rappelled down the steep, rocky slope while
another constable videotaped the descent. The charred remains of
the car were wrapped in a blue tarp, and then a towtruck hauled
it back up onto the road. All involved took a half-hour lunch
break. By mid-afternoon the sx was securely tied on a flatbed
truck headed back to town.

The few teeth and larger bones that had survived the raging inferno were eventually presumed to belong to the vehicle's registered lessee – one Shelley Byron Cooper. The VPD were swiftly notified of Cooper's death, which the coroner's jury found to be a result of misadventure: high speed, low I.Q.

The jury, following a trip to the scene of the accident, recommended that forty-two feet of pre-formed concrete abutment be placed at the site with all due haste, to prevent a similar tragedy from occurring in the future.

Shelley's memory had been sullied, but he'd been given a twelve-ton headstone. It was a fair-enough trade.

29

Every time a truck roared by on the highway, the fly went momentarily berserk. Kearns had timed a dozen tantrums. The fly had an attention span of three to five seconds. At first he assumed the duration of its rage depended on the tonnage of the vehicle; but soon he realized that its anger was fuelled by a complex-but-immeasurable formula which he could never, in the time available to him, hope to penetrate. As soon as the fly calmed down it resumed browsing the dusty window ledge. In search of that special mote, perhaps.

Kearns had arrived at the restaurant a little past three, ordered a ham sandwich and a coffee, a dozen mixed donuts – the waitress's choice as long as they were fresh – for the road. He stared at the woman's fleshy calves as she tonged donuts off the glass shelves. She had told him without being asked that her name was Mandy. Kearns believed it, and not just because it said "Mandy" on her plastic nametag. He paid for his ham sandwich and box of donuts with a twenty, pocketed his change, and slid Bo's photograph across the counter. As Mandy's sad brown eyes dropped involuntarily to the colour picture, he told her he was a cop. The lie caught in his throat. He amended his declaration to private detective.

"What'd she do?"

Kearns said, "I'm not at liberty to go into that in detail, other than to say she defrauded my client of a considerable sum of cash."

Mandy looked him over. She nodded so slowly she might've been nodding off. The photo had cost Kearns a hundred dollars, no tax or GST. He'd bought it from a guy he'd met at the beach, one of hundreds of sun-addled sand dudes he'd talked to in the past couple of weeks. Bo looked gorgeous in her bikini, and any fool could see she'd look twice as good out of it. Mandy, on the other hand, was somewhat utilitarian in design and, sad to say, any future she might've hoped for had already come and gone.

But she was no dummy.

"I might've seen her," she said. "But maybe not. I need time to think about it."

Kearns spread his arms wide in a gesture that was inclusive and benign. "Take all the time you need," he said with a warm smile.

Well, that had been quite some time ago. In the interim he'd eaten five donuts including both the pink glazed ones, slurped so many cups of coffee he'd lost count, and become extremely intimate with the cramped geography of the washroom.

Kearns was new to the game. His learning curve was essentially vertical. Too late, he'd realized that it had been a mistake to tell Mandy that a large sum of money had gone astray. He'd hoped to snag her attention, and it had worked all too well. People were greedy. If they felt they were somehow instrumental in recovering money, they always wanted a piece of the action. He stared fixedly at his watch. The problem with those quartz babies was that they never needed winding.

Mandy wandered over to his booth about quarter to six. She wiped the table fairly clean with a damp rag and then sat down opposite Kearns and lit a cigarette. Looking him dead in the eye, she said, "Yeah, I saw her."

"When?"

"About a month ago."

"Was she with anybody?"

Mandy unpinned her plastic nametag. She put the nametag

down on the table midway between them, then pushed it an inch or two towards Kearns' side. "What's your name?"

"Detective Kearns."

"No, I mean what's your *name*?"

"Ralph."

Mandy smiled. Her cheeks swallowed her washed-out eyes. She said, "Yeah, she was with somebody."

"A guy?"

"Yeah, a guy. If they drove off in a car, I probably saw what kind of car it was, the colour and everything. In fact, they were acting so weird that chances are pretty good I even wrote down the licence-plate number."

"Weird in what way?" said Kearns.

"I dunno. Happy. Scared. Always looking over each other's shoulder like they expected something bad to come along."

The metal safety pin screeched softly on the tabletop as Mandy pushed the nametag a little closer to Kearns. She said, "I might've noticed how many suitcases they had, and what they looked like and how heavy they were. It's even possible I heard 'em talk about where they were headed, and where they planned to stay when they got there." She smiled. "But the thing is, I think all this valuable information should be worth something to you, Ralph."

"Fair enough," said Kearns. He lifted a hip and reached for his wallet.

"I'm not talking about a couple of hundred bucks, *Ralph*. I want to come along for the ride." A scarlet fingernail flicked the nametag. "When we catch up with them, I want half of everything we get."

Kearns reached out and picked up the plastic nameplate. He slipped it into his shirt pocket.

Mandy leaned back. Her nostrils emitted twin streams of smoke. She said, "I got to hang around until Maureen comes on at six. Then we got to go back to my place and get some clothes and my dog."

Kearns nodded. The donuts in his belly had turned into something that felt like a lump of fermenting clay. Maybe now that they were real close, Mandy would give him a discount on one of those little packages of Tums stapled to the faded cardboard rack by the cash register. He wondered about her dog. Barb'd had a dog, but never walked it or cleaned up after it. He bet Mandy's was small, a nipper and a yapper.

A truck shot by and the fly went crazy. Ralph Kearns contemplated the million dollars at the end of his rainbow, the cheap motel rooms and saggy beds and de-tuned colour TVs that awaited him. How many neon-frazzled nights would crawl past before he and Mandy became so unbearably lonely that they couldn't stand being lonely any more? He thought about suitcases fat with money. He tried to imagine what it would be like to scrape the scales off dead fish until the day he died. He daydreamed about the easy life of a millionaire, in the runaway lands of palm trees and greased palms. A semi roared by. His thoughts turned once again to life on that hard and winding road, a life shared with Mandy and her flea-bitten dog. The fly buzzed maniacally.

So many choices. So little to choose.

Heartbreaker.